PRAISE FOR *SWAN LIGHT*

"There is nothing not to love about Phoebe Rowe's debut novel. Flawlessly researched and wholly immersive, *Swan Light* is a story about the importance of honoring the past. Rowe writes beautifully and takes readers on a journey to places both old and new, reminding us that sometimes the things we're looking for are looking for us too."

—Barbara Davis, bestselling author of *The Keeper of Happy Endings*

"Phoebe Rowe expertly interlaces the fascinating world of competitive shipwreck searching with a wonderful mystery about a vanished lighthouse. Two protagonists and two timelines can be tricky to pull off, but Rowe does so with aplomb in this excellent debut—I adored both the lighthouse keeper Silvestre Swan and the intrepid diver Mari Adams. I highly recommend this delightful novel."

—Ann Napolitano, *New York Times* bestselling author of *Dear Edward*

"Phoebe Rowe's descriptive writing in *Swan Light* transports readers to the harsh Newfoundland coast of the nineteenth century during the time when lighthouses rose from cliffs and harbours to both welcome and warn sailors. A story rooted in love and loss, the characters' lives are woven together like a fishnet, drawing to the surface secrets that were buried beneath the waves for generations. *Swan Light* drew me in from the first stone dropped into the sea by the young Silvestre Swan and carried me through Mari Adams's journey to unravel the mystery of the light and the people whose lives were intricately connected to its fate."

—Jean E. Pendziwol, bestselling author of *The Lightkeeper's Daughters*

T0026890

"A wonderfully absorbing story that swept me away to Newfoundland and the mystery of a lost lighthouse and secrets hidden beneath the ocean. With a gentle narrative and rich atmosphere, Rowe creates subtle tension, keeping the reader guessing as the dual timelines and cast of characters tangle and entwine. *Swan Light* is an accomplished debut by a writer I look forward to reading much more from."

—Hazel Gaynor, *New York Times* bestselling author of
The Lighthouse Keeper's Daughter

SWAN
LIGHT

SWAN LIGHT

A Novel

PHOEBE ROWE

LAKE UNION
PUBLISHING

Published by Lake Union Publishing, Seattle

www.apub.com

Amazon, the Amazon logo, and Lake Union Publishing are trademarks of Amazon.com, Inc., or its affiliates.

ISBN-13: 9781662507434 (paperback)
ISBN-13: 9781662507441 (digital)

Cover design by Kimberly Glyder
Cover image: ©Ezra Bailey / Getty; ©shaunl / Getty

Printed in the United States of America

For Mom
My lighthouse

Swan, 1913

Silvestre Swan's earliest memory was of losing something to the sea.

His mind filled in years later what must have come before that memory: another bitter spring morning restocking in St. John's, wharves salt-slick and thrumming with creaks and shouts and splashes, harbor air heavy with the almond taste of ice. There was Tomas Swan, dark and wide, hauling netting through the street toward the water. There was Nico Swan, scrawny and fierce, scooping up the bits that dragged. And there was Silvy Swan, tiny, dawdling behind them both. He dragged his feet through puddles. He stopped to pet stray cats. He picked up cod-wet newspapers and poked them with his tongue. Somewhere in all of this, he must have found the stone. It was pale orange veined with gold, perfectly round, and he must have squatted in the mud to study it, unblinking and reverent, until—*"Silvy! You want to swim home, then, yes?"*—he ran to catch his father and brother.

But the memory itself came just afterward: an instant where he was pressed against *Sea Split*'s bow, holding the stone out over the whitecapped bay, breathless at its bright against the water's black. It was so bright he was sure it would float. And so Silvy closed his fingers around his beautiful orange stone and he turned his hand upside down and he let it fall.

There wasn't even a ripple. There was just the hiss of raindrops on the water and the crying of the gulls and the silence of the towering cliffs, *Sea Split* moving so quickly past them and into the harbor that he couldn't tell where the stone had vanished. And hanging there empty-handed, Silvy didn't have the words for what he'd done.

There were stronger memories of that same water later. There was its solid presence through the kitchen window of their leaky little house, his mother's berry-stained hands soft on his own. There was its shape at the edges of summer days with Nico, making serpents out of seaweed and kingdoms out of coves. But now, as he looked out over the bay from the cliff high above, it was the orange stone that came back to him. It always did, on days like this one, in a particular kind of storm-ready gloom. Days when the wind was light and the birds were loud but the sea was a restless, hungry black.

Now Silvestre Swan stood with his hands on the iron rail of his lighthouse, watching the water and wondering how that little orange stone had slipped eighty years away.

The October sky was heavy, hiding a sun he hadn't seen since Monday. In his logbook, during the darkest of it, he'd written STORM COMING IN. Yesterday he'd added a question mark. Today he'd decided to wait until later to dare to comment on the weather at all.

There was always a storm coming in here, the notorious St. John's winters trickling their way down Newfoundland's eastern coast to Norman Cliffs. But something felt different about this—a menace in the air that made Swan uneasy. He could feel it in the gulls, fidgeting in their roosts, and in the crash of waves far below his feet. To his right Highs Harbor was busy with day-fishermen eager to get out and back in, their masts cluttering the docks. The town of Norman Cliffs sat calmly on the hillside behind it, its bright clapboard houses smudged by smoke from their chimneys, gray shores dotted with dories and weathered wooden fishing stages. To his left the land was wilder, tumbling cliffs and wind-beaten brush stretching empty out of sight. Everything else was the sea, endless and churning, broken only once by the white foam of waves catching on the bar, the half-circle sprawl of shoal and sand and rock that ringed Norman Cliffs Bay like a hook. It hid below the surface, watching and waiting just like the rest of them.

Yes, there was a storm coming. But there was nothing to do about it until it hit.

That much, at least, never changed.

Swan turned from the ocean and stepped back into the warmth of the lantern room. He wiped down the door pane and the rest of the windows, dripping and icy now without the flame they guarded, hoisting himself onto creaking rails with his creaking knees to reach their tops. He cleaned the brass and each bull's-eyed prism of the lens, his cloth turning black from the soot, and the iron base the lens stood on. He trimmed the wick and wiped splashes from the oil reservoir, and in the clockwork room on the floor below he cleaned the gears that kept the lens spinning, then cleaned his tools. He hummed as he went and the tower hummed along, thin notes coming from the white stone walls and the iron beams of the ceiling and the water-warped wood floor.

And then, when his stomach started growling and he could no longer put off leaving the tower, he turned his attention to the banker lurking in his wife's hyacinths, peering in his side window.

In fairness, Cort Roland probably didn't realize that the dirt he stood in was a garden. It had sat brown and flat beside the keeper's house in the five years since Grace's death, despite Swan's occasional efforts. Once, the wild pink hyacinths had been everywhere, turning the cliff into a beacon of color, and had so inspired the town that they'd named Highs Harbor after them in homage to a feature they loved but couldn't spell. Those flowers had died out decades ago, but Swan's wife had resurrected a single patch, coaxing them back through the rocky soil. With her gone, the hyacinths were too, for good.

And in more fairness, Swan himself had invited the banker to his home. It had seemed like a good idea two days ago, when, fired with intention, he'd sent the dog into town with the invitation tucked under his collar. But faced with the prospect of actually speaking with Cort, Swan balked, and as he descended the tower stairs, he considered the ways in which he could cross the lawn to the house without being seen. The tower chuckled around him in the narrow stairwell, a deep wheeze that stirred soot from the ceiling, and Swan rapped his knuckles against the wall in reprimand. "I'm doing this for you," he said. "No need to make fun." He paused in the doorway at the bottom of the lighthouse stairs to catch his breath, still debating whether he could get to the back door in time to simply lock the banker out, leaving Swan free to eat his leftover berry tart and take his nap and go about his morning in peace. But Cort Roland had already spotted him and turned with a smile made of too many teeth.

"Mr. Swan," Cort said, stepping away from the window without a shred of embarrassment and following as Swan trudged resignedly around his house to the front door. "Glad to see you up and about so early. I thought you might be having a lie-in in this wretched weather. Storm coming in, I'd think."

"Yes," Swan said to the second part, mildly offended at the first. He opened the door and stood back to let Cort Roland enter first, using the time to survey the rest of the cliff. Swan's aging Labrador, Stay, was splayed in the center of the yard. Cort Roland's horse, judging by the angle of the cart, had been forced to swerve around his unmoving form to enter the yard, and was now huffing and stomping far too close to the dog's head. Stay did not seem at all concerned. "Stay!" Swan called, and the dog's head came up with a soft *boof*. The dog had been Grace's doing too. She'd named him the first time they saw him, a bedraggled stray chasing their cart home from town like an angry bear cub, fearless under the wheels. "Get out from there," Swan had said, waving a hand at the dog, who had met his gaze and sat with a thump. "Stay," he ordered.

But at his word the dog shot up and leapt after them. "He thinks it's an invitation," Grace said, laughing and pulling the reins. She climbed down and the dog put his head to the ground, bright eyes glued to her, tail wagging furiously. "Stay!" she said.

He galloped into her arms. The dog and the name both stuck.

Now Stay ambled inside and gave Cort a quiet *huff* before flopping down beside the kitchen table, his graying belly exposed. Swan stepped over him into the warmth of the two-room keeper's house, the coals in the oven crackling merrily where he had lit them at dawn, the dark curtain that hid his bed ruffling in the sudden wind. Cort pulled the door closed behind him, rubbing his gloved hands together.

Swan took a deep breath. This had been a terrible idea. Best to get through it as quickly as possible. "Thank you for coming," he said formally. "I asked you here in regards to the lighthouse. I've sent several letters to the bank, but I haven't heard—"

But Cort was already waving one hand, reaching into his bag with the other. "No need, Swan, no need," he said. "I've read your letters." From the bag he produced a stack of paper—not the letters, something more formal, with the Norman Bank crest at the top—then another. Then a third. Swan thought wistfully of his breakfast tart, getting farther and farther away. But the yearning flickered out when he saw the paper at the top of Cort's stack. The swath of dark ink, the flourish of a sure hand. *Denied.*

Swan let out a breath, and outside the tower grunted in an indignant echo. He raised his eyes to watch it through the kitchen window, its steady comfort of a presence, the way its glass-and-iron top reflected the sky behind it, the way its white stone glowed against the sea.

The sea that crawled closer year after year.

Once, it had taken minutes to walk from the tower to the edge of the cliff. Now Swan could cover the distance in half a step, the lighthouse tilting ever so slightly toward the waiting water.

He didn't like to think about it. When he thought it too often or too loudly the tower overheard, and for days he wouldn't hear the end of it in the wounded creaking of the stone and offended groaning of the walls. *Who are you calling old, old man?* The tower had moods as real as any person's, could carry on a conversation if you knew how to listen for it. It was how Swan knew there was still time. The tower would warn him when the end was coming. And there didn't have to be an end at all, not if the tower could be moved back from the cliff's edge. It was expected, customary—lighthouses all along the Atlantic roped and lifted and rolled every few decades, tucked safely away from the water they watched over.

But until now Cort Roland, the wealthiest and most well-connected man in Norman Cliffs, the grandson of the town's last living Norman, had given only his regrets. And now, this piece of paper. *DENIED.*

"Norman Bank is sympathetic to your trouble," Cort Roland said, and Swan looked away from the cliff, back at the banker. Cort wasn't looking at him, his blue eyes instead drifting appraisingly over the rest of the room. "Truly, we'd love to help. But I'm afraid we simply can't justify the cost of relocating Swan Light."

All of Swan's carefully prepared arguments fluttered just out of his reach. "It's less than a third of the cost of maintaining the harbor," he said. "Surely it's worth—"

"I'm sorry," Cort said firmly. He still wouldn't meet Swan's eyes, his own now raking over the windowsill, where Swan kept the letters he'd saved from Grace. They still smelled to him like St. John's mornings, her yellow desk below a rain-flecked window. He felt a flash of annoyance. As if he sensed it Cort turned, his gaze finally settling. "Like I said, it's just too big an investment without getting anything in return."

Your town's safety in return, Swan wanted to say. *A clear light to shore, a guide for every harbor-bound ship whose money and goods you're so happy to take.* But before he could speak any of it aloud, Cort continued. "However," he said, his fingers drumming a light pattern on his paper, "I spoke with my grandmother about your situation. She was eager to help too, as you can imagine, given her own history with this lighthouse. And she had an interesting proposition."

Outside the tower creaked again, deeper this time, a threat. Swan barely heard it, Cort's sky-blue eyes transforming in that moment to his grandmother's, bright and innocent against the rock of the cove. He could almost hear her voice, mocking: *If you were ready to give them to Silvy, I thought you were done with them.*

After all this time, what did Abigail Norman want with the lighthouse?

"What kind of proposition?" Swan asked, cautious.

"She told me about a deed she once gave your brother, Nico," Cort said. "If it were rightfully returned to the bank, we'd consider funding the relocation of the lighthouse."

Caution turned to anger at her nerve. *She once gave your brother, Nico.* Abigail didn't deserve anything from Nico now.

There had been five of them, once, on this same cliff, long before there was a lighthouse. Silvy, Nico, Sophie, Peter, Abigail. Lying on their backs in the grass, the sun dropping thick as honey behind the trees, Newfoundland salt all over their skin. In summers they watched the birds, the terns and murres and kittiwakes frolicking along the shore, and farther out the whales, their black rubber sides lithe and lazy. In spring they watched the icebergs, floes of white so vast they looked like ships of their own, moving slowly under sails of frozen water ages old. Blissfully unaware that they were heading for the doom of warmer waters.

He doubted Abigail remembered.

"So she's holding the money ransom," Swan said. "You won't help me unless I give you this deed? I don't have any of Nico's things, Cort. My brother died almost seventy years ago."

"Even so," Cort said absently, his eyes now trained on the lighthouse behind Swan's shoulder. Greedy blue eyes. His grandmother's eyes. "Perhaps I could have a look around myself."

But Swan had heard enough. Again he thought about those five children on the cliff, watching birds and whales and ice. They'd been taking care of Abigail Norman and her mistakes even then, even when they didn't know it, even when they didn't mind. None of them ever guessing that her greatest mistake would lead to the building of this lighthouse.

All he'd wanted out of today was his breakfast tart.

"I believe we're done here, Mr. Roland," he said quietly, standing and moving for the door so quickly that Stay yelped. "Thank you for your time, but I'm not interested. You should be getting on with your day now, before it gets too late. Like you said, there's a storm coming in."

Mari, 2014

Sixty-one and a half miles from the southern tip of Greece, the Mediterranean Sea curled around the R/V *Mercury* lapis-blue and lazy, snug against the ship's rust-streaked sides. Past the ship's hull and humming cables the sea spilled into a glittering blanket, fluttering below clumps of sun-browned seafoam and pods of eager dolphins and several distant, languid cruise ships. The June breeze caught on every tiny peak of water, coating the ship with the smell of brine.

Mari Adams, hunched in the dim purple light of *Mercury*'s makeshift lab, fingers tense on the joystick that controlled the robot churning toward her from the seafloor, saw none of it.

"Tim," she called through the open shipping-container door, without taking her eyes from her screens. On her right was the sonar display, a yellow line moving over a steady blue-green scatter. On her left, a view of the silty darkness of the ocean four thousand feet below. "Everything still attached out there?"

"I promise you'll know if it's not," came Tim's reply. "Mostly from the loud splash and the screaming."

Mari grinned and chanced a look out the lab door toward where Tim stood beside the winch, keeping watch as it pulled in the umbilical cable foot by endless foot. He was wearing his favorite vintage Scripps Institution of Oceanography shirt today, the ship-and-trident design on the back marred by a black grease line slashed through the mast, a souvenir from some other long-ago cable. The mark looked like a waterline, like the top of the ship was sticking up above it, and it always reminded Mari of the poster in her childhood bedroom, a cartoon galleon wreck covered in algae and draping barnacles, nestled underwater with its masts poking above the surface. Its doors still had hinges, its cannons still had fuses, and a pirate in a nearby rowboat pointed at its still-flying flag in delight. Mari had spent hundreds of nights falling asleep with her eyes on its lines. But shipwrecks were rarely like that, she'd learned later, proud and upright, perched whimsically on the seafloor. Wrecks were wrecked, sure and violent. Shattered and flattened, rotting edges under sand. There was no lovely way for something meant to conquer the sea to instead be torn apart by it.

At the other end of Tim's winch and umbilical was their remotely operated vehicle, a deep-sea robot so old and finicky that Mari was convinced it would one day ignore her commands and hurl itself headlong into the seafloor. They'd already lost one ROV at the start of this trip, six weeks ago, when its cable had snagged on their first wreck and snapped like dental floss. Losing it had been a gut punch, had sent their cash stores from faint green to dark red. Losing two could sink the mission completely.

Mari tapped the control panel, teasing it closer.

Next to the ROV's video feed the sonar screen glowed, coating her hands neon green. Its scatter was a telltale sign of something man-made on the sand, sharp lines and dense mass in a place nature left only mottled curves. On the screen it formed the shape of a cherry, concentrated in a single bright blot with a stem spewing out from it. That was her nickname for their current dive site, Cherry, to avoid tempting fate by calling it what she hoped it really was: the wreck of the SS *Californian*.

Californian, the white whale of Mari's two-decade career. *Californian*, a British troopship torpedoed during World War I, her soldiers evacuating onto a patrol boat and leaving the steamship to sink away from the war and her own notoriety.

Because three years before a missile had ruined her, *Californian* had ruined herself.

On one routine timber transport from Liverpool to Boston in April of 1912, her captain stopped her early in the North Atlantic, wary of the field ice littering the way forward. Her radio operator, Cyril Evans, sent warning messages to all ships in the area, most notably the White Star Line's towering new marquee liner, the RMS *Titanic*. Then Evans ended his shift and went to bed. Not long afterward, *Californian*'s crew members saw white rockets going off nearby. They woke their captain, Stanley Lord, and on his orders they attempted to contact the ship with Morse lamps of their own. But their radio operator was already asleep. And so their radio stayed off through the rest of the night.

Californian's signaling went unanswered, and eventually the other ship's lights disappeared from view as she sailed out of their sight. All, they hoped, was well. But the next morning would confirm the unthinkable: that the mystery ship had been *Titanic*, sinking while *Californian* slept, plunging her passengers into the sea, her lights vanishing not because she was steaming safely away but because they'd gone out when her last boilers flooded. And soon the entire world would blame *Californian* for not coming to her aid. Captain Lord took the bulk of the blame, a fact he contested until his death. After all, *Titanic* was one of the ships *Californian* had warned about ice the night before—twice. It wasn't their fault she had ignored them to charge ahead. And so in the end *Titanic*'s supposed unsinkability brought *Californian* down with it, because in their wildest nightmares neither ship had imagined that what would happen to *Titanic* was even possible.

Mari first heard the story one midnight when she was in middle school, watching *Disasters: Exposed!* curled against her mother on the couch, and had felt it slide like a hook right into her gut. She'd never forgotten it, not through three marine archaeology degrees and countless hours underwater with Scripps, *Californian* lurking behind every tidal analysis and iron oxidation study and equipment salvage. Behind dozens of other projects, many objectively more important, it was the ship that stood still that kept pulling her back.

It had been so easy, at first, to find investors, the glamor of *Titanic* unlocking every expensive door even though *Californian* had been a different ship by the time she herself sank. It was never going to last forever, as evidenced now by her geriatric equipment and borrowed ship. But Mari didn't care.

She'd come back in a rowboat, if she had to.

Eventually the ROV broke the surface, and Tim and the rest of their five-man crew hoisted the robot aboard as Mari grabbed its two plastic bins full of debris from the wreck site. Cherry had been good to them so far. Four days ago they'd found a massive cultural deposit in what must have been the crew quarters, buttons and cutlery and even a warped picture frame, the photo inside long gone. They'd been sending the ROV back and forth to it ever since, dropping what they found into the freshwater tanks in their lab and flying more of it to Greece and even back to San Diego for further analysis, the CT scans and electrolytic baths and geochemical compositions that would tell them exactly what they'd found. Cherry was the second of four wreck sites they were exploring on this trip. The first had turned out to be a bust. Mari could only hope that if Cherry was too, they could prove it quickly and move on.

"Well, it's definitely a steamship," she said as she slid the new pans under the dim purple light. The gunk coating their insides was black, fragments of rock scattered through the sludge. Coal. Promising, but not proof.

"Sure is." Tim tipped the first pan's contents into the bath, and Mari watched the coal dust balloon upward and settle on the surface, where Tim scooped it off with a net. She used a plastic ruler to prod at the contents. It would take the water a while to clean the barnacle-encrusted metal, corroded beyond recognition, but some of her spoils were obvious: half of a ceramic plate, a jacket clasp and a handful of buttons, a silver cuff. Then she stuck the ruler into the second pan and groaned. Beyond the shards of wood and iron, two gold half eagle coins were shining at the bottom. She'd spotted them on the ROV's camera, but she'd hoped she'd been wrong. The holy grail of most shipwrecks was damning here, because there was no reason for American gold to have been on a British troopship. If Cherry had even one thing it wasn't supposed to have, the odds of proving it was *Californian* got lower.

Tim caught her eye and grimaced sympathetically. He was officially retired, arthritis creeping into his hands and his back, here with *Mercury* only as a favor. Mari hated that she wasn't making it worth it. Hated taking him away from his husband, Hector, Mari's mentor and the kindest person she'd ever met. They both told her it was fine, but she knew it wasn't fair. "Don't rule anything out yet," Tim said. "Let's send it all back to Hector. You never know."

Mari eyed the gold. "Maybe Hector will conveniently misplace them."

"You don't mean that," Tim said. "Besides, we still have two more wrecks."

"I know." Mari looked back at Cherry's shape on the screen, their three other sonar maps pinned below it. Their first target, Hero, was the bust, its iron predating *Californian* by nearly two decades. After Cherry would come Ursula and Skyline, both promising for their own reasons. That they had four sites at all was astounding, these finalists emerging after years of ruling out dozens of other shapes on the seafloor.

Tim was right. They had plenty of time.

"Dr. Adams," one of their techs said, sticking his head into the lab. "Stuart Noble's on the phone for you. He doesn't sound happy."

"Great." Mari stepped away from the bath.

"Be nice," Tim called after her. "Remind him we know what we're doing."

"I will," Mari said, and hoped it was true.

~~~

When she was younger, Mari Adams had a recurring dream where a shipwreck emerged from the deep and swallowed her whole. First came darkness, then rotted wood opening like jaws to sweep her up inside. The poster's fault, maybe. Or maybe her mother's, Scripps's first female diving instructor, a tiny powerhouse who was faced with a world that told her she didn't look right, sound right, think right, and had pushed on anyway. Deeper, always deeper. There was always something new to find, and Mari had been held in the thrall of her hunt. But then there had been the car accident, a bad storm and a skid. An empty house and a funeral, food Mari couldn't remember tasting. The wreck dreams had gotten darker after that: caught in the beams of something there and then gone, her body always sinking farther from the sky.

So she swam headlong downward, both in the dreams and outside them. What did it matter if the beams cut her skin or blocked the light? *Be careful*, other divers cautioned her. *Slow down.* But careful was no guarantee of safe. And slow, she'd learned, could never get her nearly as deep as she wanted.

It didn't usually impress investors, though, not that that was a particular goal of hers. And this one, Stuart Noble, was already having a lot of thoughts about her competency. Mari held the satellite phone away from her ear as he wondered, loudly, why she couldn't simply equip the ROV with a stronger flashlight, and had she tried sending a human diver instead, and surely she could just add a few extra hours here and there to wrap this all up. It made Mari want to both laugh, which she suppressed, and cringe, which she didn't. Luckily, Stuart Noble had always been easy to deter. She'd already calmed him down once, a few weeks ago, by telling him about the gold when they'd first seen it on the ROV camera, vastly misrepresenting its meaning for the project. She didn't mind bending the truth to buy herself time.

Playing nice with the millionaires had never been her strong suit. An interest in science was one thing. An interest in fame was something else. She needed people like Hector for that, people whose faces didn't immediately give away what they were thinking. Hector could convince a hunk of rusting metal to give him money. Hector had been the one to convince Stuart Noble to sign on with his three million in the first place. It hadn't felt right to keep using him for that when she was already using his husband and his boat. Still, she missed his easy, infectious charm. It worked on everyone. She'd been there the instant it had worked on Tim: a fundraiser at the aquarium, a spilled drink. Tim had been a goner, and she'd seen it in his eyes. Now the two of them made it work, all of it: the trips and the distance and the time zones, never asking too much or too little of each other. It astounded Mari. It had never been that way for her. For her it was men acting as though they were saving her from something, as if diving was a hobby she'd picked up to impress them, waiting to drop it as soon as it worked. It was relationships ending because she "worked too much," and she'd never known what to say to that. How could you work *too much* at something you'd wanted since before you'd had the words for it? She'd heard it about all dives, not just *Californian*, though *Californian* certainly hadn't helped. But she'd never regretted any of it. The Hectors and Tims of the world could have their aquarium meet-cutes. Mari had always done better right here, on the water. Even right here in the electronics closet, specifically. The ocean was unpredictable and the equipment could fail, but neither of them ever pretended otherwise. Mari never had to convince currents or circuits of anything.

"Dr. Adams," Stuart barked, and Mari snapped back to attention. "Do you understand me?"

"Yes," Mari said automatically, then—"Actually, could you repeat that? Satellite phone, sorry. Bad reception."

So she had no one but herself to blame when Stuart spoke his next words loudly into her ear. "I said that I don't feel comfortable loaning my money and equipment for a third year and getting nothing back. I will honor the rest of this contract, but I won't be renewing after that."

Mari's brain stuttered to a halt.

This can't be happening. Not again. Not now, when she was so close.

"If you find something in the next two weeks, I will of course reconsider," Stuart said cheerfully. Two weeks was nothing. She'd been banking on three months. If Cherry wasn't *Californian*, they'd lost their chance to move on. If it was, they'd lost their chance to prove it.

"Stuart," she said. "We really are making progress. We even found gold coins today. If I can just send you my notes, you'll—" There was a click, and the phone calmly informed her that due to a poor connection, her call had been dropped.

～～

Back in the lab Mari felt herself sink into autopilot. *Deeper, always deeper.* This was Mari's project. Funding it was her job. So she'd find a way to fund it. One way or another. But as she looked out the doorway to the expanse of the sea, she wished for a moment that she wasn't here for a wreck at all, that it was just her and an ocean that would fill any space she gave it, that left no room for thoughts like the ones that had captivated her about *Californian* in the first place. Like how there was such a small space between being the ship that saved and the ship that slept. Like how two things could be so close together in the darkness, one bright below the stars, the other sinking slowly away from them.

Swan, 1913

Abigail Norman stayed like a splinter in Swan's hand long after her grandson Cort Roland departed, leaving behind his stack of papers— *You just hold on to that, how about? Take a closer look whenever you'd like*—as Swan woke from his nap and tried to enjoy what was left of his morning.

He should read them, he knew; should make his way through the beehive of paper to see what Abigail wanted. Whatever it took to save the tower. But hearing her name had been so jarring that he couldn't bring himself to touch them, busying himself instead with the food left in the icebox. Even the berry tart was tarter than it should have been.

Now the Norman family had ruined his breakfast.

He didn't like it, this departure from sameness. Sameness was safer, especially here, where it was so hard to come by. Routine was a luxury on an island that lost things so regularly to the sea. He'd felt that way even more strongly since Grace died, even though her death hadn't been the water's fault. The only evidence of that night now was the thinness of one of the tower's lantern-room panes. Swan had put a rock through its predecessor, furious that the tower could show him miles out to sea but not two inches into the person beside him, could light up hidden rocks and terrible waves but not the clumps of blood inside her that would stick and swell and stop. The glass he'd put in to replace it had never been quite as strong.

But he'd made his peace with his wife's passing, and now it lived as a dull ache, almost a comfort in how it lodged beside his heart. That kind of missing felt safe, now. What was different was the sharp-edged loss that Abigail had stirred up. He tried to put it out of his mind. He cleaned the kitchen and the bedroom. He inspected the stable door and the cart's wheels and made a note of the rusting latch on the oil shed. Then he and Stay sat at the back window napping and staring out to sea, as they did at the end of every morning.

But this time, it wasn't the same. This time, Abigail Norman was there too.

~~~

For many long, languid summers there were five of them, tumbling through silent spruces and bogs turned bright with wildflowers and cloudberries past quivering rabbits and tight-limbed deer, spilling out breathless wherever the wind took them. Nico and Silvy Swan, Peter and Sophie Mettle, and Abigail Norman, all running as fast as they could.

Even then Abigail had been different, above the rest of them. The man who'd built Norman Cliffs a century before had made sure of that. Andrew Norman was a businessman. A bank owner, a boatyard owner, a landowner, all things he held but never touched. One day he swept into the lonely little cliffs south of St. John's and dropped his big boats and his big house and his big name and then moved on, leaving a mansion on a hill and an unremarkable fishing community in his wake.

And for a while, that's how it stayed.

But years after Andrew Norman left, a local fisherman returned from the Grand Banks with his hold full of more fish than anyone had ever seen. He was done with the sea, Captain Charles Mettle announced. He was retiring and would be moving into the mansion on the hill. Hero-struck, no one stopped him. Mettle turned the mansion into a restaurant that gave the local fishermen the best prices for their fish. He turned the unforgiving rock into a garden seared with pink and purple hyacinths. The port at Norman Cliffs became known for both, and Highs Harbor began to flourish.

Farther down a different coast, on the East River of New York City, Andrew Norman was married with three children. The youngest was a difficult boy. He would not sleep; he would not eat; he only cried. *He needs sea air,* the doctors advised. *Better for his nerves.* So the Normans sailed back to Norman Cliffs, the boy screaming all the way, only to be greeted by the surprising sight of several dozen strangers enjoying lunch in their side yard.

Andrew Norman wanted to be angry. But something stopped him. The instant his son's eyes caught on the rows and rows of hyacinths, he stopped screaming, popped his thumb into his mouth, and stared thoughtfully down to the sea.

He was a model of quiet and composure for the rest of his childhood.

And so Andrew Norman built a twin mansion on the other side of the hill and said nothing. But Andrew Norman did not like people who took what was his, and so he kept a careful eye on Captain Mettle. Captain Mettle, meanwhile, did not like people who abandoned things until they were convenient, and so he kept a careful eye on Andrew Norman.

The two houses flourished over the years, Highs Harbor below growing swollen with ships. By the time Silvy Swan was born, the second mansion belonged to Francis Norman, a giant, hard-eyed man known for slinging rocks at rabbits who came too close to his garden but who doted on his daughter, Abigail. His only child. Until she married, she would be the last of the Norman line.

The five children had favorite places all over the shore. There was the quarry with its pale rock walls, and the thickets of dense red brush that hid creeks and dips and burrows, and the beach with its gravel and grasping waves. But their favorite place of all was the cove. It sat at the foot of the tallest cliff, the little beach and the rock face above it perfectly round. There was no ladder in the wall then, not yet. Just gaps in the rock perfect for children wedging in fingers and toes with abandon until they reached the bottom.

One summer day, as usual, Nico got to the cove first, the oldest at eleven and a sea captain in his mind, already deep in the water when the rest of them caught up. Then came Abigail, ten; then Peter and Silvy, both seven; then poor Sophie, only five, always the last one down.

"Abigaaaaaiil!" she called, her tiny voice bouncing down the side of the cliff.

Abigail Norman pressed herself into the corner of the cove, out of Sophie's sight, hands clamped over her mouth in silent laughter.

"Hey," Peter Mettle said. "Wait up. She's smaller, that's all."

Abigail eyed him. "That's not my fault."

There was a skittering above them and Sophie Mettle's legs came into view. She fell the last few feet and skinned her shin, sucking in her lips to keep from crying out. "I wanted to show you a flower," she said uncertainly.

"Here, Soph," Peter said, ducking underwater and emerging with half a teacup, its sides patterned with green roses. "A gift from the cove." His sister's frown vanished. The cove was full of gifts. The pattern of the tide at its entrance, the way shoal-strengthened waves collided with the cliff, made this the final resting place for hundreds of pieces of wrecks and lost things. Norman Cliffs Bay was a terror for ships that didn't know it. Some captains were so afraid of wrecking on the bar that they came in too far trying to avoid it and ran themselves into the cliffs instead. The wrecks were rarely fatal. Most ships simply needed Norman Cliffs fishermen to tow them limping into the harbor, fix them up, and send them on their way. Their cargo, though, was not always so lucky, and most things that ended up in the sea ended up in the deep pool of the cove. The locals all knew about it and would flock in after wrecks to see what they could salvage and sell, from timber and rigging to ceramics and silver. But in the time between wrecks, the cove only belonged to the five children.

Nico dove into the pool, surfacing near the rock archway that led out to the bay. "Count me off, Sophie!" he shouted, treading water, his long hair slick to his neck, his gray eyes bright.

"One," Sophie began exuberantly, counting the waves crashing into the rock as Nico dove under each. "Two . . . three . . . go!" And Nico was up, poised on top of the fourth wave, always the strongest. For a glorious second he was suspended, untouchable, rock at his fingers and water at his feet. Then he seized the cliff and climbed out of reach of the next wave as Sophie, Peter, and Silvy clapped and yelled and Abigail *hmphed*. The only time Silvy had tried to mimic the move, he hadn't even made the first handhold when a new wave swelled in and tore the cliff from his fingers, pulling him out to sea in a rush of froth before Nico dove in and pulled him back to shore. But Nico could make the jump in his sleep.

"Here's part of a different one, Soph," Silvy said, dipping to pull another half teacup as Nico meandered around above them, singing *Waiting for me, down by the sea, hold tight your lady and count your lucky stars* loudly and off key. "Bet they're from that trader last week."

"Father said they came in with a gash in the hull," Peter said. William Mettle was the Norman Cliffs bar pilot, sweeping the coast in *How'd She Take It* to lead ships safely past the shoal. Peter had inherited his caution and his watchful eye. "They were tossing cargo to shallow up their draft."

"Didn't take long to fix," Nico said, breaking his song. "She was moored near *Sea Split* for a few days. I saw them."

Abigail, feigning disinterest by passing a stone back and forth between her hands, looked up at that. "*My* father said they didn't need to do that," she said. "He said they should have just waited for the tide to go back up."

"*My* father said," Peter mimicked, teasing her. "When was the last time your father actually went near any of his boats?"

The others laughed—it was true, Francis Norman had always preferred to direct his ships from the house on the hill rather than get his own feet wet. "It's true, they could have waited," Nico said kindly as Abigail's mouth went tight. "But even so, they never would have made it back over the bar."

Silvy peered out toward the bar as the other boys continued chattering about their fathers' ships. It frightened him, though he'd never admit that to Nico and Peter. He didn't like to think about rocks so close below the waves, the mass of something immovable in something that otherwise never stopped. He wondered, sometimes, if that's where his orange stone had landed, if the little rock had taken Silvy's softness as a sign that it was far from home.

"Silvy," Sophie panted, leaning sticky and heavy into his shoulder, and he turned to take in her huge eyes, her hands behind her back. "Pick." He squinted in thought until she giggled, then tapped her right shoulder. She squealed as she pulled out an empty hand, and Abigail raised narrowed eyes toward them. The older girl sat up, her face going soft. "Can I see them, please, Sophie?"

Sophie hesitated. Her fear of the older girl was matched only by her worship. Reluctantly she handed Abigail the two half teacups in her other hand. And in a swift motion Abigail stood and hurled them toward the rock.

By some miracle one didn't shatter, bouncing and landing on a slim outcropping as the other one cracked and fell back into the pool. Sophie's eyes filled with tears. Abigail blinked innocently. "If you were ready to give them to Silvy, I thought you were done with them."

"Abigail," Peter groaned, scraping his fingers through his hair.

Sophie's jaw was set. She was going to try it, she always did, convinced she could keep up, and Silvy's heart knocked as she tried to hoist herself onto the rocks, wobbling precariously above the pool. But then:

21

"I'll get it, Soph," Nico called, and he made his way lower, then over, descending too close to the waves. Peter raked a nervous hand through his hair. Abigail's eyes were bright with glee. But Nico was close and then he was there, lunging for the teacup, losing his grip, and tumbling into the pool. He surfaced into the sunlight grinning and holding it aloft, to three cheers and a glower.

Over the years this scene would play out over and over, Abigail starting fires and Nico putting them out. Gardens mysteriously squashed and new crops mysteriously planted. Hard words screamed and soft ones whispered. Swan would wonder, later, if that was where it had started. If it was why she'd chosen Nico, in the end. But at the time, in the cove, Silvy only saw the sun on the water.

~~~

The rest of the morning sank mercifully back into its pattern. Swan and Stay took a slow lap of the cliff, then returned to the kitchen to sit. Stay fell asleep, his huffing snores sending dust dancing across the wooden floorboards. The tower outside was asleep too, its white stone dull, and Swan took advantage of its slumber to study it, noting the rust on the roof and the peeling paint and the wind-worn plaque and its nearly imperceptible list toward the sea. Then his eyes moved beyond it to the clouds swelling on the horizon, gray and getting grayer. This storm wouldn't carry in anything good. He could only hope it didn't carry anything out.

Before long there was a huffing sound on the slope of his yard, and Peter Mettle appeared out of the woods, bundled and clutching a hand to his chest. "Jesus, Silvy," he called, his voice a wheeze. "What do you keep moving this place farther away for?"

Swan grinned and stood to open the door. "Keep you strong, that's what for."

"Keep me on the edge of a heart attack, more like. Hello, Stay." Stay woke and *boofed* as Peter collapsed into his chair with a long moan.

Peter's head was completely bald now, spotted and wrinkled from decades in the sun, but he had kept the habit of scraping his fingers over it. He did so now, the skin around his fingernails scabbed black.

"Will left cloudberries yesterday," Swan said after a moment. "Said you'd be around later and to share. They're over on the sill."

Peter swiveled to the basket in question, then turned back with a grunt. "Too far."

"Stay," Swan said, and the dog lifted his head. Swan pointed his chin toward the windowsill. Stay ambled over and hoisted himself onto two legs, grabbed the basket between his teeth, and turned to drop it in Peter's lap.

Peter chuckled and patted the dog's head. "Good trick, that." He popped a berry into his mouth, gazing thoughtfully out to sea. "Storm's coming," he said. Swan hummed in agreement. "Everyone getting in okay?"

"Yes," Swan said. "Not many yet, but it's early still." The two old men lapsed into comfortable silence, another sameness Swan valued. Peter and his grandson, Will, both came by regularly to bring him groceries and supplies, the only form of payment he received for this job. The tower didn't have a supply ship like other lighthouses did, without government oversight and so close to its town. When Swan did go into Norman Cliffs himself, he used the cart and horse he kept in a one-stall stable deeper in the woods. But most days lately he didn't even do that, instead writing what he needed on a piece of paper and sending it to town tucked into Stay's collar. It was how he'd reached out to Cort. The Labrador knew the woods better than any human, and even in his old age could cover it faster.

"Cort Roland was here earlier," Swan said eventually, and Peter swiveled in surprise. "I thought if I spoke to him directly instead of going through the bank, he might have a change of heart."

"How'd that work?"

"Not well. He's getting Abigail involved now too."

23

"Abigail?" Peter asked. "She doesn't even work for the bank anymore."

"No," Swan said. "But she's Abigail. She's sniffing around about some paper of Nico's. Cort dropped off a pile full of nonsense about it. I haven't read it yet, but she'll probably send him back to make sure I do."

Peter leaned down to scratch Stay's head. "The Normans aren't the only ones who can help, Silvy," he said. "Half the town would be glad to. Or write to the van Goorens; there are still plenty of them in St. John's."

"I don't want to bother them with this," Swan said. "And the town barely remembers me. Anyway, it shouldn't be up to people. The bank has more than enough money to do it without putting anyone out."

"Well, if you're dead set on the bank, there is someone else you could talk to," Peter said. "Abigail's other grandson. Lou. He's newer to the bank than Cort, and kinder. Paid off a few shipping fees for Will the other week without making a fuss about it."

"You think adding a third Norman is the answer?" Swan asked. "Two is quite enough, even if those two don't share that last name."

"Trust me, Silvy," Peter said. "If you have to deal with one of them, Lou's the best of the lot. If it were me I'd go around Cort and the bank both, go straight to him."

They whiled away the rest of the morning with stories and silence, the sun straight above them by the time a cart clanking outside announced Will Mettle's arrival to pick Peter up. Peter groaned loudly, hoisting himself from his chair, and clapped Swan on the shoulder as he moved toward the door. "At least talk to Lou," he said. "Keep Abigail off your back for a bit. She'll just show up here if you don't, and then you'll miss the days it was only Cort."

Mari, 2014

Mari stood on *Mercury*'s deck, her skin buzzing. The air around her buzzed too, waves and mechanical whirs mingling into the strange ancient-new chorus of a dive. It made the ship feel like a city. It made it easy to forget that they were on an ocean all alone.

She hadn't said anything to the tiny crew about Stuart Noble's decision to pull their funding. With the exception of Tim they were all just here to do their jobs, not because they cared about *Californian* specifically. Somehow, that made it worse. She didn't need a ship full of strangers feeling sorry for her.

She had, though, told Hector. Mari's mentor and Tim's husband worked at Scripps too, running tests on what its field teams sent back, and at Mari's news he'd kicked it up a notch to get her information on Cherry's materials almost supernaturally quickly. She looked down at it now, rotating her phone so that the words took up more of the screen. He'd confirmed that the iron from what they thought was the superstructure dated to 1900 and was likely Irish, both of which matched *Californian*. The cutlery and ceramics were promising too, but everything else was frustratingly inconclusive. Their most recent finds, including those damn gold pieces, wouldn't even reach Hector for another week. By then it would be too late.

"Hi." Mari looked up as Tim came to stand beside her at the rail. "Everything okay?"

"Everything's great," she said.

"Okay." Tim paused for a moment, running a hand over his short gray hair. "You know how Hector's a terrible liar?"

Mari laughed despite herself. She should have known. "What did he say?"

"Well, first he tried to sell me some logic about it being better to move on to our next target early because, and I'm quoting, 'the stingrays might get to it.' When I asked him what kind of stingrays, he told me everything."

"Right," Mari said, and Tim nudged his shoulder against hers.

"You know it has nothing to do with you," he said. "Noble was always a flight risk. Investors get cold feet all the time."

"I know," Mari said. "But that doesn't change the fact that we have to pull out of a half-finished job. Less than half, actually, since we still know nothing about Cherry."

"So we'll learn more," Tim said. "Hector will look through it, and in the meantime we'll make a run on Ursula or Skyline and grab as much as we can."

His optimism was contagious, and Mari felt hope clash against the jaded experience telling her that even a four-mile anchor shift wouldn't happen without snags. Privately, she'd never thought that Cherry was quite right anyway. It was promising enough to warrant a look with the ROV, promising enough among the dozens of potential targets they'd found with the magnetometer and sonar, most of which had turned out to be geology and waste and smaller ships. But as promising as Cherry was, Ursula was even likelier, with what looked like a wider debris field, consistent with a ship that had been opened up near the surface, and a more discernable hull that was exactly *Californian*'s size. Ursula's shape on the magnetometer was a bulging oval and two blobs like ears, and they'd nicknamed it after Tim and Hector's cat. If Mari was honest with herself, her frustration over Stuart Noble's decision had less to do with leaving Cherry than with never getting a shot at Ursula. Their last target, Skyline, would just have to wait for the next trip.

If there *was* a next trip.

She told all this to Tim, who nodded seriously. "Then let's get going," he said, turning back to the lab. But he paused just outside the door. "Oh, Hector's still on the phone for you," he said. "Sorry. I got distracted by the stingrays."

Hector, when Mari picked up the satellite phone, was blunt. "You need more money."

"I'm aware, and good morning."

"I'm just reminding you so that you're not mad about what I did."

"Told Tim?"

"No, that was for your own good," Hector said. "But I also told Zoe and had her look into projects nearby. The good news is that you might be able to borrow another team's equipment in exchange for helping them out first."

Zoe, one of Scripps's project coordinators, scheduled all of Mari's dive projects. "What's the bad news?" she asked.

"She hasn't found anything yet."

Mari chewed on her lip. It was a good idea, but she wasn't surprised it hadn't worked. Not here in sunny Greek waters already overflowing with divers and money. "Thanks for trying," she said.

"You're welcome," Hector said. "Oh, speak of the devil. She just emailed me a request that she was holding for you. Let's see. It's . . . nowhere near Greece, unfortunately, but it's—"

He broke off so suddenly Mari thought the call had dropped. "Hector?"

"Yes," he said, his voice neutral. "I just forwarded it. It's . . . I don't know if you . . . well. See what you think."

"You're freaking me out," Mari said, opening her email. The bolded text of a new message appeared, and Mari scrolled automatically to the information block at its bottom.

LOCATION: NORMAN CLIFFS, NEWFOUNDLAND
AND LABRADOR, CANADA

Mari frowned. *Nowhere near Greece* was right.

R/V: PROVIDED.

That was something, then. If she didn't need to pay for a ship, she could use any leftover money to rebook *Mercury*.

REQ: TECHNICAL DIVER (MARI ADAMS, SCRIPPS)

START: IMMEDIATE

ESTIMATED COST, INCL EQPT—

Mari froze.
Blinked.
Leaned closer.

ESTIMATED COST, INCL EQPT: 3,000,000 USD

COVERED VOID/PART/FULL: FULL

Three million. Exactly what she'd just lost from Stuart Noble. Mari felt her desperate heart thud into her throat. What were the odds she'd have enough left over from this Newfoundland job to use any of it on *Californian*? She scrolled back to the top of the message. But the DETAILS portion above what she'd just read said only:

REQUIRE A DIVER (MARI ADAMS) TO RESEARCH
AND REVEAL SUBMERGED ARTIFACT IN

INDETERMINATE (LIKELY POOR) CONDITION. EQUIPMENT AND COMPENSATION PROVIDED. RESEARCH ASSISTANCE PROVIDED. HOUSING PROVIDED. PLEASE CONTACT E. DEVON.

"Who on earth is E. Devon?" Mari asked.

"Evangeline Devon," Hector said immediately, and Mari typed it into Google. "It's on the intake form. It says the request came as a call. I'm trying to figure out who took it."

Benefactor Devon Unveils New Wing of Jacksonville Library, the results page said. Devon Grant Winners Awarded, Take Top Prizes in Chemistry and Biology. *Leara* Financier Devon to Fund Fourth Dive on Sister Ship *Malleta*. The few pictures showed an extremely old woman with thin white hair and green bottlecap glasses, stooped and pinch-faced but grinning.

"She lives in Florida," Mari said. This was typical. Evangeline Devon was probably the money, not the information. "Did she give a contact on the ground in Newfoundland?"

"What? Sorry, not you. Hold on a sec." The line went silent.

Mari kept searching as she waited. Evangeline Devon was a woman with money and the best of intentions, clearly, but what were these dives about? Bragging rights? Museum donations? It wasn't unusual for wrecks to turn into a playground for the rich; Stuart Noble and most of her other investors were proof of that. Dropping their millions paled in comparison to seeing their name next to a bar of pirate gold or a scientific breakthrough. But this Newfoundland wreck's price tag didn't make sense. Three million was for dives where divers had to provide their own ships and equipment, not dives where the sponsor was covering all of that. Mari did the math. A tec dive with equipment provided would be as close to free as it was possible to be. That meant the rest of the three million would be hers to keep and use as she wanted. And it was exactly how much she'd need for one more run at *Californian*. A lifeline in the dark water. She could buy out *Mercury* and Hector's time, get a better ROV to replace the one she'd lost. She could focus on Ursula, take her time, make not this mad grab with her fingers crossed but a purposeful tour of the shattered hull and the spray of debris and the—

"Mari?" Hector's voice cut back in.

"Yeah?"

"I had Zoe leave a voicemail for Evangeline Devon. She called back halfway through it. She's asking to talk to you."

"Do it," Mari said immediately, lurching over the console to grab a paper and pen. There was a brief rustle and a click over the phone, then a soft voice.

"Hello, is this Mari Adams?"

"Hi!" Mari heard her voice leap into her phone octave and pulled it down. "Yes, it is."

"Dr. Adams, it's lovely to hear from you," Evangeline Devon said. "I was beginning to think I imagined you."

Mari winced. Not the best first impression on someone waving around three million dollars. "Sorry about that, Miss Devon," she said. "I'm away on a project at the moment; they usually hold requests when we're booked."

"I understand," the woman said. "I'm just glad you called. And please, call me Evangeline. You'll forgive me for having researched you, I hope, but you are in Greece now, is that right?"

"That's right," Mari said. She couldn't be creeped out. She had the woman's Google search results open in front of her. "About sixty miles south. Evangeline, I just have a few questions about your dive request."

Evangeline laughed. "More than a few, I'm sure. Hit me." There was something charming about the colloquialism in her prim voice, and Mari grinned as she made a test squiggle with her pen.

"I see the closest location listed as Newfoundland. Do you have exact coordinates?"

"It's right off the coast of Norman Cliffs, a small town near St. John's. I do have coordinates. I'd have to go find them."

That wasn't helpful—Mari had heard *right off the coast* to describe anything from a hundred feet to two hundred miles. She wrote it anyway. "And what exactly are you looking for?"

"A lighthouse," Evangeline said. "A stone one, constructed in the mid-1800s, I believe."

Mari looked up, thrown. That really *was* right off the coast. Three million dollars was way too much money to find something that couldn't have gone very far. Mari stuck the pen between her teeth and googled a map of Newfoundland. Lighthouses littered its eastern coast, but two were closest to St. John's: one at Cape Spear and one at Fort Amherst. The map showed nothing at Norman Cliffs, which was indeed so small she missed it until she zoomed in. "It fell into the water? Do you know when?"

"About a hundred years ago, I believe," Evangeline said. "Maybe a little less."

"Do you know anything about the water it fell into?" Mari asked. "How deep it is? Is it a harbor?"

"It was at the top of some very tall cliffs and fell straight down."

Mari rubbed a hand over her eyes. Anything exposed to those kinds of waves and rocks had probably already been worn to a pulp. But before she could say anything, Evangeline continued. "I'd imagine the waves could have caused it considerable damage," the woman said. "But the sand here is very fine, and I imagine that parts of the lighthouse, at least, could have sunk into it and may have been preserved."

Mari straightened, surprised. "That's . . . pretty scientifically sound, Evangeline. What's your interest in this lighthouse?"

"Just an old woman entertaining herself," Evangeline said cheerfully. "I moved here from Florida about a year ago. Swan Light is a local legend, and I've become quite captivated by it."

Mari could see why. Her brain was already thrumming with the possibilities of it. Stone might not have survived, but metal could have, and most lighthouses had iron in their windows and their railings and their lenses. All of it could be there, lurking just below the water. She looked at the number again. Three million dollars and equipment for an inshore dive. Mari wouldn't need much equipment for this. From the sound of it, she'd barely need rain boots. She wanted the money, but it was hard to justify practically stealing it from an old woman. "Evangeline, can I ask how familiar you are with salvage diving?"

"I've funded several dozen wreck dives in Florida," Evangeline said. "I'm sure you looked them up. An old woman entertaining herself, again. But I assume you're asking specifically in terms of my compensation."

"Well . . . yes," Mari said. "You must know it's something a local team could do; you don't need Scripps for this. And you don't need anywhere near this much money."

"You shouldn't worry about taking advantage of me," Evangeline said, her bright voice going serious. "I'm well aware of the costs associated with this kind of project. We can discuss it further when you get to Norman Cliffs, if you'd like, but as we've already established, I would be taking you away from an intriguing project in Greece. I'm more than happy to cover the time and resources you could have spent there instead of indulging me."

An intriguing project in Greece. Intriguing? "You asked for me personally on this," Mari said slowly. "You've researched me. Why is that?"

There was a pause long enough that Mari could hear music playing faintly on Evangeline's end. "You are familiar with our Cape Race, I believe?" the old woman asked.

"Yes," Mari said immediately. Cape Race Lighthouse still gazed back at her from the map on her screen, the southernmost lighthouse on Newfoundland's eastern coast. The closest tower to *Titanic* when she sank, and the only one at the time with a Marconi wireless telegraph station on its property. It was with Cape Race that *Titanic* had been radioing when *Californian* had called a second time to warn her about ice. *Titanic* wireless operator Jack Phillips, working through a backlog of messages he needed Cape Race to send through to New York, had asked *Californian*'s operator, Cyril Evans, not to interrupt his transmission. So Evans ended his shift and went to bed.

Titanic struck ice not long afterward.

And it was Cape Race that then transmitted her distress calls out into the darkness. To the half-dozen ships who raced to help her, from far too far away, and toward the one sleeping ship that didn't.

"Tell me," Evangeline said. And when Mari did, she could hear the other woman's smile through the phone. "*That* is why I asked for you," Evangeline said. "I came across your name a long time ago, Mari, and I've kept an eye on you. I'm impressed by the work you're doing with *Californian*. It shows me your commitment to research, and your patience. Your attention to every part of the story. And that's who I want looking for Swan Light. Someone who will really care. Someone who will look for the whole story, not just what's down there now."

Mari held her breath, her eyes on the horizon. Taking this project meant leaving *Mercury*, meant leaving Tim and the crew to search Ursula without her.

But it also meant getting enough money to come back.

Mari put down her pen. There would be plenty of time for research on the plane. "And is there a whole story here, Evangeline?"

"Oh, my dear," Evangeline said, and Mari heard her smile get bigger. "There's only one way to find out."

Swan, 1913

Swan left right after Peter did, before he could lose his nerve. His routine today was as good as gone already, he reasoned. He might as well add confronting the entire Norman family to the list and start over fresh tomorrow.

Swan despised confrontation. Grace used to joke that he'd apologize to the wind for interrupting its progress. He'd always teased her back that she'd ask the wind to apologize for interrupting hers. But Peter's point had been a fair one. Given the choice between dealing with Abigail or with her grandsons, he'd pick the kinder grandson, Lou, any day.

His old horse made good time pulling the cart into town, Stay panting happily at Swan's feet. They passed through thickets of waist-high yellowing grass, the air sickly sweet with rotting berries and puddled rainwater, down slopes bumpy with roots and rabbit dens. Then came the old quarry, now nothing more than an overgrown hill, and then the wilderness gave way to darker, flatter ground as they passed the overturned yellow dory that marked the edge of Norman Cliffs. The town was a basin sweeping down to the sea, houses scattered along the rocky black soil among folded sails and laundry lines. The cliffs swept out to the left, the lighthouse perched small and lonely, perilously close to the edge. Swan felt his throat tighten once, and then again as they reached his childhood home. He pulled the cart to a stop and climbed out.

He could still picture every inch of the house as it had been then: damp and warm with the smell of spruce and salt water and Isabel Swan cooking cod and brewis, chowder, corned beef, anything she'd brought home from the grocery. The yellow rooms had been filled by Isabel and Tomas and Nico and Silvy and usually Peter and Sophie as well, the children clambering on the dory in the front yard, Nico automatically reaching for Silvy's hand when he leaned too close to the edge. Soon enough that dory would be replaced with real ships for Nico and Peter; and for Silvy and Sophie the stages, the red-ochre cabins where they spent hours gutting and curing and drying the fish for every local crew that came in from the ocean. Sophie delighted in the mess of it all, while Silvy was much more interested in the stages themselves and the huge, triangular flakes outside that would keep the fish drying in the sun. But it was the great schooners they both loved most, the beasts bound for the Grand Banks hundreds of miles offshore, that left the harbor bare and dry and returned heavy with fish to cries along the docks of "Here they come!" as their spires rounded the cliffs with their spoils. In this single respect Silvy had no interest in being like Nico: it wasn't the sea he loved so much as the coming home from it.

"Are you a vagrant?" came a voice in front of him. Swan looked down to see a small face peering at him from between the fence slats of his old home. He squatted until they were eye to eye, ignoring a stabbing pain in his knee.

"Am I a what, now?"

"A vagrant," the face repeated politely.

"Rose-Olive Cooper," an old woman admonished as she emerged from the house, and the girl turned to scamper toward her grandmother. "I'm sorry, Silvy. We're learning new words this week." She leaned on the fence and studied him. "Haven't seen you in town in a while."

"Stay's been doing the honors," Swan said, and the dog lifted his head at his name. "She's getting so tall." Rose-Olive gave him a gap-toothed grin, and Sophie Mettle Cooper dropped her gnarled hands onto her granddaughter's shoulders.

"She is," Sophie said. "We miss you, Silvy. It would be good to have you back more often."

"Once the tower learns to light itself," he said, and Sophie smiled. It was an old joke between them, but these days it just made him sad. He climbed back into his cart, giving Sophie and Rose-Olive a wave as he continued down the road.

He stopped next at Isabel's Grocery, which never changed, its rose walls and rows of pies and fish the same as when his mother had owned it. "Good morning, Mr. Swan," Gwennie the cashier sang out, as he picked out a dozen fish and loaded them into the icebox in his cart, along with a bone for Stay. One errand done. This wasn't so hard.

Then he reached the bank.

Norman Bank's white stone sides were sagging a little under the weight of their years, giving an impression of kindly, comfortable wisdom that Swan knew better than to believe. The same stone had gone into the lighthouse, but the bank wore it differently. It looked sharper here, rougher. The double oak doors at its center towered over him. Swan took a deep breath, looked back toward the cliff for strength, and pushed them open.

The room inside was empty except for a single teller, the high, narrow windows casting strange shadows across the floor. Across the room a hallway stretched away from him, but it was the door next to it that caught his eye:

THE OFFICE OF CORTNEY AND LOUIS ROLAND.

Swan crossed the room and knocked.

Perhaps he shouldn't have been surprised that Abigail Norman answered.

Her bright blue eyes widened, then narrowed, then relaxed. She didn't move from the doorway. "Silvestre. How can I help you?"

Swan's brain stuttered in his skull. He tried to remember the last time he'd been this close to her. Probably not since the funeral, a ship's ashes still settling in the bay. His body went heavy and clumsy at the thought. Abigail's eyebrows were raised, waiting. "I'm looking for Lou," Swan said. "Is he here?"

Abigail smiled. "He's not, but we'd be happy to leave word." She stepped back, pulling the door open wider to reveal Cort Roland and a man Swan had never seen before, all straw-yellow hair and freckled skin, a boy's ruddy face on a man's body. His smile stopped at his round nose. "Gable Strauss," Abigail said in introduction. "Silvestre Swan, the lighthouse keeper."

"A pleasure, Mr. Swan," Gable Strauss said, his voice dry and nasal with a strong southern American accent.

"Swan," Cort Roland said. "I'd have offered you a ride this morning if I'd known you were coming down."

Swan felt heat creeping up his neck. This was exactly what he hadn't wanted. He pictured his kitchen, yellow and warm and safe. "If it's all the same, I'd rather come back when Lou is available," he said. He knew that he wouldn't. Let Lou come to him. It was what he should have done all along: sent Stay to town with a note asking the younger Roland to come to the lighthouse, just as he'd done for his brother.

Alone.

He hadn't taken three steps backward before Abigail spoke again. "We're all on the same side here, Silvestre," she said. "We both have something the other wants, and there's no reason we can't help one another out."

Can I see them, please, Sophie?

"What do you mean?" Swan asked. "What is it that you want, exactly?"

Abigail settled behind the desk and gazed up at him. "I want Nico's deed."

"Land in New York City," Cort said to Gable Strauss. "Given away in a dowry; things were different back then." His voice had gone careless, but he seemed more tense than he had in Swan's house. They both did, Swan noticed, Cort and Abigail, as tense as if Gable Strauss were a snake in their midst. The American, for his part, looked amused, tracking the conversation with quick eyes.

"I told Cort this morning," Swan said, looking back to the banker. "I have no idea what happened to that deed. Have you asked Sophie Mettle? She lives in our old house."

"Yes," Cort said. "She didn't have it."

"Well, there you go," Swan said. "I'm sorry. But there must be another way—"

"But Sophie Mettle has no reason to hide it," Cort interrupted.

Swan stared at him. "And I do?"

"Sophie was kind enough to let us look through her things to make sure," Abigail said. "You have not extended that same courtesy."

"Because they're my things," Swan said indignantly. The lighthouse, Swan's old letters from Grace. He thought back to Cort's eyes sweeping over his house earlier, taking in everything, settling nowhere. "I've told you I don't have it. That should be good enough."

"It's not," Cort said bluntly. Gable Strauss looked delighted.

"Swan," Abigail said, and her grandson fell silent. "That deed is the only thing Norman Bank will accept as payment for relocating Swan Light. You were the last one to have it. If you want to save the lighthouse, I suggest you search a little harder."

"You see," Cort said to Gable Strauss. Gable Strauss nodded, and Swan had the sudden unpleasant sense of being a puppet in a children's show, performing a part he hadn't read. "By rights we shouldn't even need the deed transferred. I should have inherited it from my grandfather. But like I said. Things were different back then."

Abigail was watching Swan. "He's right," she said quietly, as Gable Strauss began talking loudly about property laws. "The deed belongs with us. It's what Nico would have wanted. Cort is his family too."

Swan felt as if he was drifting up out of his body. "Don't tell me what Nico would have wanted," he said. The rest of it waited there on his tongue. Just words, but he couldn't say them. Couldn't bring into existence something that had never been spoken aloud, not in sixty-five years: *And don't tell me that girl was Nico's when we both know it's not true.*

Abigail was still smiling, and it hit Swan how old they both were. How much they'd both aged, and how little they'd both changed.

And, more than anything, how little there was left to say.

Mari, 2014

It was dark when Mari reached Norman Cliffs, and she barely knew whether the sun was rising or setting. She'd hitched a ride with a Greek research ship to Porto Kagio and made the four-hour drive to Athens, flown from there to Amsterdam and then to New York. After six hours spent on the terminal floor reading over Hector's latest notes, it was on to Toronto, then by a smaller plane to Halifax, then by a smaller one still to St. John's. The driver waiting for her at the airport was holding her name on the back of a piece of fish-soaked cardboard, and she'd fallen asleep in his car.

She woke to him poking her repeatedly in the shoulder, and fumbled out onto a quiet stone street. Then she realized that the sun was, in fact, rising. Norman Cliffs, Newfoundland, was coming alive around her, and even in her delirium it was beautiful.

She was near the top of a bramble-strewn hill that swept down into a gray harbor, its docks hidden by a forest of spindly masts and thick hulls. The few dozen clapboard houses scattered along the slope were peeling and wide-spaced, no middle ground in their colors between demure slate and riotous red or yellow or teal. The trees and hills beyond them were as stark and taut as the sea below, lengthening the farther they got from town until they gave way to a rocky beach in one direction and a line of rangy cliffs in the other.

The building in front of her was larger than those around it, *Captain Mettle House* painted on a wooden sign above its door. She stepped into what looked like someone's nautical-themed living room, cozy and wood-paneled and covered in mismatched rugs and armchairs. A woman behind a spindly wooden desk gave her a key, with a plush sailboat on its keychain, that opened a room at the top of the stairs. It was only after carrying her few bags up that Mari realized she was one short, the silver case with her thermal layers lost somewhere along the five flights. A problem for later, she thought, and passed out fully clothed.

When she woke it was to a bird trilling outside her window and a sky that was cool blue instead of gray. The clock on her bedside table, a chunk of faded bronze set inside a giant shell, read 12:37 p.m. Mari sat up and looked around, her head now clear and alert.

It had been so long since she'd slept on land, and so long since she'd been surrounded by anything other than the search for *Californian*, that for a moment it was jarring. Her room was small and warm, its beige walls and lace curtains and wooden furniture bleached pale by the sun. An intricate model of a black schooner sat on the dresser, *Odela Blue* painted in gold on her bow. The bathroom door had a panel of glass cut into it and was filled with sand and crushed sea glass, the soap was shaped like a ship's wheel, and her window looked down toward the harbor and the languid sea. And despite her remaining whiplash, Mari immediately felt completely at home.

"You look worlds better," a woman exclaimed when she made her way downstairs. "You were practically comatose this morning—long trip? Find everything okay? Are you hungry?"

"Yes," Mari said to all of it. She barely remembered this woman from earlier, though she assumed it was the one who'd given her the room key. She looked to be in her sixties, short and sturdy with bright brown eyes. Her dark hair was cut close to her head, below which dangled gold wire earrings shaped like seagulls.

"You're welcome to eat here," the woman said as she bustled through the living room and into a dining room, Mari trailing after her, "but I won't be offended if you want to explore. Although I'll tell you that when people who *aren't* staying here explore, they usually end up here for food." The woman winked. "I'm Jo Cooper, and I'm quite happy to keep bragging if you don't step in."

Mari laughed. "Mari. Nice to meet you. I'll eat here. It's a lovely inn."

"Thank you," Jo said. "It's been in my family for generations; we've tried to take good care of it." *Generations.* Mari filed that away.

The dining room was spacious, its faded blue walls lined with white-trimmed windows and black ship's lanterns. Mari took a seat with the same view as her room, facing the water, and this time instead of looking at the harbor she lifted her eyes above it. Norman Cliffs, plural, implied multiple, and there were. The towering rock walls rose in a jagged line starting at the other end of the bay and ran for what looked like several miles along the shore. But the first one, the closest, dwarfed the rest, holding lonely court high above the ocean. Its top was flatter, an empty palm extended where its companions were all curled knuckles, and Mari felt a thrill run through her. If she were going to build a lighthouse here, that was exactly where she'd put it.

Jo plopped a mug of coffee in front of her and settled in the opposite chair. "So," the innkeeper said. Her eyes were full of frank, friendly interest. "You're the one here to see Evangeline Devon."

"That's me."

"My son's going to drive you," Jo said. "He's doing a job for Evangeline right now, working on her roof before the rain gets too bad. What are you doing over there?"

"I'm a diver," Mari said. "I'm helping her with a salvage project. Do you know anything about a lighthouse that used to be on those cliffs?"

"On the cliffs?" Jo frowned. "No, the lighthouse has been right in Highs Harbor as long as I've been here. More of a light rod, really; it's not very attractive. But I'm not much of a historian. Did she put you in touch with the library?"

"Not yet," Mari said. "I'm sure I'll find out more when I meet with her." A boy emerged from the kitchen and set down a plate of food she hadn't ordered but that smelled delicious, cod and peas and mashed potatoes. "What's she like? Evangeline?"

"I don't know her well," Jo said. "She moved here last year from the States and she keeps to herself, which you'll see is unusual, but we don't mind. She's very old. *Very* old. But Reggie likes her—that's my son—and she's already paid to have a few old buildings around here restored. So from all that, I think she's lovely. If you're not meeting her until later, how do you feel about a town tour?"

"I'd love one, but can I take a rain check?" Between her trips and her nap, Mari hadn't checked in with *Mercury* in nearly a full day, and her hands were itching for her email. "I have a few things I want to get done first."

But there was no news from Tim or Hector. The notes she'd read at the airport had confirmed that the hull and davits from Cherry had been made at the same time as *Californian*. If she assumed that Ursula was *Californian*, Cherry's proximity meant that it was most likely the SS *Swift*, a supply ship that sank when a mechanical fire broke out in her hold. It made Mari more desperate than ever to drop the ROV over Ursula. But excited as she was that it was happening at all, it was still happening without her.

One thing at a time, she reminded herself. If Ursula was *Californian*, the process would be only just beginning. And with Evangeline's funding, they'd be set. She wasn't going to miss a thing.

〜〜

Reggie Cooper was a round-faced, jovial man who scooped Jo up into a bear hug before opening his truck door for Mari. "You'll be able to walk or bike this from now on," he said as they bumped along Highs Street. "Miss Devon just didn't want to lose you from the get-go."

It was true the drive was short, full of sleeping dogs and buoys in yards and clotheslines layered with socks and neon jackets. The last one reminded her of her missing luggage, and she turned to Reggie as they puttered to a halt. "I lost part of my luggage. Is there somewhere nearby I can grab more layers?"

"Take mine," Reggie said promptly, moving to shrug out of his jacket.

Mari laughed and waved him off. "I'm not taking your jacket. I'll just get it all gross."

"It can't get much grosser," Reggie said. "But they stock some dive gear at Bergy Bits. They should have what you need."

"Berg-what?"

"Bergy Bits. Called after little nuggets of iceberg." He lifted his hand to point. "It's just down there, the orange door. Let me know if you ever need a ride again, okay?"

"Okay," Mari said. She wondered if she'd forgotten how kind people in towns like this could be, or if Norman Cliffs was just kinder than most.

Evangeline Devon's home was a small white cottage with a garden on each side of the door, tarp all over the roof, and a squat, overgrown barn in the backyard. Its owner was sitting at the kitchen table, a walker next to her chair and a plate of cookies in front of her, her lined face bright and expectant. She looked exactly as she had in the photos online: white hair, blue eyes, lime-green bottlecap glasses. But she was taller than Mari expected, even sitting, her back straight. And when they shook hands the woman's grip was strong. The one article that had referenced Evangeline's age said she was over a hundred, but she didn't seem it at all.

"Dr. Adams," Evangeline said in her honey-thick voice. "It's wonderful to meet you."

"You too," Mari said, taking a cookie as Evangeline pushed them toward her. They were delicious, chunks of chocolate and cinnamon in oatmeal, and she took advantage of Evangeline dunking her own into a glass of milk to look around the room. It was narrow and simple, beige wallpaper with a window set in the center of one wall, scalloped curtains parted to show the hill and the harbor. A thin rug patterned with white and blue squares took up most of the floor, and the only other pieces of furniture were a case full of glassware and mugs, a chair stacked with newspaper, and a shelf adorned with a dusty model fishing boat. It was much more humble than Mari would have expected from a retired millionaire. She liked it.

Their pleasantries were genuinely pleasant—the weather, her trip, the inn—but Mari could tell that both of them were rushing through it. So she just smiled when, during the first lull, Evangeline sat up even straighter and steepled her fingers. They were gray-veined and mottled, the only sign of her age. "So," the old woman said, "our lighthouse."

"Yes," Mari said, flipping her notebook open to the page she'd started on *Mercury*, five days and a lifetime ago. "I did a little research on the plane and wasn't able to find anything about a Swan Light." She almost cringed. It was true, all of her usual research avenues had come up empty. But she hadn't meant to accuse a new sponsor of being confused within the first five minutes of meeting her.

Thankfully, Evangeline was smiling. "That doesn't surprise me," she said. "I understand that it was constructed a bit off the record, so formal documents might be limited. Besides, this town is very small and very old, with lots of history besides one lighthouse. Things get lost. But I do have someone who should be able to help." She took a piece of paper from the bag at her feet and handed it to Mari. It was a phone number labelled KEYA TALLEY—MEMORIAL LIBRARY. "Memorial University in St. John's keeps meticulous local records, and I've found them to be quite helpful so far. As for the dive itself, I've contracted a ship and equipment from a friend. He runs a salvage company in Boston and should be here tonight, if he's not already."

"Thanks," Mari said, tucking the page into her book. "What kind of equipment?"

"That's not my forte, I'm afraid," Evangeline said. "You'll have to ask Captain Henry."

"Okay," Mari said. "Well, I'd love to know more about the lighthouse. How did you hear about it?"

"When I first moved here I stayed with a woman named Katherine Mettle," Evangeline said, her eyes going distant. "We became very good friends. She came from a long line of Norman Cliffs bar pilots and knew more about this town than anyone. She told me the story of the lighthouse in addition to many others, but that one, for whatever reason, stayed with me. She said that the keeper was a kind man who built the tower himself after losing his family. He saved a lot of lives." Evangeline pulled a stack of papers from her bag. "Kat passed away not long ago, and her death was what made me start looking for the lighthouse. She'd been drawing her grandfather's stories from memory. I'd like to turn them into an exhibit, along with whatever real-life counterparts I can find."

The pages were faded and brittle, and Mari felt her throat tighten as she thumbed through them. They were all pencil drawings, amateur but achingly attentive. A pair of veined hands on a rope. A schooner tilted forward, rising with a wave, *Sea Split* stenciled on its side. A row of fishing stages. A child squatting at the end of a pier. But it was the one on the top that drew her in most, the only one Evangeline had likely meant for her to look at: a scene of the harbor, masts snarled above the water. It was a view not very different from how it probably looked today, with one arresting addition: the lighthouse poised at the curl of the cliff behind it. Mari looked up at Evangeline. "I thought you said you were doing this because you were bored."

Evangeline smiled. "It's not as scientific as the rest of what you do, I'm sure. But it's important to me, as a last favor for a friend."

"Well, I'd be honored to help you, Evangeline," Mari said, snapping a picture of the lighthouse sketch with her phone before handing the drawings back. "And you're positive it fell into the water? A lot of times, if that seems like a possibility, the lighthouse will be moved or torn down before it can happen. Those lenses weren't cheap."

"I'm sure it fell," Evangeline said, her eyes on Katherine Mettle's drawing, and Mari didn't push. Whatever had happened to Swan Light, she'd find out soon enough.

"I believe you," she said. "I just hope that there's still something left to find, that's all."

"If there is, I can't think of anyone better to look than yourself and Mr. Henry," Evangeline said. "Which brings us to our next point. I'm compensating both of you up front, since I know you need to get that money reinvested, so if you wouldn't mind writing down your bank information, that's probably the fastest way. Unless you prefer something else, which is fine."

"You're—what?" Mari was astonished. "We haven't even started yet. What if we don't find it?"

Evangeline was smiling softly, but her eyes were sharp. "The money is yours for accepting the project. Just think of me as your newest investor."

"Evangeline, I really don't want to get your hopes up here," Mari said. "There are a lot of things that could have happened between then and now. A century is a long time underwater."

"It's rather a long time above the water too," Evangeline said. "I appreciate your concern, but it's already done. The money is yours for looking. But I would ask you to agree to one condition. If you don't find the lighthouse, if there is nothing left to find, I do understand. I just ask that you pursue every possible avenue before coming to that conclusion. Do the research. Find the people who knew it. In addition to the lighthouse itself—or instead of, if that's the case—I ask that you find out what happened to it."

The tightness was back in Mari's throat, something offended and humbled and tender all at once. "Evangeline, I may need the money for *Californian*, but I promise you that I'm still a scientist. I'm not going to phone this in for the paycheck. I would never do that."

"I know," Evangeline said. "I wouldn't have called you if I didn't trust you. I simply meant that history can be complicated, even in a little place like this, and sometimes it's just as important to search above the surface as below it. Learn about the people too. Not just the wrecks they leave behind."

~~~

Night was falling and Mari's head was spinning by the time she left Evangeline's, and she followed Reggie Cooper's earlier direction to Bergy Bits barely paying attention to where she was going.

Evangeline Devon had more invested in the lighthouse than she let on, that much was clear. Mari didn't doubt that her friendship with Katherine Mettle had inspired something, but—*learn about the people, not just the wrecks they leave behind*? What was *that* about? What people? What wrecks? How did Evangeline know there was anything to find at all? Mari didn't know what to make of the woman. But she also couldn't help feeling a certain kinship with her. The way Evangeline talked about this lighthouse reminded Mari of how she'd first felt about *Californian*. Something that sank its hooks deep. How would she handle it, when she was Evangeline's age, not being able to explore the sea herself? Having to do it through research and other people? She thought about Katherine Mettle's drawing, the lighthouse sitting calmly atop the harbor. Looking at the cliff now, you would never know. Evangeline was looking. That was worth something, regardless of why. And Mari had meant what she'd said. She'd look for the full story, whatever was left to find.

Still, she wasted no time in texting Tim about the money. He responded with a row of exclamation points—immediately, even though it was the middle of the night on *Mercury*, a graveyard shift. How's it going??? She responded.

Bergy Bits was empty except for the cashier, an olive-skinned, serious-looking man in a black T-shirt. He glanced at her, then went back to typing something on the computer. Mari walked along the aisles, thumbing through socks and gloves at random. Her phone dinged. Tim: Finished up on Cherry. Hull almost totally flattened. I'll send you the readout + keep an eye on H's notes. Ursula Wednesday.

Tell my love hello, she sent back. Then: This job is shallow. But interesting.

She grabbed the thickest jacket she could find and tossed it over her elbow, followed by a long-sleeved shirt, a hat, and a pair of gloves, all from a sale rack. A bottle of Advil. A few Clif bars. She paused next to an ice cream freezer when her phone dinged again. It was a picture of the sonar, Ursula's bulky shape at the center, Tim's hand waving at it. Then: Shallow is good, interesting is better. Do us proud, kid.

Mari breathed out a laugh and put her phone away, this time resolutely zipping her pocket. Thinking about *Californian* wouldn't get her back any faster. For that to happen she needed to focus on the job in front of her.

And then, as if she'd manifested it, she saw it. The ice cream freezer was set against a wall covered in faded newspaper clippings and photographs, sepia-tinged and curling. And there it was, near the top of the wall, just below the heating vents.

A photograph of a lighthouse.

Mari set her purchases on the freezer and leaned forward on her tiptoes, but the picture was too high. She hooked a leg onto the glass and climbed up, balancing carefully on the sliding panel. Even then she had to stretch as far as she could, but when she got close enough her heart sank. She was wrong. This lighthouse was on a hill, not a cliff, one that sloped gently downward until it reached the sea. Ferryland Head Light 1940, the print at the bottom read. Disappointment thudded in her chest.

"Can I help you?"

Mari nearly tipped off of the freezer. The cashier was below her, arms crossed and eyebrows raised. She eased down into a kneel.

"Hi," she said brightly. "Hi. Sorry. I was just . . . looking."

His dark eyes flicked up, then back to her. "At the vents?"

"Um. No. At your pictures."

"Pretty sure you're supposed to enjoy them from a distance."

Mari couldn't tell whether he was amused or annoyed. She slid off of the freezer. The cashier looked a few years younger than she, but his curly black hair was flecked at the temples with gray. There were faint lines of sunburn above the stubble on his jaw and below the sleeves of his T-shirt, Mari saw as he leaned forward against the freezer to study the pictures too.

"Looking at the vents?" she chanced, and he met her attempt at a joke with a neutral stare. She winced. *Right. Annoyed it is.*

"Are you by any chance here for Evangeline Devon?" he asked.

"Yes," she answered, surprised. "How do you know that?"

He nodded at the picture of Ferryland Head Light. "You were look-ing at the only lighthouse." He had a faint Boston accent, and Mari made the connection.

"You're the salvager," she said, and he nodded again.

"Julian Henry."

"Mari Adams," she said. "So I'm guessing you don't actually work here?"

"No," Julian said. "I'm staying in the owner's spare room. I just thought he might not like divers climbing all over his ice cream."

"Sure," she said. His face was still so serious she couldn't tell if he was joking. "Well, can I still pay you for these?" She picked up her gear from the freezer and hefted them hopefully, but he was already shaking his head.

"That register is way more complicated than a sonar," he said. "Just take them; I'll start us a tab. Knowing how most of Evangeline's projects go, we'll need one."

～～～

She arrived back at Mettle House just as a large, lively group was leaving from dinner. The air that wafted out with them was warm and smelled like toffee and fish, a combination that was somehow intoxicating rather than nauseating.

"Welcome back," Jo called from the dining room. "Need food?"

"Always," Mari said, shrugging out of her new jacket. She glanced at the menu, with its *Captain Mettle House* logo at the top, the letters around a ship's wheel. "Was there a Katherine Mettle involved with the inn at any point?" she asked. "Evangeline was friends with her."

"Probably," Jo said. "The Mettles and the Coopers are both quite large families. I couldn't possibly name all of my relatives."

The dining room was dark now, the ship's lanterns casting dancing firelight over the walls, and it was so quiet that Mari could hear the waves in the harbor through the open windows. The only other patrons were a pair of old men on the center sofa, one with his boots up on a chair, each with a bowl of soup in his lap.

"Gentlemen, this is Mari Adams," Jo said, motioning to the chair not currently holding fishermen feet. "Mari, Theo van Gooren and Bill Baxter. They're our local gossips and are responsible for about half of my annual booze bill. Mari is here helping Evangeline Devon with a project."

"Nice ta meet ya," Theo van Gooren said, a strong Newfoundland accent turning the words rough and musical. He looked like a fisherman straight out of a children's book: an unlit pipe stuck out of a gray beard so long it touched his chest, his face sun-spotted and lined, an anchor tattoo fading blue across his forearm. "What's the project, then?"

"Looking for a lighthouse," Mari said. "It used to be on the cliffs south of here, but it fell into the bay."

Theo and Bill exchanged a look and chortled. "Oh, sure," Theo said. "Heard the stories about that growing up, didn't we? *Clean your room this minute or you'll slide right into the ocean while ya dreaming.*"

"You know about it?" Mari asked.

"Sure," Bill echoed, still laughing. "Right along with the fae of the wood and the ghost of *Hazel.*" Mari looked back and forth between them, frowning, and Theo cuffed her shoulder.

"We're only teasing," he said. "And you seem like a nice lass, so I'll give some advice that should help you in your search."

"What's that?"

"Stop looking. That lighthouse never existed."

The proclamation echoed in the flickering room. Mari tilted her head at Theo. "What makes you say that?"

"Just an old bedtime story, isn't it?" Bill said. "We used to go up the cliffs as kids, try to summon the fairy folk. There's never been anything up there but trees and a hermit or two."

"It's more than that," Theo said. "Maybe there was a lighthouse once. There are certainly enough stories to make you wonder. But some-one already beat you to asking, sorry to say."

"Someone else was asking about Swan Light?"

Theo nodded. "Some people were poking around about it a few years ago. Obsessed with the Norman and Roland families who used to live here, came around looking for modern relatives, and I remember that lighthouse myth got brought up." He slurped down his soup in one gulp and sat back with a contented sigh. She had no idea how he'd managed it with the pipe still dangling from his mouth. "They were all fancy types, real nice boats," he said. "If there was any truth to the lighthouse, they would have found it."

Mari flipped her notebook open. "So they thought the Norman family had something to do with Swan Light?"

"Town's called Norman Cliffs; the Norman family had something to do with everything. The Rolands married in later. I don't remember how exactly the lighthouse came up. But I know it did."

"So what happened?" Mari asked.

Theo shrugged. "There haven't been Normans or Rolands here for a long time. When they didn't find any relatives, they left."

If it was true, it was disheartening. A century was a long time, but 1914 wasn't the dark ages. Norman Cliffs couldn't just build a lighthouse without anyone knowing. There were shipping routes, there were ship's logs, there were government records. If someone had really looked into the light and hadn't found those, it wasn't a good sign.

"Hate to be the bearer of bad news." Theo stood. "But hey, I'll give you a different project if you want it. I lost the motor on my old boat to those fairy folk Bill told you about," he said solemnly. "Back in 1971. Snipped it right off the back while I wrestled with a huge fish, longer than you are tall, because they didn't want me to catch it, you see? Had to go the rest of the way back to town with nothing but my hands and that fish as a paddle."

Mari wasn't sure what to do with that.

Later, as she lay in bed listening to the ocean outside, its noise calming her restless skin, she thought about the cliff. Was it at all possible that a lighthouse had survived underwater this long? That it had really collapsed, not been moved? That it had been there in the first place? Or had Katherine Mettle's drawing come from the same place as Bill Baxter's bedtime stories, nothing but a fanciful imagining of what could have been? Still, all tall tales started somewhere, and Mari's last drowsy thoughts were of fish-guarding fairies and a lonely light sweeping across the black of the sea. What was it Theo had said? *Certainly enough stories to make you wonder.*

Swan, 1913

Swan arrived home from town just in time to light the tower.

The cliff seemed darker than it should have been, twilight catching in the trees and in the clouds going cool on the horizon, and for a moment in the cold silence of the lantern room he felt disoriented, unmoored. But his heart lifted at the sight of two sets of masthead lights out beyond the bay, and as he lit the wick and the glass walls around him flared to life he imagined those far-bound ship's lights flaring back.

Swan had only ever seen the light from sea himself once, nearly five decades ago, when he'd been held up getting supplies in St. John's and Grace had lit the tower in his absence. He hadn't even thought about it, caught up in the numbers and prices of everything on his list, hadn't considered how it would feel, but he'd rounded the edge of Norman Cliffs Bay in the dory and there it was, a beam soaring out into the sea, slicing open the darkness, fierce and strong and immovable, and Swan had felt goose bumps spring up all along his arm.

Inside, the tower felt different: mechanical, loud, nothing like the peaceful marvel that it was from afar. The beam that looked so singular from the sea was here a complex contraption of glass and brass sitting around a well of burning oil, each line perfectly engineered to amplify the flame behind it, the lens itself nearly as tall as Swan was. And seeing it from the sea captured none of the heat, the slick smell, the beehive whirring of the clockwork mechanism in the room below as it kept the lens turning, so strong it shook the floor. In the middle of the night, the only things awake here were the keeper, the tower, and the sea.

Swan didn't linger this time, giving the churning lens a pat before going back to his house and collapsing into his chair. The ride home had been a blur, his chest tight until he made it out of town. He was convinced that at any moment Abigail or Cort would come galloping up behind him. He'd raced past a startled Lou Roland, who was walking toward the bank, and even though he was the one Swan had gone to town to see, he couldn't bring himself to do more than return Lou's wave as he rattled on. It was only now, in the stuffy safety of the kitchen, that he felt his heart slow. The rest of Peter's cloudberries still sat on the table, as if nothing had changed since that morning. *You'll miss the days it was only Cort.* His friend had been right.

His logbook sat beside the berries, leather-bound and brittle, and he realized that he still hadn't written an entry for today. It was unlike him. His memory wasn't what it once was, and he found that it was easier to note things as they happened to keep the records as precise as possible. But he couldn't bring himself to start this entry, one that would start with Cort Roland and end with Abigail Norman. Swan flipped mindlessly through the week before, buying himself time.

OCTOBER 11, 1913

STORM COMING IN? W. METTLE AT STATION. THREE STEAMERS PASSED FROM ST. JOHN'S. CLEANED AND PUT NEW PIPE IN BOILER. REPAIRS NEEDED IN SIDE ROOM. SIGNAL IN USE.

OCTOBER 10, 1913

STORM COMING IN. MADE REPAIRS IN LANTERN ROOM. FULL DEGREASE OF LENS MACHINERY. REPAIRS NEEDED IN SIDE ROOM. SIGNAL IN USE.

He'd been putting off the side-room repairs for months now. It had been their guest room, back when he and Grace had guests, her parents and cousins and Peter and Sophie coming to stay and turning the tower bright and loud. Now the room was sullen and sinking, the only part of his home Swan avoided. He glanced at its closed door, then went back to his log.

OCTOBER 9, 1913

STORMED ALL NIGHT, STRONG SOUTHWEST WINDS AND SLEET. RECEIVED GROCERIES AND CARPENTRY FROM W. METTLE. REPAIRS NEEDED ON OIL SHED DOOR. REPAIRS NEEDED IN HOUSE WINDOWS. SCH NELLE GROUNDED AND PULLED INTO HARBOR. SEA SPLIT RAN AGROUND BY COVE AND NEEDED REPAIRS. SIGNAL IN USE.

Swan winced. That note was worse than the side room. Swan had given *Sea Split* to Will Mettle decades ago, after inheriting her from Nico, who had inherited her from Tomas at sixteen. *Old enough for a life at sea,* their father had said gruffly. Old enough to die at sea, Silvy had thought. But Nico had been successful, vanishing to the Grand Banks for weeks on end and returning on a ship full to the brim with cod. And Nico had been happy with *Sea Split*. At least until one summer day, his first day back after his third season gone. The two of them were in the cove, fifteen and nineteen years old, Silvy floating in the water and his brother in his customary perch in the rock above it. Nico had gotten broad and brown this trip, and Silvy found that he had to keep staring to make his brother seem real at all.

A boat passed the narrow cove entrance, then doubled back: *How'd She Take It*, the pilot boat, Peter grinning at its wheel. "Oh-ho!" he called. "Got a report of some sea monsters around here, didn't think they'd be ugly as all this." In answer Nico pulled his lips back with his fingers and stuck his teeth forward like fangs, his release of the wall sending him into the water and dousing a drowsing Silvy. Peter bobbed alongside the rocks. "Are you both going to Francis Norman's boil-up tonight?"

It didn't seem quite a boil-up, Silvy thought, but instead a much larger and grander affair, meant to celebrate some new bank opening. "Don't much fancy spending the night watching Francis Norman try to get three new ships named after him," Nico called back, and Peter gave a wry grin.

"Please come," he said. "Father says we have to, and Soph will just be following Callum Cooper around all night. Don't leave me alone with that."

"Maybe we should go," Silvy said to Nico after Peter had departed. "When's the last time you were at the mansion? I haven't been in years."

Nico looked out to sea, his eyes flashing gray to blue as if the current was flowing right through him. Then he looked at Silvy. "I was there this morning. Don't tell Mum I didn't come straight home."

"You were? For what?"

"Okay." Nico treaded to face him. "Don't tell Mum this either, or Father. But I've been doing odd jobs for Francis Norman. I've been saving to get a bigger ship."

"Nico!" Silvy felt his face glowing. "Father won't be surprised in the slightest. He'll be so proud."

Nico grinned, bashful, under his brother's enthusiasm. "I don't want him to think it's because *Sea Split* isn't good enough," he said. "She's a great ship. She'd be a great pilot ship, actually. She's just not long for the Banks; she can't take that kind of trip anymore. I've been talking to Bowen Smith, in St. John's, paid him half a commission upfront. She'll be ready in January."

"In January!"

"I think I'm going to name her *Count Your Lucky Stars*," he said—his favorite song—and whistled a quick bar.

And so Silvy had inherited *Sea Split*, used her once, and then left her dry-docked until he finally gave her to Will Mettle to repair. She didn't have to travel far as a pilot boat, but Swan still knew her days were numbered. He would be sore to see the harbor without her cheerful yellow hull. She was a brave little ship. Braver than him.

Swan sighed and picked up his pen.

OCTOBER 12, 1913

C. ROLAND AT STATION TO DISCUSS LEGAL MATTERS. P. METTLE AT STATION TO DISCUSS PERSONAL MATTERS. CLEANED INTERIOR KITCHEN AND SITTING ROOM. KEEPER IN NORMAN CLIFFS FOR PERSONAL MATTERS. SIGNAL IN USE.

∾

The night of Francis Norman's party, Nico, Silvy, Peter, and Sophie were splayed around a fire cracking merrily outside the second mansion on the hill. Silvy sat beside his brother, watching the sparks leap and skitter and feeling very much at peace.

Until Abigail strolled out of the house.

She was as absent as Nico these days, busy at her father's bank. But the town was still watching her, eighteen years old now, Abigail Norman with those morning-blue eyes and shiny black hair, her heavy-lidded way of looking at people that made them feel both like they weren't good enough to be speaking to her and like they wouldn't rest until they were.

She came right for Nico. "Bowen Smith told me he's working on your ship."

Nico glanced around for his father. "Don't—"

"He was very impressed with himself. Apparently it's quite a fine ship."

"It will be," Nico said quietly. Abigail looked at him, lip curled, then deposited herself between Nico and Callum Cooper, both of whom went slightly flushed. Sophie, who, true to Peter's guess, had been watching Callum all night, went pink as well.

"My father is looking to sign another trading vessel," Abigail said.

"Better not, Nico," Sophie spoke up. "I heard Francis's last cargo got all the way to America only to find out no one even wanted it." Silvy felt a rush of affection.

"Hmph," Abigail said, and stood again. "Well, think about it. Trading is better money than fishing." Nico watched her go, his face thoughtful, and for the first time Silvy felt a chasm open between himself and his brother. And then it started to rain.

The group scattered, losing each other in the mess of people running for the house. Silvy found himself in a room with a fireplace and a big bay window, and he sulked on its sill, looking out through the waterlogged darkness toward the invisible cliffs. He wished he and Nico were still there, that they'd never left the cove this morning, never left to hear about Francis Norman and his stupid money and his stupid trading ships. He stood to look for Nico, to ask if they could leave, and he trod directly on a taller boy's feet.

"Hey!" the boy cried. "You're dripping on my new shoes."

"Sorry," Silvy said meekly.

The girl beside him turned. "Don't be a dolt, Arthur. The whole sky was dripping on your new shoes." She looked at Silvy, her rain-soaked hair framing light brown eyes. "Don't mind my brother," she said. "I'm Grace. Do you know where they keep the hot cider around here?"

"Cider," Arthur scoffed. "We have cider at home. Why did we bother—" His eyes flitted to the side. And Silvy watched them land on Abigail, who was already watching him.

The rest of the night passed in a blur, and aside from meeting Grace van Gooren only one thing would stay with Silvy afterward. Later, as the party was ending, people stumbling out into the post-storm haze, Silvy, still looking for Nico, ended up alone on the back porch. The cold-cellar door beside it was propped open, and as he leaned against the railing Silvy heard a thump, a stream of hushed giggles and whispers, then silence. He crept down until he could peer through a gap in the wooden cover. He watched with the sinking, squirming feeling of seeing something he didn't quite understand. And then he turned and fled.

Four months after the party, on a muted November morning, Abigail showed up at *Sea Split* breathless and pink. "Come with me for a minute, will you?" she blurted to Nico. "I want to show you something." Nico was gone for an hour, and when he came back he was tousle-haired and grinning so foolishly that Silvy wanted to check for fever.

Several weeks later, during dinner with the entire Swan family and Peter and Sophie Mettle, Nico announced that he and Abigail Norman were getting married.

"What do you want to marry her for?" Sophie complained. "She's terrible."

"She's not," Nico said. "You'll understand when you're older."

"No, I won't," Sophie said mutinously. "And yes, she is. She kicked Peppercorn and she took Odela's chicken off the fire when she knew it wasn't done yet."

"She did those things when we were children," Nico said. "She's a woman now, and ready to take over her father's business. She's said she loves me. Besides"—and here his face went pink—"we're going to have a baby. She told me at dinner. She thinks it's a girl. She'll be born in April." Isabel and Tomas exchanged a look. Nico and Abigail had been seeing each other for three weeks. April was five months away.

"I hate babies," Sophie said feelingly. "And I hate her."

"You'll change your mind," Nico said confidently, emboldened by his parents' silence. "Abigail wants to name her Hazel. I've decided I'll name the ship that too."

And so they married. Francis Norman gifted Nico the deed to the property in New York City that Andrew Norman had left behind to move to Norman Cliffs so long ago. After twice almost accidently using the document as kindling, Nico gave it for safekeeping to Silvy, who wedged it under the mattress the brothers had grown up sharing, which felt too big now that it was his alone. And in return for the deed Francis requested, when the striking brown-and-white *Hazel* made her way from the St. John's shipyards into Highs Harbor, that Nico use its first trip as a trading vessel in his name.

Francis and Abigail rushed him through her sea trials, sent *Hazel* on her maiden voyage a full two months ahead of schedule. Every time Nico protested, his eyes wary on the sea, Abigail would grab his hand and pull it to her face. *You need to go now,* she said, *before the baby comes.* And Silvy bit back what he knew he should say, because *Hazel* was beautiful and Nico was happy. What he wished he hadn't seen in the cellar that night at the Norman house, months before Abigail had come to find Nico: two shapes in the moonlight, two ragged breaths in the silence, Arthur van Gooren on a crate and Abigail Norman in his lap, moving together in a steady, swelling rhythm like the coming of the tide.

~~~

The night before Nico was due to return from his first trip on *Hazel,* Silvy woke suddenly, violently, to someone banging on the door.

It was Odela Pike, her face ashen, and Silvy's heart plunged with thoughts of Tomas, the way he'd rubbed at his chest at breakfast before setting out with Ivan Pike on *Odela Blue.* "What is it?" he gasped, grabbing at her shoulders. "Is it my father? Is something wrong?"

Odela shook her head. Her whole body was shaking, he saw now, her eyes full of tears. "Your brother," she croaked. "The harbor, come quickly. Something's happened to *Hazel*."

The night was utterly serene, Silvy would remember later. There had been a winter squall, violent but gone as soon as it had come in, leaving the tide high and restless behind it. Now the sky was open and bright with stars, the water choppy but clear, everything perfectly calm.

Everything except for *Hazel*, which sat snagged on the bar, her foremast engulfed in flames.

How'd She Take It and *Odela Blue* were already out, wheeling and bobbing as they tried in vain to get a line around the larger ship's mast. Silvy could imagine *Hazel*'s crew sawing at it from below—one good tug and it would fall, sparing the rest of the ship. A mast could be repaired. But as he sprinted down the dark road to *Sea Split* and cast away from the dock, his first time at her wheel, he knew that it was already too late. He took a breath, forced himself to hold it. The water was calm. Nico could swim. Nico would make it out.

But no.

Nico was a captain. Nico had a crew. Nico would never go into the water without them.

"Come on, come on, come on," he chanted under his breath. As if she was drawn by the need of her former owner, *Sea Split* had begun to race, faster than Silvy had ever seen her go. "Nico!" he yelled when he got close enough, coughing on the stench of kerosene. The sea was on fire, smoke as thick as water burning his eyes and throat. It torched the darkness, lighting the faces of the men swimming and sinking around it. Silvy searched them, but Nico's wasn't there. *Odela Blue*, already piled with survivors, had turned back toward Highs Harbor, and as it passed Silvy saw Tomas on her deck, his face in his hands.

"Swan!" someone yelled, and Silvy turned, light-headed, to follow the voice that had spotted his brother. But the call was meant for him. It was Peter's father, *How'd She Take It* banking hard as he lifted an immobile form from the water. Too big. Not Nico. "You need to clear back. She's going down."

Silvy ignored him and pushed *Sea Split* closer to the flames. "Nico?" There was something moving behind the cabin, a figure stumbling through the smoke. "Nico?" The shape was undulating, a terrifying creature of fire and shadow. "Nico?" The figure raised a hand. Waving. Begging. Praying. And then it disappeared. Silvy's heart was in his throat. He threw his anchor and let go of the wheel, and as *Sea Split* dipped and wheeled around to pull up flush with the larger ship, *Hazel*'s topsail finally snapped. There was a bone-deep crunch as the ships collided, and shouts rose behind Silvy as his brother's beautiful new sail scraped along his father's old bow and vanished into the water. It sent *Sea Split* rocking and Silvy pitched forward, his legs gone out from under him as he reached toward the fiery figure, and as he hit the water he could have sworn he heard the whistled melody of "Count Your Lucky Stars."

Mari, 2014

The next morning Mari woke at seven a.m. and propelled herself out of bed, alive with the feeling of a project about to start. She pulled her wetsuit on up to her waist and folded the top down, tying the arms together, then tucked in the long-sleeved shirt from Bergy Bits, which, upon closer inspection, said *Downtown St. John's Buskers Festival 2005* on the back and *Team Puffins!!!* on the front.

Her room smelled like fresh laundry and herbs, such a warm, summery scent that she was shocked when she pulled back the curtains to see fog lying gauzy over the town, hiding the sea and the cliffs from sight. She felt a stab of disappointment. There would be no exploring the cliff today. As she stared out into the gray, a single foghorn reverberated from the direction of the harbor, overlong and yolky, as if it came from the air itself.

Downstairs, Jo was bustling between the kitchen and the dining room already loud with several young families. "Nice shirt!" she called to Mari. "That festival is coming up again next week. Help yourself to coffee, and mind the cat." Mari looked down just in time to avoid stepping on the fattest cat she'd ever seen, all gray fluff and gut stretched out along the entire length of the bottom stair. "She's called Bedlamer," Jo said. "That's a baby seal. Beddy for short, Bed, Beddybear. Call her what you like, just don't expect her to ever move out of your way." Mari scratched the cat's head as she stepped over, and Beddy opened bleary green eyes and purred.

Mari poured coffee from a fresh pot in the dining room into her own metal cup, glancing out the window as she did—then stopped and stared. The view had changed completely, the fog lifting to reveal glowing blue, and Mari blinked, remembering a line about weather in the Fodor's travel guide she'd skimmed at the airport: "If you don't like the weather out your front door, go look out the back." Maybe today wouldn't be a waste after all.

"Take my bike," Jo said, as if she'd read her mind. "The cliffs aren't terribly far, but no reason to tucker yourself out before you get there."

"Are you sure?" Mari asked.

"Of course," Jo said. "I'm not going to ride it to the living room and back, am I? And mind you grab the helmet from the shelf; the birds can get aggressive this time of year."

This time Mari bypassed Bergy Bits for a general store Jo recommended, a cottage with gray clapboard siding and black sailboat-shaped shutters called Isabel's Grocery. Its shoulder-high wooden shelves were stocked with produce, herbs, jams, mustards, and pies. The rose-colored wall behind the register was, like the one at Bergy Bits, covered with beautiful old pictures. But this time none of them included a lighthouse, which saved her the trouble of climbing onto anything else, and she left with only a sandwich.

The weather was so beautiful now that she couldn't resist making her way down to Highs Harbor, following the pull of the water and the sound of boats knocking in their slips. The charcoal water was ringed with a smattering of cars and the skeletal remains of half a dozen fishing stages. There was also the new lighthouse Jo had mentioned, a squat iron box at the edge of a jetty that was empty except for a man with a metal detector walking along its edge.

Mari dropped her dive bag onto a bench at the end of the jetty and leaned against it, looking toward the cliffs. "Let's see," she said, and the man with the metal detector glanced up at her. She ignored him, doing the math in her head. The sturdiest cliff looked about eighty feet tall, and one hundred years ago it would have stretched farther into the ocean. How a lighthouse fell would depend on its size and shape. A taller tower was more likely to hit the cliff and splinter, cutting its momentum on the way down. A stouter tower could theoretically stay in one piece and hit the sand hard enough to sink. Mari found Katherine Mettle's drawing of Swan Light on her phone and held it up, comparing its view with the one in front of her now. But this was an artist's rendering, not a scientist's. Visiting the cliff would have to wait, she decided. She needed to know more about Swan Light to figure out the best way to go about finding it.

Still, it was a lovely day and she was already wearing her suit. It wasn't Swan Light's fault that Julian Henry's ship wasn't ready yet. Mari stepped to the edge of the jetty and looked down. The water was gray and thick with loose sand, and Mari wondered if Evangeline had known, when she suggested that the lighthouse could have sunk into it, how frequently that actually happened. The stories were everywhere. Windy beaches giving sudden shape to the brittle sticks of a hull, exposed and then buried again. Superstructures appearing out of silty lake beds, gone by the time the divers who glimpsed them returned. One pirate wreck, *Whydah*, had eluded discovery for centuries only to be found under a few feet of sand right off the coast of Cape Cod. If the stone from the lighthouse was heavy enough, the sand could have easily sucked it out of sight.

Mari zipped up her suit and leapt into the water, and when her feet hit the bottom she was immediately rewarded. The sand pulled at her bare skin, and she laughed, bubbles racing from her mouth. The sand was loose and fine, just as Evangeline had said. With any luck, the bottom of the cliff had done her work for her, sucking the lighthouse safely away from the rocks and waves.

"Uh . . . excuse me?" Mari glanced up, up to her shoulders in the harbor. The man with the metal detector was looking down at her. "Did you lose something? I have a net you can use, if you want."

But Mari was already slogging her way out. "That's okay," she called over her shoulder. "I think I can find it myself."

~~~

Norman Cliffs Library was a peeling wooden building with only two rooms. One was for popular releases and beach reads, boating and fishing books, and children's books; the other was for local history.

The sole librarian, a cheerful old man named Daniel, had taken her apology for her still-dripping wetsuit with a wave of his hand and "It's Newfoundland, love, everything's a little wet," and was now making it his mission to bring her anything she asked for. Sitting cross-legged at a bare wooden table, Mari went through volume after volume, her laptop open to Memorial University's archives to cross-reference, feeling the town's history pull her in the same way the sand had. She read about Andrew Norman and a hill of pink flowers, about twin mansions—one of which, she realized, was her own inn. She read about boating and banking and fishing, Mettles and Coopers and van Goorens and generations of lives that revolved around the sea.

But in all of it one thing was missing.

Any reference to a lighthouse on a cliff.

Of the few results available from searching Swan Light along with the name of the town, most of them belonged to Isabel's, the store where Mari had gotten her sandwich. Started by a woman named Isabel Swan, the mercantile had been written up in half a dozen Newfoundland guidebooks. But other than this dubious tie, there was no proof to be found. Mari felt the challenge of it quicken in her blood. Sometimes research was like finding wrecks: you chipped away at what didn't fit until you were left with what did. History under memories, iron under sand. It was how she'd found every wreck she'd ever dived on. You just had to know what to push aside to find it.

Thinking about shipwrecks gave her an idea. She pulled her laptop closer and searched the archives until she found a list of shipwrecks recorded near Norman Cliffs. The list was almost shockingly long, wrecks of all sizes and levels of damage common up to 1850. A barque grounded here, a schooner dashed by the sandbar there. Seventeen in 1845, twenty-one in 1848, two in 1849. Zero the following year. One the year after. A chill crept down her spine. 1849, she wrote and circled.

Only a few wrecks in the next hundred years had listed fatalities. She pulled out her phone and dialed the number Evangeline had given her, running her eyes over their names as it rang in her ear.

SS *Tennerd* (Tennerd Shipping)—2

RMS *Ontario* (Royal Canada Line)—11

Sally Anna—3

SS *Saint Gray* (Vettrey Shipping)—20

Evernett—7

"Memorial University archives." The woman who answered her call did so in the breathless way of one who had lunged for the phone to snag it on the last ring. "Of course, hi," she said when Mari introduced herself. "This is Keya Talley. Miss Devon told me to expect you. How can we help?"

"I'm looking for information on a Swan Light that used to be in Norman Cliffs," Mari said. "It looks like there was a big drop in shipwrecks in 1849, so I'm thinking that's when it was built. Could you look into ships' logs from about 1845 to 1920? Anything going to or from St. John's should have commented on it."

"Of course," Keya said. "I'll get started right now."

But two hours later, with no call back and no sign of the lighthouse in her own research, Mari sat back from the table and rubbed her eyes. It was still glorious outside, and now it felt as though the weather was taunting her, reminding her that she'd passed up her first chance to see the cliff to sit in this dim room instead. She stood and stretched, taking a lap of the tiny space to give her eyes a break, and moved toward the only piece of art on the wall. It was a black-and-white photograph of the fishing stages outside in their glory, before overuse bled the Grand Banks dry and Newfoundland closed its fisheries. A sticker at its bottom read For sale—from the collection of local historian Charlie Quentin.

"Huh," she said, and went back to the computer.

Charlie Quentin's website had an impressively well-categorized collection of art, organized by year and dating back to the early 1900s. Mari clicked as far back as she could get and scrolled slowly through a mix of paintings and photos. She stared for several moments at a painting of the cliff at sunrise with a white smear at its top that could have been a lighthouse but could also have been an errant cloud. She moved on: there were snapshots of families and picnics, fishermen, beaches, trees. Paintings of deer poised to run and dogs shaking water from their fur. And three-quarters of the way down the page, from the dawning months of 1904, there it was.

Mari leaned so close her nose practically touched the screen. It was a photograph, a group of people at the edge of the woods, food spread around them, the ocean low in the corner. It was badly backlit, but the location was unmistakable. This would have been taken from the cliffs farther past the tall one, looking back toward town, Highs Harbor and the bar just visible at the edge of the frame. And there in the background, nestled among the trees, was the iron ring and crisscrossed glass of a lighthouse.

There was a line of text penciled at the bottom, loopy and faded:

St. John's summers, a boil-up in the woods at Swan Light.

A picture. A lead. Grayscale-solid proof. It settled into her rib cage, blurry but perfectly clear. "Hello, Swan Light," Mari said. "Where have you been hiding?"

Swan, 1913

The next morning dawned wet and bleak. The cliff was windy, the waves below it black. Farther out the water was rising, the ever-present white foam of the bar now invisible against the churn. The storm was on its way, and it would be bad.

Swan did his best not to think about it. He had slept poorly, dreams interrupted by visions of *Hazel* burning on the bar and Abigail Norman striding across the cliff to push the lighthouse into the sea. As he took extra care cleaning the kitchen and dusting off the few things from his past he kept in a box below the icebox—a receipt from the grocery, Isabel's looped handwriting on the back; a shard of rose-patterned teacup; Grace's letters, from when she'd lived in St. John's—Swan wondered how much Cort and Lou Roland knew about their grandmother's history with the lighthouse. To them it must have seemed as old as the cliffs themselves, necessary and everlasting.

But their family had once felt differently.

There had been two funerals, in the end. Nico Swan, lost to the sea. Tomas Swan, lost to grief. The call for a lighthouse had come up almost immediately after *Hazel* sank, and a town council had been called together at Norman Bank. "A lighthouse?" Francis Norman had said, his voice lifting in disbelief. "To what end?" The crowd murmured, and he caught himself. "It was a tragedy, of course. But Nico Swan knew this water better than anyone. What would a lighthouse have done to help? Given them something pretty to watch on their way down?" He looked around the room. "It's a waste of money, money we could spend on other things."

Like stronger ships, thought some in the crowd.

Like funerals, thought others.

Their British government, as it turned out, agreed with Francis. So the townspeople took it upon themselves. They dug gleaming white stone from the quarry and carried it on carts while others lifted supplies and iron and the lens itself up from the cove, nailing wooden planks into the rock wall to form a ladder that splintered the toeholds Nico Swan had used to climb the cliff all his life. From Silvy's bedroom window it seemed like the lighthouse was willing itself into existence, growing taller every day and painting itself cloud-white against the sky. Norman Cliffs had gained a watchman.

And when, three years later, the lighthouse was finished and it came time to choose a keeper, only one voice had volunteered.

Swan wondered how much Lou and Cort Roland knew about any of it. About the ship with their mother's name sitting at the bottom of the bay. Hazel Roland had died when the boys were young, he knew, and their father not long after, leaving Abigail and her own father, Francis, to raise them. Abigail had never remarried, even as the town whispered that it was Arthur van Gooren she still wanted, Arthur van Gooren who'd left her behind, and eventually the fact that her name was legally Abigail Swan was all but forgotten. Nico, *Hazel*, the tower, none of it meant anything to Cort. He didn't care about saving it. Swan knew that. He'd only thought dangling the offer to do so would get him the deed he wanted.

Peter was back in the afternoon, his breath silver in the air. Swan saw him coming and propped the door. "Two visits in a row," he called. "Should I be worried? Are you dying?"

"If only," Peter said, falling again into his chair. "Ingrid has shooed me out of the house again. I'm meant to be getting more wood before the storm, but I wanted to check on you. It's going to be a bad one, Silvy."

"I know it." Swan looked past the tower to the bar, the surest way to measure bad weather. The mound of shoal and rock and sand rose high enough from the seafloor to create waves that could rise to monstrous heights during a storm. It was starting already, water catching to create a froth of foam that made the bar look like a surfacing sea creature. Above it the clouds were heavy, blurring the horizon into an unbroken mass of gray.

"Promise me you'll be careful tonight," Peter said. "You know the lighthouse makes me nervous in this weather; I wish you'd come stay with us. Swan Light is not as safe as it used to be, Silvy, I hate to say it."

"I know it," Swan said again. The tower tutted. "We'll be careful. There may be ships out there that need us. But the tower won't go anywhere without telling me."

Peter eyed the stone dubiously. "Whatever you say."

They took up their customary spots on the back porch, Stay sprawled out between them, watching the sky grow darker. "Well, I'd better be off," Peter said eventually, pushing himself to his feet. "Ingrid will have words for me." Swan followed him back around the house, and Peter paused by the oil shed on his way to his horse, stooping to fiddle with the latch. "You'll want to replace this," he called back to Swan. "Don't want it to blow open in the gale."

Swan had noted the rusting latch in his logbook, and cursed himself for forgetting. He should have gotten a new one yesterday in town. Foolish. Still, the lock had held through worse. It would be fine. He raised a hand in acknowledgment.

"Head down behind me if you want," Peter said as he climbed bodily into his cart. "I'll tell Gwennie to keep Isabel's open late, keep an eye out for you."

"I'll be all right," Swan said. "I'll see you next week?" Peter waved as his horse trundled off into the woods.

But no sooner had Swan closed the door than there was a gust of wind and a loud bang from the yard, and he moved to the window to see the oil shed door swinging open. Swan cursed and pulled his coat tight as he strode out to examine it. The lock had shattered. He couldn't risk leaving the kerosene open to the coming rain. It looked like he was going back to town after all.

Swan hitched his horse to the cart and set off. After only a few minutes he realized that he hadn't blocked the oil shed door, and that if the rain started while he was gone the oil would still be at risk. He groaned and stopped the cart. Maybe he really was getting too old for this. "Watch the horse," he said to Stay, and climbed out to trek back to the shed.

He heard them before he saw them.

There were hushed voices, and the soft thumping of rope. Swan drew level with the end of the woods and froze there to see Cort Roland and two other men standing by the tower, peering up. Cort pushed open the door and vanished. The tower let out an angry keen.

Swan's first reaction was surprise. What kind of coincidence was it that Cort was there right after Swan himself had left? He must have come up from the sea, climbing the ladder from the cove. How long had the men been sitting out of sight at the top of the path, waiting, on the chance that Swan would leave? Cort couldn't be that bold, could he, with a storm approaching—what if Swan hadn't left at all? Because he wouldn't have, hadn't planned to, if it hadn't been for—

Swan closed his eyes.

Peter fiddling with the latch. *Head down behind me if you want.* "Oh, my friend," Swan said softly, "what have you done?"

"Hey!" one of Cort's men called, and Swan shrank back into the trees. "The old man left the oil room open."

"Block the door," the other one said, and the first man wheeled Swan's handcart over and wedged it against the door. "Last thing we need is all of this going up in flames."

~~~

But the storm was on Swan's side, the threatening wind forcing Cort and his men back to the cove not long after they'd arrived, their dory vanishing into the rising mist. Once they were gone, the cliff quiet again, Swan left the handcart where it was and did what he should have done all along, writing a note to the smith that he'd send to town with Stay after the storm had passed. He collected Stay from the woods and returned the horse and cart to their stable, then stepped into the lighthouse. The stone creaked, and he laid a hand on the wall in apology. "These are strange times, my friends," he said, and Stay *boofed* his agreement. But the lantern room was undisturbed, no sign of Cort having been there other than the still-affronted stone and the bad taste in Swan's mouth.

He lit the oil earlier than he needed to, tipping an extra layer of kerosene into the well and lingering a moment before cranking up the clockwork and climbing back to the lantern room. He watched the way the prismed glass threw red and yellow patterns against the windows and the bruise-yellow sky behind them. A frozen sky, a golden one. And out beyond the bar, the thunder finally began.

Swan, 1913

The storm was so loud that he barely heard the crash.

Its tail end woke him, a screech still fading when he jerked upright in the moaning, buckling clockwork room, where he slept during storms to keep an eye on the oil, and for a moment he was a boy again, Odela Pike banging on the door. *The harbor, come quickly.* He shook his head and stood. Stay was awake too, crouched at his feet, ears up and eyes wide.

The noise came again, a hideous animal scream. And Swan's heart plummeted, because he knew that sound.

Metal on rock.

A ship on the bar.

He pushed open the hatch to the lantern room, head bowed against the violence in the air. The flame was steady and bright behind the shelter of the lens, but wind rattled the windows and slammed against the roof. Swan pressed his face to the shaking glass, but all he could see was the fire reflected in the furious rain. He had to be farther from the light.

Outside the wind and rain were worse that Swan had ever seen. The tower was swaying, dancing, baring its teeth into the storm. *You'll have to try harder than this,* it said. Swan pressed both hands hard against its side and turned away.

The edge of the cliff was invisible, and Swan dropped to his hands and knees and moved slowly along, driving his fingers into the mud until he felt it give way. He waited as the beam swung around: three seconds of darkness, three seconds of glow, three seconds of scorching bright light. But even through the mess of the night he could see that there was no telltale gleam of metal on the bar. Was he too late? Was the ship already lost?

Then the sound came again, so loud he jumped. It was close. Too close to be the bar.

Close enough that it could be directly below him.

Holding his breath against the wind, Swan stuck his head over the edge. And in the moment the beam above him swung from a hint of light to a full glow, he froze.

There was a ship at the bottom of the cliff.

A steamer, all wet metal and fire, clung to the rocks just before the cove. Its heaving side was garish, indecently out of place, like rolling over in an empty bed to find a face two inches away. It bucked once, vomiting smoke.

And as the lighthouse's beacon continued on across the sky, the ship faded back into the dark.

Swan threw himself backward and crawled until he hit the keeper's house, his heart thumping painfully. He tore a page from the log and scribbled out CARGO WRECK AT CLIFFS, NEED IMMEDIATE HELP, folded it in a flap of rubber, and slid the note into Stay's collar. "Go get Peter," he said. But the dog was frozen, trembling nose fixed toward the sea. "Stay!" Swan barked. "Peter!" Stay bolted for the door. Panting, Swan crossed the lawn and took the stairs two at a time back to the watch room.

And there in the darkness, he faltered.

He'd brought in bad wrecks before. But not even in the worst of them had he ever stopped the spinning light. It could be a death sentence to any ship still out there. But this ship was here, now, at his doorstep, the taste of fire and metal in the air, her symphony of creaks getting louder as she fought her losing fight. And there was only one way to give her rescuers a chance.

Swan grabbed hold of the lever beside the clockwork mechanism and wrenched the whirling gears to a halt.

The ceiling sighed and strained, and Swan climbed back through the hatch as the spinning lens slowed. It was impossibly heavy, but Swan used its own momentum to guide it until its bull's-eyed panel caught the light at an angle that threw the beam directly over the cliff. He pushed hard and it stayed there, motionless and resolute. Swan fed the oil and threw up a prayer to any saints who might be watching.

And he climbed down the stairs and back into the storm.

In this steady new light the ship seemed smaller, vulnerable, and as the sea lifted her screeching against the cliff Swan felt a surge of protectiveness, seeing her in that instant through dozens of eyes that weren't his own. Her builder at her sea trials, her owner choosing her cabin paint, her crew passing her berth and counting down the days until she would carry them away. None of it mattered now. From here, Swan couldn't even read her name.

He felt the swell, the ocean drawing in a breath, and he went cold. The fourth wave, always the strongest. *Count me off, Sophie!* The water hurtled backward and the steamer fell, metal sparking on rock, coal dust billowing out behind her, as the wave crested high. High above the ship and all she'd been, above the sea and all she'd done, above the single pale figure Swan could see clinging to a port-side rail.

"No," he breathed.

The fourth wave came down.

Metal screamed as the steamer was torn in two. The stern plunged below the surface, coal embers still glowing through the waves, leaving the bow alone to slam again and again against the cliff.

Swan felt every inch of his eighty-three years on an island telling him what to do. Telling him what not to do. This wreck was far beyond him, it had been all along. He'd done his part in alerting the town, alerting men with younger bones and stronger ships who would come and do everything they could. It was far better to be here when Norman Cliffs arrived, waiting it out, waiting for help. *Waiting for you, under the moonlight.* The ship was lost, and there was no sense losing himself with it. *Waiting for me, down by the sea.* The sea took and it took and it rarely gave things back. *So hold tight your lady.* Except to the cove. Whatever the sea took, it returned to the cove. And he was the only one close. *Hold tight your lady and count your lucky stars.*

Swan was moving before he meant to, hoisting the long coil of cable from just inside the house and stumbling along the cliff to the top of the ladder. He didn't let himself think about the height or the wind or the rain or the fact that he hadn't climbed these rungs in nearly forty years or the fact that the waves waiting for him at the bottom had just ripped a giant into pieces. One hand over the other. *Count me off, Sophie!*

Swan lashed one end of the cable to the top rung and heaved the rest of it over the edge, where it vanished into the black. The ladder bars were sturdy under his gloves, and the curve of the cove protected him from the worst of the wind. Still, it felt like a century before water crashed against his feet. He stopped, holding tight to the cable, and turned.

The bottom of the cove was gone. There was no silver sand, no hidden treasures, no curve leading into the sea. In its place was a seething well of water, higher than Swan had known it could be, waves crashing spectacularly against the stone. The arch that had always risen high above the sand now had only a few feet of empty air beneath it. He hastily climbed a few rungs back up to safety, his heart thumping painfully and a curious tingling crawling along his left side. Through the arch he could see the gleam of the steamer's bow, and his heart sank when he realized how much space it was blocking. The only way a person could get into the cove was to dive under the arch intentionally. And none of these sailors knew it was here. The smell of smoke was so strong he could barely breathe. "Hello?" he choked out. The wind snatched it away.

Above him there was a smash of thunder that sounded like the sky itself falling, and with a stab of fear he thought about Stay, finding his way through this alone. Then lightning splintered across the sky, lighting the cove day-bright, and Swan closed his eyes against it, his vision searing red, before opening them into blessed darkness.

And a figure crouched atop the water.

Swan sucked in a breath. It couldn't be. But there he was, long hair tied back, shoulders hunched bashfully, smiling, and Swan's mind went blank. "Nico?" he whispered.

His lightning-scorched vision cleared, and the smiling boy was gone.

Swan clung to the ladder, his heart thumping erratically, eyes locked on the arch. The screeching outside the cove had reached a new pitch, but Swan barely noticed. Music wafted by, another trick of his terrified mind. *Waiting for me, down by the sea . . .*

Then a shape broke the water. A real one this time, Swan knew. A man's hand, pale and thick-fingered, reaching up from the depths.

Swan snapped back to himself. "Over here," he bellowed. It was no good. He could barely hear himself. He looked around, wildly. The cable had been cut to reach exactly to the bottom of the cliff, but since the water had risen so high, there were a dozen yards of slack bobbing in the water. Swan reeled it in and threw it, but the cable was too heavy and the waves pushed it right back, and Swan could only watch helplessly as the hand sank again.

But as he clung there, a second shape broke the water, heading straight for the first. A boy, surely not much older than a child, heartbreakingly small against the waves. Swan watched as this new boy dipped below the water, then resurfaced, holding the first man close. They bobbed there together, fighting for space. The first man was unconscious, or at least had stopped moving. The small boy was making a tremendous effort to pull him, but the waves were too rough. They wouldn't last long.

Swan reeled in the cable, tied it as tightly as he could across his chest. He took a deep breath.

And he leapt into the water.

The cold was shocking, brutal, and he fought for air as he kicked toward the arch. The child had seen him and braced a hand against it, keeping his companion above water. It took agonizing minutes for Swan to reach them and push the remaining cable into the boy's waiting hand. The pressure of the water was immense, suctioning Swan's leg painfully against the stone, and he could only hope the boy was behind him as he turned and followed the cable back to the ladder. When he reached it and hauled himself up he turned to see the child still there, the end of the rope tied around his chest, the man sagging in his arms, and Swan was suddenly light-headed. This was going to work.

Swan wrapped both hands around the ladder and pulled himself to his feet. One rung. Then another. Another. Another. One hand at a time.

A wave came down.

Swan's chin slammed against the rung and he tasted blood, saw stars. Reeling, he clung to the ladder, hoisting himself three more rungs until he was free of the water and could safely turn. The next wave swept the two sailors into the rock, and Swan watched in horror as the child's head cracked against the cliff. The boy went limp, the cable still tied around his chest. And free from his grip, the man vanished into the churning pool.

Swan felt a sob rise in his chest. "Nico!" The child bobbed up on a wave, his body waterlogged and prone. Swan pulled the cable as hard as he could but there was too much slack swirling through the water. The child's face dipped below the surface. *Waiting for me, down by the sea.*

Swan untied the cable from his chest and looped it over the ladder, clinging so hard to its metal that he could see the bones of his fingers.

With his other hand he pulled to make the loop larger, over and over until he felt a body hit his back. The child was still motionless, his eyelids purple, his wide lips bloodless. Unconscious? Dead? Swan didn't know. He barely knew the same about himself. He looped the cable over his shoulders, lashing the boy to his back.

And slowly, slowly, Swan began to climb.

Once they were away from the waves the journey was featureless, all black air and stone, giving no sense of how far was left. If it weren't for his arms screaming in pain every time he clenched a new rung, Swan would swear they weren't moving at all. On they went, one hand after the other, until finally, astonishingly, his hand went up and found only air.

A last surge of strength propelled him over the edge, where he lay gasping on the rocks, on his side, staring bleary-eyed at the beam of light still shining into the rain. Francis Norman's voice came back to him in the wind. *What would a lighthouse have done to help? Given them something pretty to watch on their way down?* It really was something, he thought. Glass and fire could do so much and so very, very little.

And then there were hands on him, someone yelling his name. A moment of weightlessness, the light of his home, a bed. "Thank God, thank God, you foolish man." Peter. Behind him the town doctor, Amos Wright, bending over a motionless lump on the kitchen table.

"Cliff," Swan said thickly. "Ship."

"We're there, Silvy," Peter said. "*Sea Split* is on her way out, more behind her. It'll be rough work, but they'll do what they can. Thanks to you."

But to Swan the world was swimming now, dark and gray and white. Something cold and wet moved along his forehead, and he turned with great effort to receive a mouthful of Stay's fur, soaked and freezing. The dog laid his paws on Swan's chest, a growl rumbling as he bared his teeth at Peter. "You did it," Swan said, his tongue too soft under the words. "Good dog."

And then everything went black.

Mari, 2014

Mari emerged from the library feeling like she'd lived decades. She was almost shocked that it was still daylight, that modern cars still trundled through the streets, that the sun was still so soft on the water.

The printer in the Norman Cliffs Library had needed a new cartridge and a stern talking-to from Daniel the librarian before it agreed to work, but now Mari had a blown-up version of the photo from Charlie Quentin's collection. It was clear enough that she could gauge Swan Light's dimensions, based on the people and trees in front of it. She guessed the lighthouse had been about twenty-five feet tall, which was taller than it needed to be for already being elevated on a cliff. That placed it more probably in the camp of having splintered as it fell, leaving behind pieces that might have been too light to sink into the sand. Its lens, though, would have been heavy, what looked like six dense feet of iron and glass. She'd learned all she could without diving. Now it was time to see the cliff for herself.

She was so preoccupied as she grabbed Jo's bike from where it leaned against the wall outside—when she'd asked for a chain and lock, Jo had looked at her as if she had three heads—that she physically jumped at the brassy chirp of her phone ringing. **Evangeline Devon**, the screen said. "Evangeline, hi."

"Good morning," her sponsor said. "I don't want to be one of those investors who constantly checks your progress, but I did want to let you know that Captain Henry is all set and ready to start tomorrow. I told him to meet you at the inn later."

"Great." Mari pulled her phone away from her ear to check the time. "I'm at the library now. I'm going to try and make it over to the cliff. But I'll be back soon."

"Perfect," Evangeline said. "Well, then, I'll let you get back to it."

"Thanks, Evangeline."

"Excuse me," came a voice behind her as she hung up, and she turned to see the man with the metal detector from the harbor, the one who'd offered her a net.

"Hi," she said, surprised.

"Hi." He smiled sheepishly back. He was young, probably in his midtwenties, curly blond hair puffing out from below a baseball cap. He had a faded scar over one eyebrow and a gold ring in the other, and those, combined with the design on his hat—a human-faced squid wrapping two tentacles around a sailing ship—gave him the look of a very fresh-faced pirate. "I'm sorry, I didn't mean to eavesdrop, but I couldn't help overhearing. You need a boat to take you to the cliffs? I'd be happy to take you."

Mari was immediately wary. People had been outrageously friendly here, yes, but this man didn't seem like a local. His jacket was too expensive, his detector too shiny. "I don't need a boat," she said. "I was talking about the top of the cliffs, not the water."

"Oh. Sorry." He paused for a moment, then hefted the detector. "Can I ask what you're looking for? I won't pretend to be on your level, but I do have a professional curiosity and, again, I do have a boat."

"What makes you think I'm looking for something?"

"Your bag. I noticed it while you were in the water earlier." Mari glanced down at the Scripps Institution of Oceanography logo looking back at her. "If you're here on a project I'd love to hear a little about it."

The man's face was open and eager, and he seemed harmless enough. He was probably just a rich kid with too much time on his hands. But

Mari was still cautious, twenty years of competitive diving in the back of her brain. If she were to find something while using his boat, or even tip him off that there was something to find at all, she had no idea what he'd do. And if he heard that Evangeline had so much money to spare on the search, there could be a legal battle before she knew it. Her fingers were itching to dive, but there was only one more day to wait for Julian. Better safe than sorry.

"I actually shouldn't talk about it," she said with a smile she hoped looked commiserating. "It's not a wreck dive or anything. Just some research before heading back to a different project." That, at least, was true.

The man's face fell, but he nodded. "Fair enough. If you change your mind, I'm usually down near the harbor. My name's Sam Beauregard. Feel free to stop by any time."

"I'll do that," Mari said, with no intention of doing that. "Nice meeting you."

"You too," Sam Beauregard said. "Good luck with whatever you're looking for."

〜〜〜

There was no road to the cliff. Mari pedaled over rocky soil and past wind-battered spruce trees until the ground jumped into a hill and the greenery was replaced with prickly yellow grass. It grew taller and denser as she climbed higher, giving way to straggly gray woods as the hill evened out into a plateau.

And then she burst out of the wilderness to a view off the edge of the world.

Mari gasped and braked hard, letting the bike tip to its side, and walked the last few feet to the edge of the cliff. She'd seen every ocean from dozens of angles, from ships and from land, from their edges and their centers and their depths. But she'd never seen anything like this.

Newfoundland soared out around her like something alive, a vast bird thrumming with energy, the shore its wings and the water its endless crackling core. A warm breeze fluttered along her skin, bringing with it the smell of wet soil and salt water. To her right Norman Cliffs sat in a postcard-perfect curve around the harbor, its moored boats scattered out to sea. The waves hitting the harbor bar mirrored its curl, like two cupped hands holding the bay between them. Beyond the bar drifted an iceberg, blindingly white against the gray sky.

She stared out at the sea for so long that she nearly forgot why she was there, lost in the view until gathering storm clouds reminded her that her time might be limited. Then she finally looked down. "That is a *long* fall," she said to no one, kneeling carefully at the edge. Waves lapped against the base of the cliff, turning the rock black where the water fell away. Even from here the water was silty, impenetrable, and it made an orange buoy that had come loose and was bobbing along the rock look even brighter by comparison.

Mari sat back on her heels, studying the rock between her shoes and the sea. Based on the rates of erosion she usually saw in her work with Scripps, she estimated the cliff's face could have lost up to fifty feet in the last century, which meant that if it had indeed fallen, and had indeed survived, Swan Light could be fifty feet from its base now.

Mari swiped open her camera and took photos of the rock face and the water, walking slowly along the edge. When she reached a point where the ground dipped low enough to be dangerous, she turned. And it was then, on her way back, that she saw it.

There was a house in the woods.

It was almost fully hidden by the overgrowth, the amount of green within its walls giving it a strangely two-dimensional look, as if someone had hand-drawn it over the trees. Mari approached it cautiously, climbing around a particularly large bush that had smashed through one of its windows, and found a door facing away from the cliff, the frame tilted forward, the wall above it splintered and sagging where the gray-shingled roof had caved in. What looked like a porch off to one side had collapsed completely, taking the left wall with it, bushes snaking up over its piles of broken wood. Mari stepped inside. What was left of the walls was streaked with mold and moss, the ceiling chittering with bugs, a bird's nest tucked into the eaves where the fourth wall had been. The wooden floorboards were uneven, warped by roots and rainwater, stripped away in a patch at the end closer to the sea to expose the dirt, which had somehow given birth to an explosion of pink flowers. A brick oven sat beside them, and a gray stone icebox. In the center of the room was a thick wooden table missing a leg, leaning down on its corner, a backless wooden chair lying beside it. Beyond a smaller opening to her right there was a pile of timber and a scrap of orange cloth.

And Mari knew what it was. What it had to be.

A keeper's house.

She hadn't even thought about them, all the lighthouse keepers Swan Light must have seen. She'd thought this project would be different from her other wrecks, but lighthouses had captains too, and suddenly it wasn't just a piece of stone anymore. If the light had stood sixty years it likely would have had several different keepers, and Mari wondered how many of them had known what was coming. The lighthouse would have already been decommissioned by the time it fell, but its last keeper must have known. How it must have felt, watching the end getting closer, being powerless to stop it. Had that keeper returned to some faraway home, or had they stayed in Norman Cliffs? Had they been forced to watch years of dedication go plunging into the sea?

Mari could have stayed there thinking about it forever. But it was getting late, and Julian Henry was probably already waiting for her at Mettle House. She took a green flag from her pack and went back to the cliff's edge, then hammered it into the rocky overhang, level with the house, as a point of reference for tomorrow. The fog below was thickening, soupy and featureless. The buoy she'd noticed earlier had reached the cliffs, its orange glow the only thing cutting through the mist, and she watched it, soaking up her last minutes for now looking over this strange new sea. It trundled along the rocks, bowing to the current as it rolled and dipped and bobbed—and disappeared.

Mari frowned. She knelt and inched closer, stupidly close, and peered along the rest of the shore. If it hadn't been such a bright orange, she would have missed it. The buoy seemed to have sunk right into the rock, and as she peered closer she saw something else she'd missed: just past the cliff there was a break in the rock so narrow it was like an optical illusion. And through it was a cove.

Mari grabbed her bag and followed the edge through a patch of trees, their roots hanging exposed and sinuous over the edge, and over a swath of rocky black ground. And then she was staring down into the guts of the cliff. It was like looking into a well, a deep pool of gray water at the bottom, the buoy now bobbing calmly at its edge. The fog hadn't fully crept in here, the cove protected by the wall of rock surrounding it, and she could see a thin strip of sand ringing the pool. And leading down to it . . . was that a ladder?

It was, though it was possibly in worse shape than the house. Individual metal rods protruded down the cliffside in groups of two; she could tell that there had once been rungs between them, but most of those had deteriorated away, leaving behind only these fist-sized metal corners. It didn't look particularly safe. But a closer inspection revealed that the corners had been driven deep enough into the cliff that they were still sturdy, and that there were plenty of natural toeholds in the rock. And this cove was so close to where Swan Light had been that it would be stupid not to check it out. Mari slung her bag over her shoulder and started climbing.

The metal rods were stronger than they looked, the rock that held them sheltered by the sea-facing wall across from it, but it still took almost half an hour to reach the sand. She brushed off her hands and looked around. The far wall didn't open to the sea until close to the bottom, in a natural archway now thirty feet above her head, which was what had made it so hard to see from above. That wall protruded farther into the sea, catching the current as it flowed past, which explained how the buoy had ended up here. And it wasn't just the buoy. She was standing at the center of an I Spy book.

The sand and shallow water were littered with wood and netting, and more interesting things too: a ceramic horse and an ornate lampshade and a blue window frame and what looked like the rusting slab of an outboard motor. This last one was half submerged in the sand at the edge of the pool. With some heaving and the use of one dive flipper from her bag as a wedge it came free, and Mari tugged it back to the sand. It was in very good shape, and the scientist in her wanted to examine it. But it was too heavy to pull back up the ladder and she had no idea what high tide looked like here. Anywhere she stashed it could leave it in danger of being swept back out or buried.

So she called Mettle House. "I found something cool," she said when Jo answered.

"Ooh," Jo said. "About the lighthouse? Where are you?"

"Not about the lighthouse," Mari said. "It's an old motor. I'm in a cove near the cliff, but I can't carry it back up. Any chance there's a Julian Henry there waiting for me?"

"There is, actually. He's eating soup. Should I send him out?" Before Mari could answer, Jo shouted into her ear: "You there! Do you have time to stage a rescue?"

"It's not a *rescue*," Mari said.

"We get no excitement around here. Let me have this. He's on his way."

It was almost too dark to see by the time an inflatable Zodiac boat slid into view at the mouth of the cove, Julian Henry behind the wheel. "Hello again," he called, easing the boat onto the strip of sand and sticking a leg overboard to anchor it in place. "Finding more things to climb, I see."

"Very funny," Mari said. Together they hoisted the motor into the Zodiac, and she climbed in after it, making a mental note to return for Jo's bike, still at the top of the cliff, in the morning. "I'm hoping this isn't the ship you've needed all this time to get ready."

"Very funny." Julian gunned the engine to take them against the current and out of the cove. "No, *Shanty's* in the harbor, loaded up and ready to go. My friend Otis is going to be our dive supervisor."

"Great," Mari said, swiveling as they sped away from the dark cliffs. From down here they were massive, a towering wall of earth, and even though they were still just rock and dirt it seemed different now. She couldn't keep her eyes off the tallest. It was otherworldly in the dusky glow, its top gray and shadowed, nothing but faint stars behind it, and Mari again pictured Swan Light standing there shining bright. The tower that was instead somewhere below her shoes. Something had changed, and now it was all inside her. Something about Swan Light had burrowed under her skin.

"So what are you getting?" Julian Henry asked, interrupting her thoughts.

"Excuse me?"

"Evangeline," he said. "I'm assuming if you had to come to Bergy Bits for clothes, you didn't have much time to pack either."

Mari studied him in the waning light. He wasn't like the divers she was used to working with, she could tell that already. He seemed relaxed on top of the water, for one, not itching like she was to get underneath it: one wrist was draped sure and lazy over the wheel, his sleeves pushed to the elbow to show muscular sun-ruddy skin. He was on her team. Unlike Sam Beauregard with his metal detector. But it still might not be a good idea to talk about a dollar amount. "She's funding another round of the project I was on before this," she said carefully.

Julian's dark eyes didn't leave the water. "Did she say why she picked you?"

"Not really," Mari said. "She said she's been following me because of *Californian*—my other project—and that she wanted someone who was going to look for the whole story."

"*Californian*?" Julian asked. "As in *Titanic Californian*?"

"Yeah." She shrugged. "I told her she should use a local crew, but she wasn't interested. What about you? You've worked with her before?"

"I have," Julian said. "Three times now." He glanced over at her. "This isn't going to be one of those things where you turn out to be her long-lost granddaughter or something, is it?"

Mari laughed despite herself. "My grandmothers were Delilah and Ami, both from Texas. I think we're good."

"If you say so."

As they entered Highs Harbor and the sun finally vanished behind them, the streetlamps that lined the wharf flickered to life. They danced there, orange and merry, soft smudges of light in the gloom. Julian brought the Zodiac up to the dock and hefted Mari's motor onto his shoulder. "Okay," he said, grinning wryly. "Let's hope the rest of it is this easy too."

Swan, 1913

Waves slid lithe and lavender over Silvy's bare feet, their cold a shock he didn't mind. The cove was soaked in dusk light, the foam of the bar glowing in the dying sun. A final resting place, Silvy thought. A menace and a comfort, an unchanging line in the sea. And above him, something new. A great white beam swinging across the sky, steady and sure. Measured and strong. Completely in his care. Silvy felt wild with the pressure of it, untethered by all he still had to learn. He dug his toes deeper into the water, letting its weight hold him to the earth.

"Hello, you." Silvy turned to see Grace hop down the last few rungs of the ladder, grease staining the bottom of her hair. She puffed it out of her face and crossed the sand to wrap warm arms around his waist. "Did you know that soot gets truly *everywhere* when you try to fan it away from you? We're going to need more towels."

Silvy laughed and pulled her closer. "'We?'" he echoed. "You said this was just a weekend trip."

"It is," Grace said. "But there's a funny thing about weekends. There are more than one of them." She pressed her cheek to his shoulder. He smelled sunlight and ship rope. More than one thing holding him to the earth. "You're not getting rid of me that easily, Silvy Swan," she whispered.

Silvestre Swan opened his eyes.

Daylight was splashed across the walls, so bright that he simply stared at it for a moment, transfixed and confused, Grace's voice still soft below his ear.

Until the night before came back to him.

The wreck.

The cove.

The boy.

And then: the tower. Its beam hanging frozen, its terrible, wrenching moans.

Swan propped himself upright, gasping with the effort, and forced himself to look toward the back window before he could change his mind. But his clanging heart eased when he saw the midday sun glowing on the white stone. The lighthouse rumbled in greeting, strained but clear. *One piece,* Swan thought. *We're all in one piece.*

As memories of the night returned to him, pain did too. His bottom lip was swollen where it had hit the ladder, the taste of blood still thick in his mouth, and his body felt heavy and impossibly fragile. He brought a hand to his face, not sure where to start, and at the motion Stay's head appeared over the edge of the bed. They stared at each other for a moment, and then the dog leapt into his lap, howling.

"Easy," Swan laughed, collecting the dog's face and rubbing his ears. Stay flattened himself against Swan, licking and sniffing and pawing like a puppy.

"Easy!" Dr. Amos Wright echoed him, hustling into view from the kitchen, a pan of steaming water in his hands. He slid it under the blanket at the edge of Swan's bed, pulling another from below his feet. "Welcome back, Silvestre," the doctor said. "We were worried for a minute there, weren't we, Stay?" He swatted at the dog's tail, then picked up a mug from Grace's chair, which had been moved from the kitchen to his bedside, and pushed it into Swan's hands. "Finish this, please."

Swan gulped it down. It tasted like dirt. "The steamer?"

"Still down there," Wright said. "Well beyond saving. The lads got ten more crew off her; they say around twenty more were lost. She came from America—Massachusetts—fighting weather the whole way. It's a wonder they found us at all."

Swan closed his eyes. Twenty lost. *Something pretty to watch on the way down.* "And the boy from the cove?"

The doctor smiled slightly and stepped aside. "See for yourself. No boy, as it turns out, but doing well and asking the same things about you."

"I owe you my life, Mr. Swan," someone said, and Swan looked over Dr. Wright's shoulder as a figure emerged from the side room and limped toward them. It was a girl, small and wounded. Her head was heavily bandaged, her left eye purpled and swollen shut. But her good eye was set resolutely on Swan. "I'm Clara," his survivor said. "Clara Vettrey."

"Does this mean my sedatives are wearing off?" Wright asked her, his voice severe. To Swan he said: "I thought she was going to try to drag the steamer up here with her own hands this morning. She woke and immediately tried to run back down there."

Clara ignored him, still watching Swan. Up close she looked impossibly small, hardly more than a child. Her forearms were bare even in the cold, skin riddled with blood and burns and bruises. "I can't believe you did that."

"Did what?" Swan asked.

"Got me up here," she said. "By yourself, in the middle of a storm like that."

"That's my job," Swan said gruffly, avoiding her guilt-ridden eyes.

"No," Clara Vettrey said. "It's not. I've never seen waves like that. And it was so dark, and you're so *old*—no offense meant—and even if you *weren't*, that could have killed you, and I—"

"It's my job," repeated Swan, who in that moment had never felt older. The effort of talking to her now was much greater than the effort of carrying her up the cliff. He tried to remember the last time someone so young had been in his home.

"I'm just glad you were here," she said, and went mercifully silent.

"The whole town is," said a new voice, and Swan balked at the number of guests who were apparently in his home. It was Peter, stomping in from outside, his hands full of baskets. "You're a popular man today, Silvy. These are all thank-you gifts."

"It's a good thing I was here to see it," Swan said, still ornery. "Good thing I wasn't in town, getting a new latch for the oil shed."

Peter's face fell. "Ah, Silvy. I'm sorry. Don't be angry. I would have told you after, I was going to. It was for your own good. All Cort wanted was to look for the deed himself, and then he'd believe you. I hated seeing you so upset over it."

But Swan wasn't angry, he found, not really. His energy to be anything other than astonished to be alive had faded. Well, astonished, and eager to have his home to himself again. His energy was waning quickly. He threaded his fingers through Stay's fur.

"I hope some of those thank-you gifts are fruits and vegetables," Dr. Wright said. "You'll almost certainly have pneumonia, Silvestre. I don't like the sound of your lungs at all." Clara's face filled again with guilt, and Swan decided not to mention the tingling in his fingers and the way his heart kept leaping and crashing. Dr. Wright looked at Clara. "And you, you need to be lying down. You had no business working on that ship in the first place."

Clara narrowed her good eye. "What, because I'm a woman?"

"No, because you seem to be about ten years old."

"I'm seventeen," she said defensively. Then she collected herself, her eye flicking to the window. "Where is this, anyway?"

"Newfoundland," Wright said. "Norman Cliffs."

"Newfoundland!"

"Yes. Where were you bound?"

Clara seemed to wilt. "Halifax," she muttered, and Swan looked at Peter, shocked. Halifax was hours away, back in the direction her ship had come from. The storm must have been terrible for them to veer this far off course and keep sailing in the chaos. "Where is Norman Cliffs?"

"On the eastern shore," Swan said. "Below St. John's. You're lucky you curved in. You came just short of missing land completely."

But Clara was frowning. "The lighthouse below St. John's is Cape Spear."

Swan was surprised that she knew it. "It is. We're below that too."

"Below Cape Spear is Bay Bulls."

"Cape Spear, Norman Cliffs, Bay Bulls."

Clara shook her head. "I don't remember seeing a lighthouse between Cape Spear and Bay Bulls."

Swan and Peter exchanged a glance. This still happened sometimes, their little local-built harbor lighthouse missing from older or grander maps. Islanders knew what the light meant, that was all that mattered. "Take that up with our government," he said.

"Miss Vettrey, I really am going to have to insist that you sit down," Wright said. "You're bleeding through your bandage again."

"Won't I do that sitting down too?"

"Sit," Wright said firmly, and Clara reluctantly complied.

"Is everyone else okay? Will?" Swan asked Peter. Wright handed him another glass of dirt water, and Stay leaned forward to lap the bits that dripped from Swan's chin.

"All fine," Peter said. "Will's back piloting; we're expecting a few ships in off the Banks tonight. Lord knows what shape they'll be in."

"He'll have his hands full keeping an eye on the cove until then," Dr. Wright said. "If it hasn't been picked dry. It was already swarming when I came back this morning."

Peter chuckled. But Clara stood up again, frowning. "What do you mean, picked dry?"

Peter glanced at her, then away. "Nothing."

Clara turned her gaze on Swan. "You mean looters."

"Yes," Swan said. "It's the current. It pulls things onshore at the cove."

Clara stood frozen for a moment. Then she wrenched her chair backward and took off. The room sat in stupefied silence until there was a thump at the door and her bandaged head reappeared. "Which way is the cove?"

"Miss, your bandages," Wright protested.

"It's to the left," Swan said over him. "Down the black stone path."

"Swan," the doctor reprimanded.

Swan shrugged as Clara vanished again. "It's her ship."

"Well, if you're feeling well enough to send wreck survivors running off through the wilderness, my work here is done," Wright said. "I'm going back to town to see to the rest of them. Abigail Norman has offered to send them all home on *High Noon* next week."

"Of course she has," Swan said.

"I'll be back to check on you later," Wright said. He gave Stay a last pat and pointed to Swan's mug. "There's more on the fire. Keep drinking it. I'll know if you've dumped it."

And then he was out of the room, Peter behind him, casting one last anxious look at Swan before he went. The door closed and Swan let the blessed silence ring in his ears, his chest tight, his head pounding. "All right?" he asked, and the tower across the yard keened. "I know," he said. "Rest now." He wondered vaguely who had put its light out while he was unconscious. He realized he was once again behind on his logbook. The tower chirped again. *You rest now too.*

Swan obediently closed his eyes. And there in his own heaviness, he finally thought about Nico.

Because it had been his brother in the arch of the cove last night, he was sure of it. Swan had lived in the wild long enough to know that he couldn't understand it. He'd seen lights with no source and heard voices from nowhere. He'd heard the stories growing up. The town had always talked of fairies in the woods. But last night was the first time he'd seen something he knew: Nico rising from the depths to shepherd the wreck about to join him. It was only in the stress of the wreck, he knew, the years blurring the losses together. But Nico had shown Clara Vettrey just where to go. And the look in his eyes, earnest but unyielding—Swan had almost forgotten that expression. Had his mind simply summoned it up? Or had something about it been real? Outside the tower chirped again, and Swan tried not to think about the next loss coming, the next thing joining Nico in Norman Cliffs Bay. Then he pictured Grace again, windblown and soot-streaked and smiling. *You're not getting rid of me that easily.* More than one thing, tethering him to the earth.

We're all in one piece, he reminded himself. And he drifted back to sleep.

Mari, 2014

The morning after finding the cove and the keeper's house, Mari woke to a text from Tim reading **HAPPY URSULA DAY!** She sent back a heart, then shook her head. It was the first dive day for Swan Light, and it wouldn't work if she was distracted. Her trip to the cove had shown her how many things could end up on the bottom of the bay. She needed to be fully focused to interpret them—and to see whether Swan Light was among them. She pulled on leggings, a sweatshirt, and sneakers, and crept down the stairs for a run, resolutely leaving her phone behind.

Outside, fog still sat heavy on the harbor, but the sky over town was crisp and clear. Mari jogged along Highs Street until she reached Isabel's Grocery, which wasn't open yet so she continued on, taking a long lap of town, past Evangeline's quiet house and Bergy Bits and the other rows of houses that were quickly becoming familiar. Somewhere a church bell tolled, six gongs long and deep. She continued her run down to the harbor and along the water, the cold air clearing her head and her lungs, looping back to the grocery just as it was opening. But the photos she'd noticed on its wall didn't seem to have anything to do with the sea. Instead they displayed town landmarks, with very few people in them at all. She spotted Captain Mettle House, a line of fishing stages, a white stone bank. No connection between Isabel Swan and the lighthouse, then, at least not here. She'd have to find something else.

By the time she retrieved Jo's bike from the clifftop and returned to Mettle House, the kitchen was bubbling with activity, a few families enjoying their breakfasts as Jo completely ignored them, entranced by the rusted motor now sitting between her, Julian Henry, and Theo van Gooren.

"I was only joking," the old sailor rumbled as Mari joined them, meeting Julian's amused eyes. "You really went and did it."

"Did what?" Mari asked.

"Found my motor from 1971," Theo said proudly. "Thought I lost it forever when that fairy tried to take my giant fish."

〜〜〜

Julian's ship, a sturdy blue-and-white 54-footer called *Shanty*, was berthed at the end of Highs Harbor. It sliced through the whorls of fog still dancing on the water as they made their way out to the cliff, the flag Mari had pinned still flapping at its top. There was only one other ship in sight, red-hulled and larger than theirs, cruising slowly much farther along the shore.

"All yours," Julian said after he cut their engine and threw down their anchor, and Mari nodded and pulled on her tank. They'd talked about this last night. Mari would do a recon dive first, to take stock of what was below the shallow surface in case any of it could endanger their equipment. Next would come the sonar, to paint a thorough picture of the seafloor, then the magnetometer to show them any spots of metal hiding below the sand. *Shanty's* lab was stocked and set for whatever they found. All of it filled Mari with joy. No matter the project, this was always her favorite part. The question mark, the edge of knowing, the Schrödinger's shipwreck of something that was only real if you proved it.

She kicked slowly toward the cliff, sweeping her light back and forth. The seafloor was murky but surprisingly smooth, and only one rock near the cove stuck up high enough to potentially be a problem. She attached a marker to it and followed its ballooning yellow flight to the surface. "All clear," she called, and Julian hefted their four-foot, torpedo-shaped sonar towfish in a salute.

They wouldn't be able to pull the towfish behind them with a cable the way Mari normally did; the water was too shallow, and they'd have so little slack that the piece of scanning equipment would end up dangling too close to the propellers. Instead Julian affixed the sonar to one end of a thick plastic rod that he dropped into the water, the other end mounted on the ship. They followed the coordinates Mari had set, mowing hundred-foot lines back and forth across the face of the cliff. Their first four tracks showed nothing unusual, the only abnormalities bits of fishing gear and obvious trash. As they wheeled around for their fifth track, Mari saw that the red-hulled ship had turned and was coming back toward them, moving at a crawl. She noticed the flag high on its mast, a pennant with three circles on it, one white bordered by two red. It was a combination more commonly seen in masthead lights, warning that a ship had equipment in the water. She nudged Julian and pointed at it. "They're towing something too."

"Bit dramatic," he said, eyeing the flag. "As long as they stay over there, they can do whatever they want."

It took Mari and Julian another hour to finish mowing. Most of the hits that showed up were easy to identify: a bicycle frame, a cut lobster trap, and boating remnants. The area near the cove was interesting, busy and mottled almost like a shipwreck's debris field, probably due to rocks falling from the cliff over the years. But two things stood out as soon as they hit the screen, pushing Mari and Julian upright in their seats. Twenty feet from the cliff, directly in front of Mari's flag, were two strong lines. They weren't long, but they were perfectly parallel, and darker in the middle. And a few dozen feet farther was a mangled half circle that looked at least seven feet long.

"The rest of it could be buried," Julian said, running his finger along the space where the parallel lines disappeared, and Mari nodded. If it was, it was an extraordinary stroke of luck that the sonar had picked up the lines at all. The constant storms here probably uncovered and covered things so quickly that any given scan could look completely different an hour later. She stared at the bright yellow hits, thinking. The two lines could easily be part of a stone tower. And the circle could easily be part of a railing. The stone wouldn't show up on the magnetometer, but the iron would. Her fingers itched to get started.

But by the time they finished with the sonar, the sky was turning dark behind them, thunder growling at the tops of the trees. Julian chewed on his lip. "Those clouds are coming in quick," he said. "Wind's already at twenty knots. It's not worth it."

They couldn't use the magnetometer from *Shanty*, not in water so shallow that their own metal hull would interfere with the reading. By the time they returned in the smaller, inflatable Zodiac, the water could be too dangerous. "Fine," Mari said. The red-hulled ship was trundling back too, its tow pennant gone, and she cursed inwardly that she'd missed seeing what they took out of the water. *New Providence*, her bow read. Mari craned to see her deck as she passed, and one figure leaning out over the port side toward them caught her eye: floppy blond hair under a green baseball cap. It was Sam Beauregard, the man with the metal detector. He raised a hand in greeting as they passed, though Mari couldn't tell whether he recognized her or was just being polite. "I met him yesterday," she said to Julian, surprised. "He seemed like an amateur with a metal detector. I didn't think he was actually looking for anything."

She checked her phone as they trundled back toward Norman Cliffs and saw two missed calls from Memorial University.

"Mari!" Keya said when she called back. "I hit a gold mine on your lighthouse. I looked into logs, like you asked, and there were a lot of references to it up until November 1913, mostly from local ships.

'Passed Swan Light in good weather at zero three hundred.' 'Light north of Norman Cliffs was lit in heavy fog.' Things like that. But then—on November twenty-fourth a ship called *Meridian* logged that they 'near hit a shoal coming around Norman Cliffs, no light at cliffs.' There are more like it later, day and night. 'No fixture.' 'Cliff light dark.' 'Lighthouse gone.' But November twenty-fourth was the very first one."

Mari sucked in a breath. "That's great, Keya."

"I know," Keya said. "And there's more. I found some great info on its namesake. You were right. It was Isabel Swan's son."

"No way."

"Way," Keya said. "Swan Light only had one keeper through its entire sixty years. I present to you one Silvestre Swan, born 1830, year of death unknown. He helped build Swan Light with stone from a local quarry and stayed on afterward. I emailed you a few articles from the time that mention him by name. I also sent his keeper's logs. The physical book is at Eastern Archives, in Mount Pearl, but they scanned most of it as part of a lighthouse summer-camp series a few years ago. It isn't terribly interesting, and it stops before the last ship log noting it, which is odd. But regardless, you have it."

"You're the best," Mari said, scribbling it down.

"Hold that thought," Keya said. "When I was talking to Eastern they also told me who donated them. A man named Gerald Cooper, who still lives in Norman Cliffs. I just sent you his address."

"*Now* you're the best," Mari said. She hung up, staring at NOV 1913 and 1830 circled in her own handwriting. Silvestre Swan had been a teenager when he'd helped build Swan Light, and over eighty when it fell. She'd been wrong. Swan Light's last keeper hadn't just seen years fall into the sea. He'd watched his entire life disappear below these waves. And this new information ruled out the lighthouse being decommissioned and dismantled, which would have taken longer than those few weeks in between its last sighting and the first notice of it being gone. If ships were still reporting its light up until November 1913, it had kept working until the day it fell.

"Anything good?" Julian asked, and she realized that he'd been waiting as she stared silently back at the cliff. She still wasn't used to working this closely with anyone on a dive. Even on *Mercury* the crew didn't necessarily care about *Californian*, just how their own skills applied to it, and she wasn't used to other people asking about her research. She handed Julian her notes and entered Gerald Cooper's address into her phone's search bar, where it showed up on a map under a dot labelled HORIZONS COMMUNITY. "It's a nursing home," she said. "If we're losing today anyway, we can head over and talk to him now."

"No, thanks," Julian said, and she looked up in surprise. He shrugged. "I'm getting paid to steer a boat and fly a towfish. Let me know anything you find about the lighthouse, but the story part is all you."

So much for working closely. Mari watched the salvager as he returned his focus to *Shanty*. She'd had so many dive partners on so many projects that she'd almost stopped paying attention to them as individuals. Most projects were so quick and focused that they rarely interacted about anything but the work, and the crews blurred together over the years, one project indistinguishable from the next, an endless line of faces behind masks and oxygen lines and computer screens. But there was something unusual about Julian. Last night at Mettle House he'd ignored the fishermen trying to pull him into a drink or out on the town, even as Mari herself had joined Theo for a beer, and several times already she'd been seized by an urge to act like a tourist in front of a British guard to wave and pull faces in front of him to see if he'd crack. She took diving seriously, took her projects seriously, but never at the risk of losing time or speed. She threw herself into the deep end; Julian plotted carefully before wading in to his knees.

She wasn't sure yet whether that was a good thing.

"Okay," she said. "But if the weather clears up, don't go back out there without me."

～～

Horizons Community felt less like a nursing home than some kind of retreat for former mariners. Mari followed the manager, Beth, along a gravel path through a series of cabins, each one's yard scattered with buoys and model lighthouses and little handcrafted boats. It was raining now, but not as hard as she'd expected. They probably could have stayed on the water. The weather was going to keep them on their toes, she could already tell. Still, Evangeline had been firm with her, if not with Julian: find Swan Light, and find out what happened to it.

"Here we are," Beth the manager said, rapping on a cottage door with *GERALD COOPER* written neatly beside it.

Gerald Cooper was a stooped man with fierce eyes but a kind smile who immediately invited Mari inside as he limped around preparing tea, swatting good-naturedly at Mari's hand when she tried to help. She thought about asking if he was related to Jo, but given what Jo had said and what Mari had read herself about the sizes of the families here, she guessed he would have no idea either.

"I haven't had the pleasure of meeting Evangeline Devon," Gerald said as they settled onto his couch. "What kind of project are you two doing?"

"I'm a marine archaeologist," Mari said. "Evangeline wants me to look into Swan Light."

At that, Gerald Cooper's friendly smile vanished. "Swan Light?"

"Yes," Mari said. "I heard that you donated Silvestre Swan's logbook, and I was hoping you could tell me where you got it."

But Gerald was squinting at her, his eyes cold. "Where did you say you were from?"

"I didn't," Mari said, thrown. "I work for Scripps Institution of Oceanography, in California, but I'm here separately for Evangeline."

"Do you have credentials?"

"Sure." Mari rummaged in her bag for a business card. "Mr. Cooper, is everything okay?"

Gerald peered at the card, his eyebrow furrowing and his eyes darting back and forth across it. After a moment his face relaxed marginally. "You're a diver?"

"Yes."

"And you're really only here about the lighthouse?"

"Yes."

The old man sat back, tucking the card into his front pocket. "I see. My apologies, dear. Diving is fine. I was just worried you were part of that Norman group."

"Norman group?"

Gerald nodded. "Some lawyers were coming around a few years ago, looking for people descended from the Norman family. Some estate tax redistribution thing. Something. A lot of big words. They were asking about that lighthouse too. I thought they might be back."

Mari frowned. It was the same story she'd heard from Theo van Gooren at Mettle House her first night. "What's wrong with asking about the Normans?"

"Nothing, if you do it politely. They weren't polite, they were in everyone's faces. They nearly broke Esther's walker accosting her on her way to lunch. One of them damn near broke my door down, and it took me taking pictures of him and threatening to send them to the police for him to leave."

"That sounds terrible," Mari said. "I promise I'm not with them."

"Okay." Gerald leaned forward, apologetic. "You can never be too careful, you know." These Norman lawyers must have scared him, she thought, for those words to be coming from a member of a community that she knew never locked its doors. "And I'm sorry, but I don't know much about the logbooks. They were in a box I cleared out of my sister Rose-Olive's house when she died."

"I'm sorry," Mari said.

"Thank you," Gerald said. "My grandma Sophie was close to the Swan family and bought their house when the mother died. It stayed in our family until Rosie died too."

"The mother—you mean Isabel Swan?" Mari asked.

"That's right," Gerald said. "I have no idea how long the logbooks had been in the attic when I found them. Grandma Sophie and her brother, Peter, tended to hoard things. They both left things up there over the years, and I know Rosie never touched it. It took forever to sort through. I gave most of it to Eastern."

"Do you remember hearing anything about Swan Light when you were a child?" Mari asked, even though her hopes weren't high. Gerald was old, but he didn't seem a hundred. The lighthouse had probably been gone by the time he was born.

But the old man leaned forward, childlike, his blue eyes shining with the anticipation of what he was about to say. "Yes," he said. "I have something I think you'll like." Mari thought he was trying to make up for questioning her earlier, but she still wasn't ready for what he said next. "I remember the stories," Gerald said. "My sister saw it fall."

Swan, 1913

The sky was midnight blue and clear, stars scattered across it like broken glass, the promise of winter sinking its teeth into every breeze. Far below, waves crashed white against the sagging metal hull of the American steamer. The entire cliff still smelled like coal fire. Yesterday it had rained, and the droplets pinging off the metal had made the cliff sing. Swan would have found both of those things beautiful if he hadn't known the source.

It had been three days since the shipwreck. The water below him was peppered with smaller ships from Norman Cliffs and St. John's and even farther, there to raid the wreck and the cove for anything they would give up. It was just as it had been in Swan's youth, before the tower, when wrecks on the bar were more common. This one, though, was more gruesome. There were twenty bodies down there somewhere. Swan didn't know if any had been recovered. He didn't care to, even though it should go in the log. Thinking about them made him think of *Hazel*. They'd never recovered any bodies from that wreck either.

Since the morning after the wreck Swan hadn't spoken a word to anyone other than Stay and the tower. He had a feeling that Peter was behind this lack of visitors, guilty about the oil shed, keeping Abigail and Cort away to give him time to rest. The calm of the cliff was a salve, but his heart was still skittering, its muscle contracting in galloping fits and slowing to tentative thuds so often he was already getting used to it. It was as if that night in the cove had shaken something loose inside him, something that was now rattling around with no need for rest. It had shaken something loose inside the lighthouse too, a new weakness in the walls that made them clatter in strong winds, as if the stone was thinner now, more brittle.

Swan was trying not to think about it.

He sat on the edge of the cliff with his legs dangling down, his eyes on the black hull, visible only when it reflected the light swinging past above it. He didn't know what he was looking for. For bodies? For looters? For his brother, still climbing around above it and whistling his favorite song? Nico was still clearer to Swan than anything else about that night. Clearer than pulling Clara Vettrey up a ladder, clearer than swimming all the way across the cove. Looking down now, he couldn't believe either of those things had been his doing.

He still didn't know the ship's name. He'd left a blank when he'd noted the crash in the log, reminding himself to ask Peter or Will about it. And now, looking down on the steamer in all her fierce and fragile luster, it made him sad, too aware of all the life lost below his feet, not just on this ship but on all of them. It had pulled him back here night after night, watching the glow on the metal until Stay woke and tugged at his sleeve to pull him away from the edge. Tonight, though, Stay was quiet, his watchful brown eyes on the light.

Much as he'd like to, Swan couldn't stay out here all night, and before long he knew that it was time to feed the oil and go to bed. He rose, knees cracking, and turned toward the tower. And as he did, he saw a shadow of movement in the beam of light. It happened once, then again. Someone moving in front of the flame.

Swan froze. *Nico?* was his first thought.

And then, *Cort.*

A ball of anger settled in his stomach. So this was why the Normans hadn't come after him again. They were, as usual, just waiting for the right moment.

He pushed open the tower door and climbed the stairs, his feet finding each step comfortably even in the utter darkness, and he'd made it to the clockwork room before he realized something strange. The last time Cort had been here, while Swan watched from the edge of the woods, the tower had moaned and rumbled in protest.

This time, it hadn't made a sound.

Swan braced his shoulder against the hatch in the ceiling and shoved it open, the wooden door slamming against the floor as he climbed torso-high into the lantern room. And Clara Vettrey leapt away from the lens as though it had scalded her.

For a moment they stared at each other, equally shocked. "I thought you'd gone in for the night," she said finally.

Swan climbed the rest of the way into the room and pulled the hatch closed. The walls hummed around them, pleased at the company. "No such thing," he said. "I have to check the oil every few hours. What are you doing here?"

"I walked back from town."

"Why?"

Clara didn't say anything. She had on a new bandage, thinner than the first but still stiff with dried blood. New bruises had risen along her collarbone and her unbandaged temple. He was still waiting for her answer when she turned to the lens and adeptly hoisted herself onto its iron base, peering down into the flame.

"Do you want me to do it?" she asked.

"Do what?" he asked, startled.

"Top off the oil." And without waiting for a response she had leapt down and back up again, the small oil jug from against the wall in her hand. Swan didn't have time to warn her about the angle and the flare and the fact that she only had use of one eye before she was tipping the jug into the oil reservoir with a light touch, just the way Swan would have done it. Better than he would have done, if he was being honest. "There," she said, satisfied, thumping back to the floor. "That's another few hours, at least." And as she replaced the jug she tilted the windowpane, letting in more air to balance out the rise in smoke, while Swan stared at her, dumbfounded.

She met his gaze and grinned, foxlike. "I know a fair bit about lighthouses," she said. "I grew up near one. My family is . . . does a lot of shipping, in Gloucester, Massachusetts."

"So you knew I was going to have to come back up here tonight," he said.

"Yes," she admitted.

"What were you planning on doing then?"

"Hiding on the landing, probably. I thought I was keeping a better eye on you. I am sorry for being here. I just . . . I had to—" Her good eye flicked toward the window. Toward the ship Swan realized she couldn't even see from here.

And with that, the wariness drained out of him. Clara Vettrey was a sailor without a ship. That was what that look was, her dark eye fixed on the sea: hunger and pain and pride, the same way Tomas and Nico had worn it. Far be it from him to stand in her way. "Come with me," he said gruffly, and led the way down the stairs.

Clara hovered on the edge of the cliff like a bird, tiny and unafraid, and Swan heard her breath catch when the beam swung past, illuminating her ship in its glow. "You can see it better during the day," he said.

"I know," she said, then glanced at him. "I've been coming up here every day since the wreck. During the mornings, while you were inside. I've been sleeping in the cove and climbing up from there."

"You—" Swan was, again, rendered speechless. The tower creaked apologetically behind him. "You said you walked back from town."

"I did," she said. "I walked back from town three days ago."

She'd been sleeping outside, in Newfoundland, in the middle of October. "It's a miracle you didn't freeze to death."

"It's more sheltered than I thought," she said brightly. "There's almost no wind down there. Anyway, I don't mind the cold, and I had this." She hoisted something Swan hadn't realized she was wearing, some kind of thick fur coat. "Sophie Cooper gave it to me. She says hello." And Swan could do nothing but gape.

"But now you're stowing away in my lantern room instead?" he asked finally.

She looked up, her young face going serious. "You were the only one who told me the truth about the cove," she said. "About the looters. The others wouldn't have said anything."

"Because you were bleeding," Swan said. "You still are, by the way."

Clara absentmindedly pressed a hand to the red of her bandage. "I'm fine." She looked back down at the ship. "I wasn't supposed to be there," she said softly. "Captain Forsythe knew it. I snuck on in Gloucester; he should have thrown me off. But he didn't." And Swan remembered the first man from the cove in the storm, the one Clara had tried to pull to the ladder, the one who'd sunk away from them. She'd found the cove because she was trying to save someone else. Or maybe the cove had found her. "Can I stay in the lighthouse tonight?" Her voice was a whisper.

Nico. Grace. The twenty bodies still somewhere below him. Swan couldn't be responsible for another life out here, not anymore.

But maybe just for one night.

"You can stay," he said. "Only until morning." Clara beamed at him, and he pointed toward the steamer to distract her from doing anything like hugging him. "What was her name?" he asked. "I never saw." *For the log*, he wanted to say. But he could see in this girl's face that she didn't need a reason, that the asking was enough.

"The strongest ship I've ever seen," Clara said. "Until the very end. She was called the SS *Saint Gray*."

～～

Clara slept in the lantern room. And when dawn broke and Swan rose to put out the light, he found it already extinguished, with the girl nowhere to be found.

There was no sign of Stay, either, and as Swan climbed the stairs he felt a twinge of alarm that he might have welcomed a stranger into his home who had sabotaged his tower and stolen his dog. Then he heard barking and laughing from outside, and he stepped onto the tower landing to see Clara walking back from the direction of the cove, Stay trotting at her heels. She knelt down and grabbed his face, saying something that caused his tail to wag frantically. Traitor, Swan thought.

"Good morning," she sang out as the two of them clumped up the tower stairs to join Swan in the lantern room. "I brought you a gift. Pick a hand." She bounced her shoulders, both hands behind her back.

Swan glanced toward the cove. "You brought me a gift from your shipwreck?"

"Yes. Pick a hand."

Swan stared blankly, but Clara was clearly not going anywhere. "Left," he said finally.

Clara pulled out a hand-sized pane of bull's-eyed glass. "From one of *Saint Gray*'s lanterns," she said. "It matches yours."

Swan held the glass chip up next to the tower lens. They did look similar. "What was in your other hand?"

She pulled out a piece of sturdy driftwood, thin and perfectly straight. "That was more for the dog than for you," she admitted, grinning and passing it to Stay. Then she sobered. "I do truly want to thank you, Mr. Swan. For saving my life, and for letting me stay here."

"It's all my job," Swan said, yet again. "You deserve a chance to say goodbye to your ship and your shipmates before you go home."

She frowned. "Home?"

He'd forgotten she'd only been in town long enough to pick up a coat. "Abigail Norman is sending a ship to Gloucester to return your crew," he said. "You'll want to get back there soon, before they leave."

"Oh," Clara said. "That's very kind, but I'm not going back to Gloucester." *Well, you're not staying here either,* Swan wanted to say. One night was one thing. He didn't need another stray. But she changed the subject before he could say anything, leaning far over the railing to look down at the cove. "How long after wrecks do things keep washing up down there?"

113

"Weeks," Swan said. "Sometimes years."

Clara's face clouded. "Do you think I could scare off the looters if I threw rocks at them from here?"

Swan laughed. "No, I don't think so. Did it scare them to find you sleeping there?"

"Not really," she said. She leaned back, her good eye still on the water. "I hate the thought of people taking her apart."

"There's nothing you can do about that," Swan said. "If they don't, the sea will."

"I know. Still."

"They don't mean anything by it," he said. "They're just townspeople looking for something to salvage. I was down there all the time as a child."

"How old are you now, anyway?"

"I'm eighty-three."

She smiled. "My friend back home was an assistant lighthouse keeper; she was eighty. She always said lighthouses exist because people are so afraid of the sea that they forget to be afraid of the shore."

"Your friend sounds wise."

Clara nodded silently. Then she abruptly raised her hands to her head and started unwrapping her bandage. Swan had to assume it was against Dr. Wright's orders, but he said nothing as the pile of pink-stained cloth in her hands grew until her head was bare. The gash was wide and yellow-rimmed but healing, and Swan winced as he remembered the wave that had caused it, the one that had slammed both of them into the ladder. His own lip was still tender from where it had smashed into the metal. It was no soft place, this home of his. But he could see that it was softer than wherever this girl had come from.

"That's better," Clara said quietly. And together they looked out over the sea.

Mari, 2014

My sister saw it fall.

Gerald Cooper's words hung fat and almost tangible in his coral-orange room. Mari sat holding her breath, scarcely able to believe her luck.

But it was too good to be true.

Because that line, as it turned out, was all Gerald Cooper had.

It was a story his sister Rose-Olive had told over and over growing up, to her brother and her parents and anyone who would listen, a story that had burrowed into Gerald's memory the same way their own stories had for Bill Baxter and Theo van Gooren. How Rose-Olive had woken in the middle of the night to a monster sweeping across the night sky, a great winged thing that had gone straight for Swan Light and knocked it into the water. Gerald seemed to have no questions about the accuracy of the story, and Mari tried and failed to imagine reporting back to Evangeline that the lighthouse had fallen because of an aggressive night dragon. Even if Rose-Olive had still been alive, Mari wasn't convinced the story would sound any different. It was a five-year-old's memory of a hundred-year-old event. *Dragon topples tower* might be as close as that would ever get.

Not for the first time, Mari wondered how she was supposed to know when she'd found the full story Evangeline was looking for. She could find all the facts and fables she wanted, the years and the names and the logbooks, but who got to decide where the story ended? Would Evangeline be happy with Gerald's memories along with whatever they pulled from the water? Or did she know that there was more to find? And if she did, why wouldn't she tell Mari exactly what it was? Maybe Evangeline was telling the truth: that she didn't know the story and simply wanted to find it. Maybe she didn't know what was out there any more than Mari did. But her nagging need for science, for logic, told Mari that there must be more to it than that.

And something else was nagging at her as she left Horizons Community, pedaling through rain that turned to a downpour just as she reached Mettle House. She left Jo's bike under the shelter of the front porch and climbed the stairs to her room, where Beddy the cat was curled comfortably on her pillow. Mari cracked the window and sat cross-legged on the bed, her phone and notebook in front of her.

Gerald Cooper was the second person to bring up a group asking questions about Swan Light while looking into the Norman family. Theo van Gooren had said that this Norman group would have found the lighthouse if there were anything to find. But what exactly had they been looking for? Why did they think the lighthouse was connected to the Normans? And why would it matter if it was?

Mari opened Memorial's library portal on her phone and searched again for the history of Norman Cliffs. This time, instead of looking for the lighthouse, she traced the Norman family through the years. The only match she could find near the time of Swan Light's disappearance was a Cortney Roland, a local banker who'd taken over Norman Bank from his grandmother Abigail Norman. She found several mentions of Cortney: in a newspaper article about trade vessel funding in St. John's, in another article about the bank expanding into the United States, and in a series of letters between him and a merchant named Nathaniel Vettrey. The bank was still operating in the US, which was interesting, but none of the rest seemed helpful. Just like the lighthouse, the Norman family was now a ghost. It wasn't surprising, she thought, the things that no one thought to write down. Especially there at the edge of electricity and radio, of technology that would unite the world, and on the brink of a war that would divide it. There were so many ways so many things could have slipped through the cracks.

Mari emailed the names and her thoughts to Keya and let her phone go dark, looking out over the storm-hazy sea. The waves were ferocious, grabbing at the shore like hands trying to crawl in from the deep, and even from here she could see them breaking against the harbor bar, sending plumes of white into the sky. She thought back to the keeper's house, its caving roof and crumbling walls exposing it to this over and over for decades. It was a wonder that there was anything standing at all.

Then her phone lit again with an incoming call. The screen read **Maybe: Horizons Community.** She frowned and opened it. "Hello?"

"This is Beth, from Horizons," a voice said. There was another voice yelling nearby. "I'm sorry to call you like this, but Mr. Cooper is having an issue. A man was just here. Gerald says he's one of those Norman—who? Gerald, you have to—sorry, hold on, here."

"Dr. Adams," Gerald Cooper's voice boomed in her ear, and she pulled the phone away. It woke Beddy, who rolled over with a startled yowl. "You brought those Norman men back."

Mari moved to scratch the cat behind the ears. "I did what?"

"The Norman group," he bellowed. "The ones I told you about, coming around asking questions. They're here again."

"A man came in right after you left," Beth said, having wrested the phone back. "He was asking who you'd spoken to and what you talked about. I assumed he was a colleague of yours, so I brought him to Gerald."

Could it have been Julian changing his mind? Why wouldn't he have just called her? "Did you get his name?"

"He said his name was Sam," Beth said. "He was fairly young, with blond hair. But Gerald started yelling at him and he took off."

Mari lifted her hand from Beddy. That sounded like Sam Beauregard again. Seeing him on the water could have been a coincidence, but now he was following her, asking about her? "Can you put Gerald back on?"

"Doctor!" Gerald boomed. Beddy sniffed at the speaker.

"Gerald, that man wasn't with me," Mari said. "But I think he might be following me. You're sure he's the same person who was bothering you last time?"

"No, he's not," Gerald said. "I've never seen him before. But he's with them, that same group."

"How do you know?"

"His hat," Gerald said. "I looked back at my pictures from last time to make sure, the ones for the police. Never sat right with me, that squid with the human face."

~~~

"Do you think he's dangerous?" Evangeline asked, her hands shaking slightly as she poured Mari a cup of tea.

The old woman looked somber, and Mari immediately felt bad. She hadn't wanted to scare Evangeline. All she'd wanted was to see whether her sponsor had spoken to these people or knew who they were, and now Evangeline was worried about Mari and the Swan Light project.

"I don't think he's dangerous," Mari assured her, swirling her tea. "My guess is, since he saw me on the water after I said I wasn't here to dive, now he thinks we're after the same thing and he's getting territorial. I'm sure I can clear it up if I run into him again."

"I would be surprised if he was also looking for the lighthouse," Evangeline said. "There's no money in it. And as you're learning yourself, most of the town doesn't even remember it."

"I thought the same thing," Mari said. "I'm not sure what he's looking for. But Gerald Cooper recognized the symbol on his hat from a group of people who were here years ago asking about the Norman family who founded the town."

Evangeline frowned. "The Norman family? Do you know why?"

"No idea," Mari said. "I'll ask him that when I see him too."

Evangeline nodded and looked away, down toward the harbor. The reflection of the sunset caught in her lined face, and for the first time she actually looked her age, the light leaving deep shadows in each of her lines.

"What made you want to move to Norman Cliffs?" Mari asked impulsively.

Evangeline looked away from the window and the impression was gone, her face back to its normal youthful animation. "I was here once when I was very young," she said. "I don't remember it, but my mother kept the pictures on our fireplace. I loved it. I've always loved the water."

"There's water in Florida," Mari said. "Most people migrate the other way around."

"They certainly do," Evangeline said. "I think my street becoming retiree central is part of what made me leave." They grinned at each other, and then Evangeline shook her head. "The water is different here. There's just something about it."

"I get that." Almost without meaning to, Mari looked back toward the cliff. The other cliffs lost their shape early to the fog gathering below them, but the largest still stood in stark contrast to the sky, towering alone. It made the cliff look lonely in a way it hadn't during better weather, as if instead of guarding the town it was being left behind by it.

"What did Captain Henry think about this Norman fellow?" Evangeline asked.

"He wasn't there," Mari said. "I don't think interviews are his wheelhouse."

Evangeline chuckled. "Go easy on him," she said. "I was a little surprised he took this job at all, considering my dives haven't been kind to him."

"What do you mean?"

"Because of his ex-wife," Evangeline said. "He met Vanessa on the very first dive I hired him for." Surprise must have shown on Mari's face, because her sponsor frowned. "He hasn't said anything about that?"

"No," Mari said. "I didn't know he'd been married."

"It's probably not my place to tell you," Evangeline said. "I just thought he would have mentioned her. Maybe that means he's moving on."

"What do you mean, your dives weren't kind to him?"

"Well, they were engaged three months after that first dive, and by their second project with me they were no longer speaking." She shook her head. "I had no idea when I contracted that second project, or I wouldn't have forced them to work together. They were both very professional about it, of course, but I felt for them. I worried when I reached out about this job that it would have left a bad taste in his mouth. I'm glad it didn't."

Mari thought back to Julian refusing a drink with Theo that first night, his insistence on doing what was asked of him for Swan Light and nothing more. Was this where that rigid professionalism had come from? Overcorrecting for a past dive with too many lines crossed? "Me too," she said aloud, then cursed the way it sounded. "What about you, Evangeline? Were you ever married?"

"No," Evangeline said, cheerful. "The idea of settling down never appealed to me at all, I'm sorry to say." She looked as if she was about to say something else, then closed her mouth and gazed thoughtfully out the window. Again Mari was filled with the urge to press her for information, to ask for the real story of what Evangeline knew and what she wanted to find. But something about the old woman's fragile sincerity made it impossible every time. So Mari just followed her gaze toward the water.

~~~

When she left Evangeline's the streets were dark and slick with rain, but the air was clear and surprisingly warm, and when Mari reached the split in the road that led back to Mettle House she turned the bike toward the cliff instead. She had more emails from Keya to read. And something told her they'd have a bigger impact if she read them in the place they were about.

She sat on the ground just beyond the keeper's house, heedless of the mud. It must have been a lonely life up here, she thought. The cliffs were close to town, but here it felt much farther. Here, the miles might as well have been oceans. And it would have been worse with the bright light of a lighthouse, outshining the glow of the town. A person's eyes would never really adjust. And as she finished reading through Keya's articles the feeling got worse. Because Silvestre Swan had helped build the lighthouse after he'd lost his brother, Nicolas, in a shipwreck on the very shoal that sat below her now. And then Swan's wife, Grace, had died at seventy-five. Mari's heart ached at the loneliness that must have bookended his time here, even before the lighthouse fell.

She opened Keya's next email, titled simply Logbooks. The pictures looked older than their hundred years, brittle beige paper under dusk-blue charcoal. Mari started to read, each entry quick and factual, bare of much personal information.

JUNE 11, 1873

KEEPER ASSISTED IN GUIDING ASHORE A STEAMER FROM ST. JOHN'S AFTER IT RAN AGROUND AFTER DEPARTING. MADE REPAIRS IN TOWER ROOF. SIGNAL IN USE.

MARCH 28, 1890

HEAVY WIND. SIDE ROOM IN DWELLING IN NEED OF REPAIR. SEVERAL STEAMERS PASSED FROM THE SOUTH AT 0300, 0345, 0550. SIGNAL IN USE.

The entries continued in the same format through the years up until the last one:

OCTOBER 12, 1913

C. ROLAND AT STATION TO DISCUSS LEGAL MATTERS. P. METTLE AT STATION TO DISCUSS PERSONAL MATTERS. CLEANED INTERIOR KITCHEN AND SITTING ROOM. KEEPER IN NORMAN CLIFFS FOR PERSONAL MATTERS. SIGNAL IN USE.

Mari sat up straighter, her eyes going back to the first line. Here, unexpectedly, was a tie between the Norman family and Silvestre Swan—surely C. Roland was Cortney Roland, the banker who had come up in her research. But "legal matters" did little to clarify the relationship between the family Sam Beauregard was looking for and the lighthouse Mari was. October 12 was still several weeks before the last recorded sighting of Swan Light. But that wasn't entirely unexpected, she supposed: there were entire years missing from these scans, in places, likely lost to weather or age as they sat in Rose-Olive Cooper's attic. These logs would be a great addition to Evangeline's exhibit. But they didn't tell Mari anything new.

Keya had also included a medical evaluation from a man named Amos Wright, dated October 19, 1913.

Benjamin Forsythe III is in good spirits after I have re-set his injured leg. I advise him to elevate it and to drink plenty of water. Mr. Forsythe marks the last of his companions that I have found to be in suitable condition for their journey home, with the exception of Clara Vettrey, left at Swan Light but due back for evaluation soon.

Mari studied the words as the wind picked up behind her, sending leaves and sticks and flowers fluttering over the edge. October 19 was closer, but still before the date Swan Light had vanished. Though it mentioned Swan Light by name, this evaluation read more like a town doctor noting a casual, everyday encounter. Nothing dramatic, nothing unusual. Nothing that explained why Sam Beauregard was asking questions about the Normans and the lighthouse, or why, if he was truly only looking for Norman descendants, he was towing equipment by the cliff. What exactly was the link between C. Roland and Swan Light? What was Sam Beauregard looking for that was worth following her around town? And how far would he go to find it?

Swan, 1913

Swan woke just after the sun rose. The sky was dusty blue, the water dark and calm, and he lay there for a moment listening to the wind and the gulls. Then he hauled himself out of bed and made himself tea. He ate a slice of leftover berry crumble for breakfast. He wiped the condensation from the back windows and wrote out a note for Stay to deliver to town, requesting a delivery of new hinges for the windows.

And then he went outside to make sure his houseguest hadn't accidentally drowned herself in the cove.

Because, somehow, Clara Vettrey was still here. He'd woken at dawn every day the past week to the sound of the tower's clockwork going silent. It had offended him to his core the second morning, when he'd rushed to the tower and pulled the lever of the clockwork mechanism from her hands. But later he'd noticed how much lighter he felt after not doing the heavy job himself. He'd be glad to have his home to himself again, but he had to admit the respite had been nice. And she was certainly excited enough to do it.

She still spent most of her time in the cove, only returning to eat and sleep, and he couldn't guess what she was doing. Maybe she really had started to defend the wreck against looters. He didn't ask and she didn't offer, and as the days passed they settled into a new rhythm, coming and going around each other, the tower murmuring happily along between them.

"Abigail's been asking about her, you know," Peter told him one morning while Clara was at the cove. The sky was peeking bright blue through the clouds, the sun warming the frigid air. "She's sent the rest of the survivors home and knows she was one short, and she's friends with Amos Wright. I wouldn't be surprised if she comes looking."

"Why does Abigail care?"

Peter studied him. "You don't know who the girl is, do you?"

"What, Clara?"

"Clara *Vettrey*," Peter said. "Vettrey Shipping, out of Gloucester, near Boston. Picked up a fortune in dry goods; her father is nearly royalty. He owned *Saint Gray*. And now his daughter is just living in your spare room?"

"She's living in my lantern room. She didn't want the spare."

Peter chuckled. "Well, it certainly says a lot if you trust her up there. Just be careful, Silvy. The Vettreys are Gloucester's version of the Rolands, but even richer and less accommodating."

But another week had passed since then with no sign of Abigail or Cort. Now, Swan leaned back against the base of the tower, scratching Stay's ears. When Clara reappeared from the cove, red-nosed and windswept, she had a leather bag in her hands that she dropped inside before coming to join him. She plopped herself comfortably beside them, and Stay rolled over to put his head in her lap. "Can we have fish for lunch again?"

"I thought you ate it all last night," Swan said, and Clara mock-gasped.

"I would never," she said. "I did feed some to Stay, though. So if it's gone, it's his fault."

Stay yelped, making them both smile, and Swan hauled himself to his feet and trudged back to the house with the dog and the girl at his heels. There was plenty of cod left, and he was just setting about putting it on the fire when there was a knock at the front door. He opened it to see Cort Roland. "Good afternoon, Mr. Swan," he said.

"Mr. Roland," Swan said. "Can I help—"

"I have good news," Cort said, stepping past him into the kitchen, where Clara and Stay looked up expectantly. "My family and I are having dinner with an investor who may be able to help you with your lighthouse problem."

"My *lighthouse problem* . . ." Swan echoed, but Cort was already focused in on Clara.

"Ah," he said, extending a hand. "You must be Miss Vettrey. I'm Cortney Roland, owner and executor of Norman Bank."

"Hello," Clara said.

"I'm sorry that you missed the family's ship back to Gloucester," Cort said. "We didn't realize you'd come back here. You're more than welcome to stay in town while we arrange another one. There's plenty of room if you'd like better accommodations."

"I like it here," Clara said quickly, and Swan's chest warmed.

"I see." Cort's eyes lingered on his pile of legal papers, stained with berry juice. Clara had been using it as a place mat. "Well, join us for dinner, at least. As I said, we'd like to speak with Swan anyway."

Clara looked at Swan, who couldn't think of a less obvious way to shake his head in time. "Okay," she said politely, and Swan almost groaned. But outside the tower murmured, talking to itself, and beyond it he could hear the lapping, searching waves. His *lighthouse problem.* To this, Swan could not say no.

Clara rode in Cort's cart, Swan following in his own. When they arrived Swan tried not to look at the cellar door, or at the fireplace where he'd first met Arthur and Grace during the boil-up all those years ago. The table was already covered with food and ringed by Cort's brother, Lou; Abigail; a blond man Swan recalled as Gable Strauss; and Cort's wife, bouncing a son on one knee and a daughter on the other, the older of whom was clutching a broken toy sailboat and sobbing into his mother's skirt. No one looked at Swan except for Lou, who gave him a half smile. Every other eye was turned to Clara.

"Philip," Cort said, and his son gulped back tears and sniffled into silence. "Why don't you see if Mr. Swan can help fix your ship?" It was not lost on Swan where the two empty chairs were. One was next to Cort's wife and children. The other, on the opposite end of the table, was between Abigail and Gable Strauss. *An investor who may be able to help you,* Cort had said to Swan, but the man's eyes had not left Clara. There was something eager in them, greedy. Swan remembered how he'd felt the first time around the Normans and Gable Strauss: as though Swan himself were just a puppet in their larger show. Swan shifted uneasily in his seat, and Abigail met his eyes through the steam rising from a plate of cod.

"It broke," Cort's son said, and Swan looked down to see the boy holding the ship toward him in cupped hands. Its single mast had snapped, the flag at the top dangling limply to one side. "Let's see," Swan said gruffly, plucking it up. The boat was comically small in his hands, the mast toothpick-thin and fragile. Swan pulled ineffectively at the string that served as its halyard, trying to wrap the mast in place.

"Hope you've been feeling all right since the Vettrey wreck," Cort said to Swan over his son's head. Swan handed the ship back, its mast still loose, but it seemed to please the boy. "What a nasty night that was."

"I feel fine," Swan said, even as his heart rattled behind his ribs. "No thanks necessary."

"Nasty night," Cort said again, and Swan looked at him, remembering that Cort had been there that night too, in the tower just before the storm, while Swan hid at the edge of the woods. He'd almost forgotten, in everything that had happened after. At the other end of the table, whatever Abigail was saying to Clara had made the girl's eyes light up, and she responded animatedly, gesturing with her fingers. Swan suddenly felt very old and stupid. She'd said she liked the tower, but of course Clara felt more at home in this house, with this family. She looked impossibly young next to Abigail. Or maybe it was that Abigail looked older than ever next to the girl. *Bowen Smith told me he's working on your ship.* Abigail had been only a little older than Clara, that night. The night of Arthur van Gooren, the night *Hazel* was still meant to be called *Count Your Lucky Stars.* The last night Nico had really been his.

Nico, climbing a rock face for a teacup, face shining in the sun.

Nico, pooling every last penny for a ship of his own.

Nico, sailing home to his pregnant wife too soon and too fast, ignoring every lesson in his saltwater blood warning him not to ride through the storm.

There were two portraits on the wall behind Cort, a man and a woman. COLIN ROLAND, said one. HAZEL ROLAND, said the other. Swan's eyes traced the lines of Hazel's face, the pointed chin and narrow nose, the thick brow and widow's peak and those bright blue eyes.

She looked just like her son Cort.

She looked just like her father, Arthur.

"What?" Clara said loudly, and Swan jerked from his thoughts as the room fell quiet. Clara turned to look at Swan, then back at Abigail. "He asked you to help move the lighthouse, and you said no?"

"It's a bit more complicated than that," Abigail said. Her voice was smooth, but Swan saw her hand shake slightly on her glass of water. "Relocating a lighthouse is a delicate and expensive process, especially one as precarious as Swan Light."

"It's been there for years," Clara said. "You had plenty of time before it got *precarious.* But now you'll suddenly be able to find the money if Mr. Swan helps you find this deed you're looking for?"

Swan dropped his eyes to keep from laughing aloud. No one had ever spoken to Abigail Norman like this, he was sure. But the look on her face made him wish someone had done it sooner.

Cort was looking nervously at Gable Strauss, who no longer looked nearly as amused as he had the morning Swan first saw him in the bank. "That's exactly right, Miss Vettrey," Cort said to Clara. "Norman Cliffs built Swan Light without any government assistance, so we don't qualify for it now. It's always been simply too much money to justify moving the light without getting something out of it in return."

Clara stared at him. "Why do you need to get something out of it? Why can't you just help?"

"The light isn't effective enough to be worth it," Abigail said. "After all, it clearly didn't help *Saint Gray*."

Cort's daughter had started crying in earnest, and his wife picked her up and carried her from the room, though not without sending a hard look at Cort.

"Clara," Abigail said. "All I'd meant to tell you in bringing up the deed was that Silvestre has been uncooperative in the deal we're trying to make, something I'm sure your family has dealt with before. I knew you'd recognize the importance. I'd simply wondered if you'd noticed anything while you've been staying there, that's all."

"You were going to have her look through my things," Swan said. Something about Clara speaking her mind so easily made it easier for him too. "Didn't Cort already do that, the day of the storm?"

Lou Roland put down his fork. "Is that true?" he asked his brother. It was the first thing he'd said all evening, and perhaps the first time Swan had ever heard him speak: his voice was softer and lower than Swan expected, the opposite of his brother's near-bellow.

"I would remind you, Swan," Cort said, his eyes hard, "that your home and Swan Light were also constructed by Norman Cliffs money on Norman Cliffs land. I'm well within my rights to search both for my own property."

"It's *not* your property," Clara said. "Have you ever thought that Mr. Swan might not want to just give up his brother's things?"

Cort swiveled, triumphant. "So he *has* said something."

"And the investor who wanted to help move the lighthouse?" Clara asked. "That was a lie too?" She looked at Gable Strauss, who let out a loud guffaw.

"Me?" he asked. "Help move a lighthouse? Good lord, no. Why would I want to be involved with any of this?" He stood, pushing his chair back from the table with a screech. "Thank you for dinner, Cort," he said. "Let me know when you have a better handle on all of your assets."

The room rang quiet after his departure, except for Cort's daughter coughing in the next room. Cort's face was thunderous, then pained as he glanced toward the sound. Swan felt like he was circling *Hazel*'s wreck all over again, his feet gone out from under him, his throat clotted with smoke. His heart sped and slowed and sped again, and he gripped his spoon so tightly he felt his blood thudding against the metal. The portrait of Hazel Roland watched from behind Cort's head, blue eyes vacant and unblinking. "Abigail," he said. "Can I speak to you for a moment?"

"You may," she said, and Swan was aware of the rest of the room's eyes on the two of them as they stood. Abigail led him into the kitchen, stopping beside a rounded cellar door, and turned to face him. "Yes?"

Again Swan was aware of how old she was. How old they both were. They'd come so far from those children scampering around the cliff. "There's no need to bring Clara into this," he said. "Let's settle it just the two of us."

Her hands were on her hips, pale and bony. "Does that mean you're ready to give me the deed?"

"Abigail, I don't have your deed," Swan said wearily. "I don't know how to be any more clear about that. If you and Cort want to search through my things so badly, fine. Come up to the tower and you can look for yourself, again. Just please put this pettiness to rest."

Abigail's eyes had gone cold. "Petty?" she repeated. "I'm not the petty one here, Silvestre. You're doing this because of Nico. You never forgave me for marrying him, did you? For taking him away from you."

"What?" Swan asked, startled. "No. I never begrudged that. Nico was his own man, and he loved you."

Something flickered across her face. But then it was gone, the hard set back in her jaw. "You resented me," she said. "You worshiped him, and you hated that I took him. But this is what Nico would have wanted, Swan. He died trying to come home to his daughter. He would want her son to have the deed."

The harbor, come quickly. Something's happened to Hazel. "He didn't," Swan said. "He died because you forced that ship out before it was ready. If I begrudge you anything, it's that."

"Nico agreed to that," Abigail said. "He signed as a trader knowing the rules and the risks. Don't you blame that on me."

"He'd crossed the bar a hundred times," Swan said. "You think he would have hit it if there wasn't something wrong?"

"You're not the only one who lost him," Abigail said, her voice going shrill. Her eye was twitching, the pulse of thinning lashes keeping time with Swan's own heart. His throat was tight again, the air too stuffy with heat from the fire. The cellar door had been propped to let out the smoke from their dinner, and Swan couldn't look beyond it because he knew what he'd see. The room where he'd spied Abigail and Arthur, all those years ago. "I know you think I wasn't good enough for him," Abigail said. "But he was my husband. And he would have wanted the deed to go to his daughter and her son."

Waiting for you, under the moonlight, waiting for me, down by the sea, so hold tight your lady and count your lucky stars. Threads of a song drifting out over a burning sea. They filled Swan's head, and his next words came without thought. "He didn't have a daughter," he said, his heart still thudding, his eyes still on the cellar. "Hazel wasn't Nico's. You know that as well as I do."

He balked immediately at his own gall, and looked up expecting to see Abigail furious. But her eyes were steady, searching. "So you did know," she said softly. "I always wondered."

"Don't pretend the deed is some birthright," Swan said. "It was a gift in a marriage you tricked Nico into."

For a moment Abigail was quiet, her eyes on the cellar door. "I didn't trick him into anything," she said, her voice a near whisper. "Nico knew about Arthur. It didn't matter to him. We'd been spending time together that summer, when he was working for my father to save up for his boat. Your brother was a good man, Swan. He was the only one of you who was ever kind to me. The only one who ever really saw me."

Swan took a full step backward, his mind reeling. Could that be true? Had Nico known about Arthur and married Abigail anyway? *We're going to have a baby.* But before he could speak the kitchen door creaked open, and he and Abigail both turned. It was Clara, shoulders set and back straight. "Mr. Swan," she said loudly. "It's time to go. It will be time to light the lantern soon. We don't want ships to be out there in the dark."

~~~

The trip back to the cliff was quiet except for the plinks of steady rain, Swan keeping his eyes firmly on the road even as he felt Clara glancing at him again and again. Abigail's words played over in his mind. *Nico knew. Nico knew. Nico knew.* All this time, he'd thought he was protecting his brother's memory, harboring this decades-old grudge. He should have remembered that Nico had never needed protecting. That had always been Abigail. And Nico had always been the one to do it.

It wasn't until the tower swung into sight, its stone gray in the lengthening shadows, that Clara spoke. "Are you okay?" she asked. "I wasn't sure how long I should give you. Lou went to find something in his study, and Cort started being insufferable again, so I thought I should come check on you. And then I heard yelling on the last bit."

"What did you hear?"

"Not much," she said hastily. "And I was the only one close enough to. About Nico not having a daughter. Nico was your brother?"

"Yes."

"And he married Abigail, and her father gave him the deed as a wedding gift, and he gave it to you?"

"Just for safekeeping," Swan said. "Not that he ever would have needed it. I hadn't thought about it since then. I left all of Nico's things with our mother, when he died. And I'm sure Sophie Mettle cleaned it out when she moved into that house."

"It is odd," she said. "Cort could have asked for the deed years ago, same as he could have moved the light years ago. Why bring it up now?"

Clara lit the tower while Swan tied up the horse, and no sooner had they both returned to the keeper's house than there was a knock on the door. Swan stood and opened it to reveal Lou Roland, bright blue eyes blinking owlishly in the dark. "Hello," the younger Roland said.

Swan opened the door wider, cautious. Rain was falling harder now, slicking the boy's dark hair to his forehead. And he *was* a boy: up close it was clear he was much younger than Cort, probably not much older than Clara. "What are you doing here?" Swan asked. Was this another ploy for the deed, already? "Did Abigail send you?"

"No, no," Lou said. He was panting, winded. Swan didn't see a cart; he must have run here, after them, alone, in the rain. "She doesn't know I'm here; she probably hasn't noticed I left. She usually doesn't."

"Why did you?" Swan asked.

"The study shares a wall with the kitchen, and I couldn't help . . ." He trailed off, pushing his hand across his wet brow. "Is it true, what you said? Nico Swan wasn't my grandfather?"

Swan felt cold and old and exhausted, guilt bubbling up between all of it like blood. Abigail's past wasn't this boy's problem. He stepped back. "Come inside."

Lou followed him into the warmth of the kitchen, where Clara had lit several logs in the oven. Lou nodded to her. "I should apologize to you too," he said. "My family shouldn't have brought yours into it. They just get carried away sometimes. They were showing off for Gable

Strauss. He won't be in town long, and he's mostly just spending his time here trying to decide whether we're worth investing in or not."

Clara said nothing, her fingers wrapped protectively through Stay's fur.

Lou Roland stood there dripping in his home, taking in the tilting side room and the rusting icebox and the tattered orange curtain, and again Swan was seized by the memory of Arthur van Gooren. *You're dripping on my new shoes.* But this boy's eyes were earnest and bright, and the tower standing guard outside hadn't made a sound.

"How much did you hear?" Swan asked Lou, pulling a chair out from the table and lowering into it. Stay ambled over and put his head on Swan's knee.

"Most of it," Lou admitted. "It's true?"

Swan wondered if he'd already done enough damage, discussing this with Abigail after so many years. But Lou was watching him, expectant. "Yes," Swan said. "Hazel's father was a man named Arthur van Gooren."

Lou made a sound of surprise. "The bank's lawyer is named Edward van Gooren," he said. "He lives in St. John's."

"A distant cousin, I believe," Swan said. "There was a whole huge clan of them." He thought about Grace, another van Gooren, her face when he'd told what he'd seen the night of the party. *Arthur would do anything to feel important,* she'd said. *Abigail probably liked that about him.*

Lou half smiled. "Cort will be thrilled. He's always admired Edward's business acumen."

"Did Cort hear too?"

"No," Lou said. "But Grandmother might tell him anyway. She tells him everything. I'm a little surprised she never told him this." He squinted out at the tower, his face going bone-white to mottled yellow as its light swung past. "I'd always kind of liked it," he said softly, almost to himself. "The idea that I was related to Captain Swan. Grandmother never talked about him, but the rest of the town did. Still does. The reason for the lighthouse. I always thought there must have been something kind about our family once, if someone like him had seen it." He pulled a small square of paper from his pocket and handed it to Swan, who found as he spread the paper over his knees that he was unable to speak. It was a charcoal drawing of the tower, a much different angle than Swan was used to. The lighthouse was visible through a break in the trees, its iron top rising above them, the horizon meeting its center in an endless unbroken line. It looked calm, safe. Strong. "I've always loved that view," Lou said quietly. "You can keep that, if you want."

And this, more than anything, convinced Swan to trust him. Sailors weren't the only people moving through the darkness, using the tower to guide them.

"I'd like to try and help you, Mr. Swan," Lou said. "I don't have nearly as big a pull in the bank as Cort does, or even my grandmother. But I'll see if I can do anything to move Swan Light without them." Outside the tower gave a hopeful, high-pitched creak, and Swan felt his own fissure of cautious joy. Lou's face was set and shining, surveying the lighthouse through the window. "I'll check the bank. There might be a way—" His voice was lost in a peal of thunder clattering over the cliff. Stay whined and lifted his head, and Clara jumped to her feet.

"I'll keep an eye on the oil tonight."

Lou stared. "All night?" he asked. "In this weather? Aren't you afraid it will—"

"No," Swan and Clara said together, and the tower chuckled.

"Well, I guess I should be going too," Lou said, casting an uneasy look outside. Another roll of thunder echoed across the sea, and the rain picked up, clattering and furious.

Swan sighed, already resigned. "Don't be ridiculous. You can stay here tonight. Only tonight, though," he said sternly. Clara, one hand on the door, stopped and tilted her head, staring Lou down.

"And you'll sleep in the side room," she said. "Stay will be sitting outside the door in case you're thinking of poking around Mr. Swan's things." And Swan almost laughed again. His stubborn, suspicious saving grace tonight.

"I didn't—" Lou started to protest, but Clara was already gone. Lou looked back at Swan, who raised his eyebrows.

"You heard her," he said. "Side room. Be careful of the far wall; it leaks."

Swan heard the boy pacing about long after he himself had climbed into bed, and he fell asleep listening to the creaking of a floor no one had walked on in years. *After all of this is over,* he thought ruefully as the house settled around him and his now-tripled home, *I'm going back to only leaving the tower once a day.*

Mari, 2014

Mari hit the bay in a plunge of white bubbles as the underwater world unfurled around her.

It was the most beautiful day they'd had yet, seventy-five and sunny, the water calm and clear. Mari moved along the seafloor, watching the sand turn gray and green and gold in the filtered light. A dozen feet away, Julian looked eerie where he floated closer to the cliff, sand swirling around his flippers. "Just blow some bubbles if you need me," came his salvage partner Otis's deadpan voice into their radios, and Mari grinned into her mask.

They were alone this time, no sign of Sam Beauregard's *New Providence* at the cliff or in the harbor. Instead of relaxing her, it put her on edge. If Beauregard thought that Mari was making a run for something he wanted, he should be watching this spot like a guard dog. Mari had been in his position before, racing to salvage something before another crew reached it. It could bring out the worst in divers, make them ruthless. Especially people like Sam Beauregard. Because now Mari knew who they were up against, if not exactly why.

Julian was the one who had figured it out.

"I need you to look something up," she'd said, the morning after talking to Gerald Cooper.

Julian peered blearily at her over the top of his cup of coffee, his curly hair disheveled. They were the only two people in Mettle House's dining room, and clearly only one of them was a morning person. "What did I say about me and research?"

"It's not research," she said. "It's a boat."

"What does that mean, 'It's a boat'?"

"Sam Beauregard's boat," she said. "*New Providence*."

"Are you still on that?"

"He stalked me to a retirement home," Mari said. "Yes, I'm still on that. He thinks we're competing with him."

"So? I'm sure he'll stop when he realizes we're not."

"Well, I'd like to tell him as soon as possible." She tapped her fingers until Julian looked up from his cup. "Honestly, I don't care what he's looking for. He's a rich kid with a fancy metal detector. I don't care about whatever Mel Fisher discovery he thinks he's making out here. I just don't want him getting in our way."

Julian laughed briefly, then sobered. "Okay. So what about his boat?"

"It had a Boston hailing port."

He looked back into his coffee, but his eyes were thoughtful. "Yeah," he said. "Yeah, I'm on it."

His contact in Boston Harbor said that *New Providence* was registered to a Sam Beauregard Sr., sixty years old, who was as much a ghost online as his son. As they'd printed their sonar sweeps from Jo's huffing old computer, Mari had googled every combination of "Sam Beauregard logo kraken man face ship" she could think of—which led to a few maritime merchandise stores and some truly bewildering fan fiction—and still came up empty. Eventually Julian looked up from studying the sonar. "You said Gerald Cooper took pictures the last time they were here, right?"

"Yeah," she said.

"So get those from him and send them to Scripps." He shrugged. "I'll send them to my team too. If these people aren't hiding their logo and are being this aggressive, someone's probably come across them before."

It was a smart idea. After she sent the pictures, Hector called her almost immediately and whistled loudly in her ear. "That's Teach," he said.

"Teach? As in school?"

"Teach International. Taken from Blackbeard's real name, Edward Teach, if that tells you anything about how they see themselves. They're officially contract salvagers, but I'd say they're more like old-school treasure hunters. Do you remember the reef survey we had to stop when someone damaged part of a galley nearby? That was them. They thought there was gold on board."

Mari did remember. It had caused an uproar, salvagers treating a wreck so poorly that they'd caused it irreparable damage. The *Shillock* galley was still off-limits to divers, under strict environmental protection. "Any idea what they'd be looking for?"

"No," Hector said. "They usually stick to the tropics. The last time I remember hearing about them was when they were looking for some pirate wreck in Boca, near a spot the bio team was working. And now that I'm thinking about it, that was the dive when Patricia said someone moved her anchor overnight. Teach swore up and down it wasn't them, but no one else was there."

Even in competitive diving, vessel sabotage was low. Mari relayed it all to Julian, who gave a dark grin. "I'd love to see them try."

Now that they were back in the water, Mari pushed Sam Beauregard and Teach International resolutely from her mind. Their sonar sweeps were pinned to *Shanty*'s pilothouse window and might as well have been pinned inside her mask, for how ingrained they were in her mind. She kicked toward the yellow flag that marked their favorite hit, the twin lines with that stone denseness between them, while Julian searched for the mangled half-circle that they hoped could be part of the lighthouse's railing.

Her handheld dredge made quick work of shifting the sand, sucking it loose in a steady stream. The past few days of bad weather and fast water had reburied the lines, and Mari was again aware of how lucky they'd been to use the sonar when they did. Any other day, and there might not have been anything to see. She worked for twenty minutes, sifting through sand and rock and mottled glass, when finally one burst of air came up against something solid two feet below the surface.

It was a piece of long, pale stone.

A chill crept along her neck, even under her wetsuit, and for an instant her childhood dream flashed behind her eyelids, the wreck watching her, waiting to strike. Mari positioned the dredge alongside the stone, sand ballooning around it as its edge slowly began to emerge. When she'd made a deep enough hole, she started moving across the stone's face. It was mottled, and badly cracked in places. But it was large, its face spanning five feet until she reached the other edge. It was far too straight and long to be natural, the ghostly pale of something that had once been white. It almost seemed too good to be true. *It's supposed to be,* she reminded herself. *This is supposed to be easy.* She'd worked plenty of dives that turned up what they were looking for right away. But something about Swan Light was so mysterious, so untouchable, that it seemed it should be harder to find.

She'd almost forgotten, after all the stories, that in the end it was just iron and stone.

She floated for a moment, taking it in, until Julian's voice came through her radio. "Negative on the ring," he said. "Just some old fishing gear."

"Roger that," Otis said. "Mari, any luck?"

Mari found her voice. "Yeah," she said. "Yeah, I found something."

〜〜

The next few hours passed in a blur of activity. Julian joined her at the stone and they photographed it, documenting every angle they could reach. Then they brought down the industrial-sized dredge from *Shanty* and navigated it in a slow circle, freeing the stone inch by inch. And what emerged was a half cylinder eight feet long and five feet wide, badly damaged along the end that had been buried farthest in the sand. That side was now bulbous and distorted by calcium carbonate buildup, which meant that there was iron somewhere inside it that had been exposed to the salt water. Mari and Julian lashed the column to a sled and winched it up to *Shanty* and into the tank of fresh water waiting on her deck, where it would stay until they moved it into the electrolytic bath in Evangeline's barn to start to dissolve the buildup. "Good thing it wasn't any bigger than this," Julian said as they lowered the slab, sending water splashing over the side.

He was right. But as big as the stone was, it wasn't nearly big enough to be the whole lighthouse. This was only a piece of Swan Light. Still, Mari tasted anticipation as she held her ringing phone to her ear. "Evangeline, it's Mari. We found it."

The old woman sucked in a breath. "Are you sure?"

Julian was leaning over the tank, passing his metal detector across the length of the rock. The machine chirped steadily, again indicating iron stuck somewhere inside. Iron that could be reinforcement from the inside of the lighthouse but could also be the remains of the equipment that had kept it running, or even its railing and lens, rusted and warped together with the stone after all these years underwater. "Yes," Mari said. "We'll have to run tests to prove it, of course. But there's nothing else it could be."

"That's amazing," Evangeline said softly.

"We're going right back into the water," Mari said. "There's a lot still to look for, and we still have to use the magnetometer. But I wanted to let you know right away."

"Thank you, Mari," Evangeline said. "Please keep me posted."

Mari tucked away her phone as Julian clambered off the freshwater tank. He was grinning, exuberant, and it occurred to her that this might be the first time she'd seen him really smile.

Then the sunburned, long-haired Otis paused in the middle of packing up the sonar. "On your three," he said quietly.

She and Julian looked over to see *New Providence*'s red hull trundling around the corner of the cliff. The other ship cut its engines several dozen feet away, and for a moment they both floated there, sizing each other up. Right of way would go to the ship with divers or equipment in the water, but *New Providence* wasn't flying her tow flag today, and *Shanty* no longer even had markers down. The smartest move would be to throw the sonar back in just to stake their claim, but before Mari could move their radio crackled to life.

"This is the inshore vessel *New Providence*," a deep, raspy voice said. "Research vessel by the cliff, can you identify yourself?"

Julian and Mari glanced at each other. Otis moved to the other side of the cabin, out of *New Providence*'s sight, and when Julian nodded he heaved the sonar back overboard with a splash. "This is the research vessel *Shanty*," Julian said into the radio. "Be advised that we have equipment under tow, *New Providence*. Where are you headed?"

"We can see your anchor line, *Shanty*," the voice said pleasantly, ignoring the question, and Mari winced. Teach was calling their bluff. "Do you have people in the water?"

It was an easy lie, one that made its way to Mari's mouth before she realized she wasn't the one with the radio. But Julian held her gaze and shook his head. "Negative," he said. "We're orienting a towfish directly below us. Our track lines run fifty feet out from the cliff. I repeat, where are you headed?"

There was a moment of crackling silence on the other end. Then, "Am I speaking to your vessel's captain?"

"Yes. This is Captain Julian Henry. Can you confirm that you'll stay clear of our track lines?"

There was another moment of silence before the voice came back brusque and businesslike. "That's a negative, Captain," it said. "Since your anchor is down we'll be moving into your box. Be alert for equipment on your port side and vacate as soon as you pull that towfish."

Julian's eyes were angry. "Stand down, *New Providence*." But there was no answer as *New Providence* whirred back to life and moved forward again, passing them twenty feet farther out to sea. Close enough that Mari could see Sam Beauregard at the rail, pulling his teeth back in a wolf's grin as he gave her a two-fingered salute.

But for once, the fickle weather was on their side. As *Shanty*'s three-person crew finished loading the stone into their tank, the dark clouds waiting behind the cliffs moved in and blanketed them with rain, turning the water rough and choppy. "Enjoy, inshore vessel *New Providence*," Julian said in satisfaction, imitating the other captain's rasp as he swung *Shanty* back toward the harbor. "You're not pulling anything up in this."

〰️

Determined to claim the cliff first the next morning, Mari and Julian were in the harbor before the sun. They were rewarded with the sight of *New Providence* sitting quiet and empty in her slip. This time they left *Shanty* behind and took the much smaller Zodiac. Normally Mari would have used the mag immediately after the sonar, but she'd been too excited about the lines on the sonar—and too aware of how easily they could disappear again—to wait. On most dives, using the sonar and the mag was like using two separate contact lenses. You needed both together to see what was worth exploring. The sonar created a picture of the seafloor but couldn't find what was buried farther beneath it. The mag, on the other hand, wouldn't show shapes or lines or find more stone, but it would pick up on iron even if it was buried below the sand. With any luck it would show them a whole host of new targets to explore, the parts of Swan Light that had shattered.

Mari watched the monitor flicker on as Julian swiveled to join her. He'd been quiet all morning, focused on setting up the ship, but now he tapped her on the knee. When she looked over, his dark eyes were intent. "I didn't love that, yesterday," he said.

"Which part?" she asked. "Teach going all pirate on our search box? Me either."

"No," he said. "I meant that you were going to tell them we had people in the water."

Mari stared at him. Was he joking? But she'd rarely known Julian to joke, and right now he looked more somber than ever. "What's wrong with that?"

"I just think that if you can't figure something out without lying, maybe you're not doing it the right way."

She shook her head. "What are you talking about? It was just lousy timing. If they'd come ten minutes earlier we *would* have been in the water. Besides, you think Teach is going to play by those same rules? If we'd been the ones coming up on them, they would have lied too."

"I don't care what Teach does," Julian said. "Teach isn't on my ship. I'm just asking you to be a little more careful, that's all."

Mari thought back to her past dives—the numbers crunched, the corners cut. These were things she believed made her a better scientist: a faster one, a more calculated one, one more willing to take risks to find the answer at any cost, all while never compromising the integrity of her work. But something in Julian's face swayed her. It was open and honest, without a trace of deeper motive. She was sure her own face had never looked like that. "Sure," she said, surprising herself, and his answering smile loosened a knot in her stomach she hadn't known was there.

The monitor beeped, then, pulling both of them away. "There's our first hit," Julian said, clearing his throat, and they lapsed into comfortable silence as the mag monitor came to life, speckled traces appearing on the screen with increasing frequency as they moved closer to the cliff. Most of the hits were tiny, more due to the sensitivity of the machine than to the metal it was responding to. But as they reached the end of their track line opposite the cove, the screen showed a larger hit, a soft yellow circle. "That's something," Mari said, marking the coordinates. For a moment the monitor stayed quiet. Then it lit again and again, a long staccato of metal reaching a dozen feet along the floor and ending in a bright smear, the largest trace yet. Julian and Mari looked at each other, thinking the same thing. Could this be the metal frame of Swan Light's giant lens?

"It really spread out," Julian said, tapping the map where they'd found part of the tower. The mag hits were nearly thirty feet away. As they crept closer to the cove the light lingered on the screen, and Julian frowned. "I'm going to go a little past our lines," he said. "Let it adjust itself."

"Sure." Mari squinted into the cove as they approached it. Depending on the forecast, maybe they could leave the Zodiac there and climb up. Much as Julian had said he wanted to stick to steering, she'd seen a different side of him today, one that was funny and invested, and she knew he'd be intrigued by Silvestre Swan's house if he saw it. They only had two more track lines to run; there would be plenty of time.

And then, twenty feet past the cove, the mag screen exploded in color.

Mari gasped as the monitor lit as though it was self-combusting, hits scattering across the floor beneath them faster than she could count them. "What the hell?" Julian said, jolting forward. "Maybe *this* is the lens, and it's coming apart?" But seconds later they knew that wasn't it. The mag hits farther out had been in one piece, sometimes two. This was hundreds. This was many pieces of something huge. This was a pattern that to divers was unmistakable, and Mari felt her arm hair rise.

"That's not a lighthouse," she said, eyes on the scatter. "That's a shipwreck."

Lou, 1913

Lou Roland did not know what to make of any of this.

He'd spent most of his twenty-two years avoiding water, and for twenty-two years, even living on a bay, he'd been largely successful. Lou had never liked the water. He didn't like how quickly it changed, how even though it was clear you could never see the bottom. He'd also never been quite comfortable with heights. And yet here he was, farther from the ground than he'd ever been, surrounded by an ocean that licked and lapped in all directions like an animal just waiting for something to drop.

He sat at the edge of the sagging bed in the lighthouse keeper's extra room, looking out a window that faced town. The storm had passed quickly, leaving the sky a harsh blue. He could see a sliver of his house—his grandmother's house, the Norman mansion that had stood since Andrew Norman sailed back to Newfoundland from New York and found his original home occupied by Captain Mettle. Lou knew the story word for word. The man who'd saved the town, raising it from obscurity with hard-earned money and well-built ships, and the man who'd stepped in and claimed its success for himself. The owners and the squatters. The Mettles were opportunists, crafty, always lying in wait. Puttering along the coast in their pilot boat, lording it over visitors, acting like they owned the shore. It had been a bedtime story, and later a barb, after Lou spent a school day with Will Mettle instead of Cort. He remembered Cort's face: *Where's your family loyalty, Lou?* But lately he wasn't sure how much he believed it.

Because the night of the *Saint Gray* wreck, Will Mettle had been one of the first in the water to help.

The Rolands hadn't left their beds.

Lou stood and crossed the room to crack the door open. Swan's dog, as Clara Vettrey had promised—or threatened—was lying flat across the threshold, fast asleep. Lou stepped carefully over him. The lighthouse keeper was asleep too, snoring, just visible behind the orange curtain that hid his bed. There was a pile of juice-stained paper on the table and a pile of fresh-chopped wood by the oven, and each pane of every window had been scrubbed meticulously clean. Lou wondered how much of the cottage Cort had searched for that deed. He stood there a moment, considering. Then he took a step outside, shutting the door softly behind him.

The air was frigid, wind buffeting the woods, and Lou couldn't help holding his breath as he moved cautiously toward the lighthouse. It really was striking, all white stone and black iron, taller than Lou would have thought. He'd never been to the top of the cliff before—water, heights—and it was shocking, up close, how near Swan Light was to the edge. It looked it, from town, but he'd always assumed it was the angle, some hidden slant keeping the lighthouse safer than it seemed. But no, there was the drop, running along below the stone square that made the tower's base. Lou was fairly sure one corner of the base was actually *hanging over* the edge, nothing supporting it at all. But there was no way he was getting close enough to find out.

Instead he squatted in the flat grass, studying the tower. As it was, trying to relocate Swan Light could be what pushed it over the edge. They'd need rope, lots of it, to keep the building in place while they shunted it backward off its base and onto a platform. Lou pulled a piece of paper and charcoal from his pocket, supplies he always kept on him, and began sketching it out, laid across his knee. Dotted lines for the rope, a quick platform with wheels. They'd have to be large, but the lighthouse's base would work in their favor there. Still, it would take lots of men and horses, and maybe a platform suspended below it to guide it from the sea. Lou chewed on his lip as he wrote out the math, lost in thought until a voice behind him asked "What are you doing?" and nearly sent him over the edge himself.

"Christ," he said, standing and turning. Clara Vettrey was standing there holding an empty leather bag, sopping wet. "What are *you* doing?"

"Fishing."

He eyed the bag, amused. "Catch many fish in that?"

"What would you know about it?" she retorted. "Bank hours let you bring in a morning haul first?"

Lou blinked. "As a matter of fact," he started, with no idea where he was going next, and Clara raised her eyebrows, waiting. Then a traitorous burst of wind swooped in, pushing him a full step closer to the edge of the cliff, and he scrambled backward as Clara Vettrey burst into laughter.

"You're afraid of it," she said delightedly.

"I think that's quite reasonable," Lou said. Her smile grew bigger.

"Is it?" she asked, moving past him toward the tower and leaping easily onto its base. Lou's stomach tightened. "This is what's so scary? A pile of stone?" Lou could have sworn he heard the lighthouse rumble.

"Christ," he said again. "Please be careful."

"Careful has nothing to do with it," she said, darting across the crumbling corner. "It's just walking, same as you'd do anywhere else."

"It's absolutely not 'just walking,'" Lou said. He held up his sketch page. "This is what I was doing, coming up with a plan to move it. It won't be easy, if it's even possible. It might already be too close to the edge."

"I think you need to have a little faith, Lou Roland," Clara said, jumping back across the base and landing smoothly on the ground. She straightened and patted the stone, as though it was the dog. It made that strange deep gurgle again. It almost sounded like laughter. Lou recoiled, and Clara smiled. "Come on," she said. "There's something you should see."

~~~

The bottom of the cliff was, if possible, worse than the top. It removed the element of height but required climbing straight down the rock face on ladder rungs that were holding on for dear life themselves, and it brought him that much closer to the grasping waves of the bay. There was nothing between Lou and the water but an impossibly thin strip of sand. And opposite it, stretched right across the arched opening of the cove like a hand over a mouth, was the black shell of *Saint Gray*.

Lou stared, cowed into silence at its size, at its ruin. "I know," Clara said softly. "And this is only half of it. The stern is underwater."

They stood in silence, staring up at the ship, and again Lou thought about the night it had wrecked. Cort had been late for dinner, which wasn't unusual, but it had been dinner with a client from Gander, which was. Cort never trusted Lou alone with clients. Lou wasn't a very good banker, something his grandmother had always made abundantly clear. Not that she'd had to. The numbers spoke for her. He brought in less than half the money Cort did, closed a fraction of the deals. Fell behind on collections, on mortgages; paid off debts he shouldn't; lost more than he took. Francis Norman, the great-grandfather who'd helped raise him, was the gold standard, still. Francis had worked dawn to dusk to dawn again, hard as any fisherman. He'd tripled Norman Cliffs' trading vessels and routes, put their little harbor town on the map. And it was a thankless job, one that set him apart. It demanded a ruthlessness that a town full of sailors could never understand. They called him hard, called him callous, didn't see that everything he did was just to keep the rest of them afloat. Abigail had inherited giant shoes, and had done her hardest to live up to them. She hadn't had a childhood, she told Cort and Lou, whenever they complained. Hadn't had true friends. Just stolen moments in coves with children who knew she wasn't one of them. Who thought her ruthless. Who could never understand.

After Abigail, it had been Hazel's turn. And Hazel had plans bigger than any of them. She made a contact in the United States, a man named Gable Strauss, something even Francis had never done. She had a better sense of when the tides were turning. *American banking is a mess,* Francis had said. *It's not worth it.*

Just wait, Hazel had told him. *Just wait,* through America's booms and busts and depressions. *Just wait, we will turn this into something yet.* Hazel had been charming, and tenacious, and driven. Hazel had planted seeds before the rest of them even saw the dirt. Hazel had married another banker, Colin Roland, to combine their budding empires. Hazel started Cort early, bringing him to the bank with her when he was five, even once to a meeting with her American contact, Gable Strauss. Surrounding him early with what it meant to succeed. The Normans before her had brought Norman Bank across the island. Hazel was going to bring it across the ocean.

And then Hazel had Lou, and then Hazel died.

And now Cort was the one following in her footsteps, or at least trying to. Lou wasn't ruthless enough. Once, Cort hadn't been either. Lou remembered their early days at the bank fondly. Cort at the helm, helping anyone who asked. A loose grip on the reins, to Abigail's dismay, but the bank had never suffered. But then his youngest daughter was born and wouldn't stop crying, couldn't stop gasping for air. A small lung, Dr. Wright had said, and Cort's grip had tripled down overnight. Gone were the help and handouts, the time for anyone who wasn't her. Every spare cent went to his daughter's medical care—first his own money, then the bank's. The latter was almost gone now, though no one in town knew it. But it wasn't enough. It would never be enough. His daughter got sicker and Cort got meaner. The deed, expanding into America, Gable Strauss's money, all of it: they were desperate grabs by a desperate man. Gable Strauss's investment, if he decided they deserved it, could keep the bank afloat for a year or so, could repay the money Cort had taken from the bank and could buy his daughter time. If Cort got Strauss's money, Lou was convinced, he would forget about the deed immediately. They were both just means to an end.

It had been Lou's job, first, to get the deed from Silvestre Swan. He'd tried once, had gotten as far as the trees. But more than the cliff and the water that had stopped him, it was Silvestre Swan himself, unaware that anyone was watching, standing on an overturned bucket to clean the windows of his house, windows that no one but him ever saw. Something about the care in that tiny gesture had stopped Lou in his tracks. *He can still clean his damn windows, Lou,* Cort had said impatiently when he returned. *Just go in and get the deed.* And so somehow Lou knew, the night of the storm and *Saint Gray*, that Cort had missed dinner and left him alone with an important client because he'd gone to the lighthouse instead. That like every other job Hazel had left the two of them together, Cort had taken this one upon himself alone.

Clara was still staring at the shipwreck, her eyes distant, and Lou shook his head and cleared his throat. "Why did you bring me down here?" he asked.

She turned to face him, her eyes going bright and fierce. "I wanted to show you what Mr. Swan saved me from," she said. "And what you're trying to take away from him."

"Take away from him?"

"The lighthouse," she said. "It's going to end up right next to *Saint Gray* if your family doesn't do something."

"It's nothing personal," Lou said. He couldn't tell this girl about the bank bleeding money, about his niece. For all his faults, Cort was his brother, and he was trying his best for his daughter.

"But this deed is a big enough reward?" Clara squinted at him. "What's so important about it, anyway?"

Lou had met Gable Strauss for the first time a year ago, with Cort. Their mother's American contact had been in St. John's on other business, and Cort had taken an entire week off to prepare. At the end of his speech—after all the numbers and figures and Hazel's hard-earned research, all the reasons Norman Bank would thrive in New York City— Gable Strauss had just looked at them and laughed. "You're nothing like your mother," he'd said.

Lou looked back at Clara. "The Federal Reserve," he said after a moment. "The United States is centralizing their banking system. I know it doesn't sound like much. But it's going to be so powerful. My mother predicted it years ago and now it's finally happening; they'll announce it any day now. And all this time we thought we'd have land waiting for us in New York, ready to go, but it turns out it's still Nico Swan's."

"Can't you just bribe someone for it? Or buy different land? Aren't you supposed to be rich?"

Years of dwindling money, of Cort dipping into the family funds and then into the bank's. Funds that had vanished once already after Newfoundland's bank crash nineteen years earlier; Abigail had fought like hell to bring them back. "It's not that easy," Lou said.

"Okay," Clara said slowly. "You know Mr. Swan doesn't have the deed, though, don't you? Your brother was here looking for it himself. Why should the lighthouse have to suffer?"

"Cort didn't have time to look everywhere," Lou said. "The storm was coming in."

"You can't be serious," Clara said. "You still think he's got it tucked under the woodpile, when he knows it could save the lighthouse?"

An old man standing on a bucket, carefully scrubbing a window, all alone. "No," Lou said. "I believe him. Swan had no use for it. But Cort doesn't think like that. To him it's like . . ." He cast around for an example and remembered the dog stretched outside his door. "Imagine you gave someone a puppy. And then years later you asked about it, and they told you they had no idea what happened to it, barely even remembered it. Would you believe them?"

"Of course not," Clara said indignantly.

"It's the same thing to Cort," Lou said. "He's not a bad person. He's just under a lot of pressure. He thought Swan might be holding back on the deed as a tactic, because it's something Cort himself would do."

Clara was staring hard at *Saint Gray* again. Then, to Lou's surprise, she started to laugh.

"Well, Lou Roland," she said, taking a step forward into the water and spinning to face him, "today is your lucky day. I think I can solve both of our problems." She waded backward, getting deeper. "Wait here," she said. "I'll be right back."

"Back?" he asked. "Where are you going?"

She smiled, toothy and wild. "Fishing." And then she was gone, fully underwater until her head reappeared at the mouth of the cove, tiny below the wreck. She stared up at the waves, ducking under one, two, three, until the fourth one, stronger than the rest, barreled in and she propelled herself on top of it. When the water cleared she was dangling from the rock face well out of reach of the water, and Lou thought he might have a heart attack.

"Ha!" she cawed. She hoisted herself upward and then, crablike, started making her way around the curve. In another moment she was out of sight.

"Clara?" he called. No answer. Several seconds later, there was a metallic clang. "Clara? What are you doing?"

"Climbing over *Saint Gray*'s hull. I'll only be a minute."

"You're . . . is it . . . how does it look?"

"Well . . ." Her voice went hollow, echoing. "It's in fair shape, actually. Except for, you know. The rest of the ship not being attached to it. But I can—*oof*." There was a thump, then a clang, then silence, and then a far-off "I'm fine."

It was only a few moments before she reappeared, sliding along the rock wall until she cleared the wreck and leapt into the water, her leather bag clutched under one arm. And when she surfaced Lou saw that it was no longer empty. But it definitely wasn't full of fish. Clara hefted it over her shoulder and marched up to him, dripping and intent. "Were you serious last night?" she asked. "You really want to help save the lighthouse?"

Lou Roland did not know what to make of any of this.

All he could do was nod, and she grinned and pushed past him toward the ladder. "Come on, then," she said over her shoulder. "I have a plan."

Mari, 2014

Slowly, what was left of Swan Light emerged from the water.

They found half the lens first, their brightest hit on the mag, its iron and brass warped and corroded, sheets of water-worn glass still stuck to each line. The hits leading up to it were other chunks of stone, shattered iron from the lens, and what must have been structural reinforcement embedded in the white rock where it had all snarled together on the seafloor for a century. Deeper below the sand they found a squat pole with turn marks worn into its base, a rod with a latch on it that looked like it had come from a window, and a pile of heavy gears. Mari and Julian dove each hit together, Julian with the metal detector and Mari with the dredge, using the larger air vent from *Shanty* when they needed to clear more space. Every piece of metal they found made its way to the freshwater baths in the darkness of Evangeline's barn, slowly shedding the decades of seafloor that clung to it.

Keya from Memorial had reconstructed a blueprint of Swan Light based on all of the information they'd found on it so far, and a blown-up print was now pinned to the barn wall, where they could try to match each sliver of stone and iron to what it might have come from. So far the light's five-foot lens was nearly reconstructed, though the beautiful bull's-eyed patterns on its glass had almost fully worn away. Also nearly complete was the mechanism that had kept the lens turning, made of six brass wheels and a weight and a drum. Other members of Julian's team were on their way from Boston to do the X-rays and CT scans and electrolytic baths that would bring each piece back to life. In the meantime Mari and Julian just kept diving, widening and deepening their search around the largest hits, hoping for more pieces of stone.

But it was pieces of shipwreck that kept popping up instead.

Mari really wasn't trying to seek them out, but they kept finding her. The wreck overlapped with the lighthouse, smaller pieces appearing well outside the concentrated mass that had so captivated them on the mag. She could only imagine what they'd find if they moved their dive closer to the cove. It was almost certainly what Teach was looking for, which became even clearer when Hector called to tell her that a claim on a ship in Norman Cliffs had appeared on the legal wires overnight. It explained Sam Beauregard's ongoing absence. Teach was in court, trying to win the salvage rights that would give them total control of the wreck. If it was a claim they won, they could sue Mari and Julian for being anywhere near it.

Julian, unsurprisingly, was opposed to even looking into it. "We're here for the lighthouse," he said. "Let Teach deal with the wreck."

"Julian, they're a group of treasure hunters known for sabotaging equipment who are going to come back any minute now and find us in their water. You really want to go into that scenario without any kind of ammo?"

And so they found themselves one morning sitting in the archive room of Norman Cliffs Library. Outside, rain poured down, thunder reverberating across the water, the mist so thick it hid the rest of town from view. It made the archive room humid, the windows fogging over as the ancient radiator in the corner clanked merrily away, releasing a slightly floral industrial cleanser scent. Mari manned the computer while Julian pored back over the town history books she'd used her first day. Based on the density and sheer space covered in the mag readings, Mari guessed that the wreck was a steamship. And the lack of huge fields of coal suggested that it either had already used its stores on a long journey or hadn't been fueled for a long trip in the first place. That much was helpful for ruling out a lot of the smaller wrecks they came across. But it wasn't enough, and after several hours of reading, neither of them had anything close to a lead.

"Their record keeping leaves a lot to be desired," Julian said absently. Her dive partner was wearing glasses for the occasion, thick and vaguely grandfather-y ones that were kind of endearing. He was sitting on the floor with his elbows propped on his knees, his back against the wooden paneling. "Anything that hit the sandbar is fair game to be called a wreck, even if the ship was totally fine. And they love listing wrecks as 'local' even if they were miles away."

"I guess you can't stop a seafarer from telling a good wreck story," Mari said.

"But look at this," Julian said, tapping a page. "This *Bretton* looks promising, but it's not clear whether it actually sank here or off of Cape Spear. And *this* one apparently wrecked twice in the same year, once here and once off St. John's. Either Vettrey Shipping was running an elaborate insurance scheme or no one bothered keeping accurate records. This one's okay; can you look up the SS *Mailehorn*?"

But Mari was frowning. Vettrey—where had she heard that name before?

"Go back a second," she said. "What about Vettrey Shipping?"

"Their steamship the SS *Saint Gray* sank in 1913. According to a letter from the shipping company, it sank in St. John's. But it's showing up twice because the *Cliffs Gazette* says it sank here in Norman Cliffs."

And then Mari remembered why the name was familiar. The doctor's note Keya had found from Amos Wright. *With the exception of Clara Vettrey, left at Swan Light but due back for evaluation soon.* At the time, Mari had written it off as unremarkable. But how many Vettreys could there be? "Hang on," she said, spinning back to the computer. Julian came to lean behind her as she typed it in, and she got a whiff of woodsmoke and mint. SS *Saint Gray* was just under two hundred feet long, she read, which certainly fit the wreck they'd found. And a trip like this would have used most of her coal.

"Vettrey Shipping carried mostly molasses and fish," Julian said, reading over her shoulder. "They had routes from Gloucester all over the Eastern Seaboard, with a line to and from Halifax for molasses and coffee. Looks like your average cargo trader, easy to throw off in a bad storm. Can I see this?"

She pushed away to let Julian type. It was looking more likely by the minute that *Saint Gray* was the wreck they'd found. And someone related to the ship's owner had been aboard, and had gone to Swan Light—why? And why did Teach care about any of this?

Then Julian tapped his finger on the screen. "Oh, shit."

"What?"

"Well, depending on how much faith you have in this message-board user named WreckFanWren91, there's a rumor that *Saint Gray* sank with treasure on board."

"You're kidding," Mari said, leaning in behind him.

"No," Julian said, still pointing. "Gold, worth millions in today's value. There's a whole fan club of conspiracy theorists about it, but it appears they're all referencing the St. John's location."

"That makes sense," Mari said. "St. John's is so close. If someone at the time described *Saint Gray* as sinking 'near St. John's' it's not surprising it got mixed up. You wouldn't know to look for references to it in another town's paper."

"Let's see if the *Gazette* has anything else," Julian said. He went silent for a moment, scrolling and clicking. "Mari."

"What?"

"Look—'Edward van Gooren puts up for sale today a set of fine ship's wheels, from the strong Vettrey Shipping freighter wrecked two months ago. Taken from the freighter after its crew was aided by the pilot and lighthouse keeper.'"

"*What?*"

"It's an article from December 1913," he said. "Silvestre Swan was in his eighties and still helping shipwreck victims."

No wonder Clara Vettrey had gone back to the light. "Wrecked 'two months ago,' in December," Mari repeated. "That means *Saint Gray* wrecked in October, right before Swan Light fell. It fits what the doctor's note said too." Mari felt her hair stand up. *Look for the whole story.* What had happened in November 1913? "Does the *Cliffs Gazette* still exist?"

"No idea," Julian said, relinquishing the computer and grabbing his phone. "I'll find out."

"And I'll tell Keya to look into Vettrey Shipping," Mari said.

By the time they were done the storm had stopped, though there was still a chill in the air. Mari pulled her jacket tight as they walked back toward Mettle House and Bergy Bits. "That must be why Teach was asking about the Normans," Julian said, shoving his hands into his pockets. "*Saint Gray* sank in Norman waters. Teach probably wants to make sure that if they do find gold, a descendant of Cortney Roland's won't pop out of the woodwork to try to claim it."

"It'll be a legal nightmare even without that," Mari said. "Vettrey Shipping and their insurer will get involved, and both the American and Canadian governments. Besides, the gold might not even be real. No offense to WreckFanWren91."

"Teach certainly thinks it is," Julian said. "They could even have come across the same references we did. That's how they know about Swan Light, and why they're the only ones looking in the right place for *Saint Gray*."

The streets seemed subdued as they walked along, the houses and stores silent, their lights dark, which was surprising. It was just now seven o'clock. But as they approached Highs Street Mari heard music and voices getting louder, and when they swung around the corner it was to what looked like a carnival running through the middle of the street. "The Buskers Festival is this week in St. John's," Mari said, delighted, remembering what Jo had said about her Bergy Bits shirt. "Norman Cliffs must be doing their own." From the Newfoundland research she'd done on the plane, Mari knew that the Buskers Festival was made up of musicians and acrobats and magicians taking over Water Street in St. John's. Norman Cliffs' version was much smaller but probably no less boisterous, though the sole performer seemed to be Theo van Gooren, who was juggling burning sticks and cackling while a group of children shrieked. Mari couldn't decide whether it was more likely that he'd been born with the skill or had decided he should try it for the first time right now. The pockets of color and fire, combined with the after-storm chill and the smell of burning leaves, made it feel like Halloween, somehow, even in summer. She sucked in a breath of air, content, watching as Theo dropped a torch on his foot and scooped it back into the air without so much as a yelp.

Food vendors had set up shop out of tents and truck beds, each one bright and delicious-smelling. "Well, she clearly doesn't need our support," Julian said, watching Jo expertly flipping four burgers at once while engaged in conversation with the Mettle House tent's waiting line.

"Especially once she starts hiring out Theo as in-house entertainment."

Julian laughed. "I'd pay very well for that."

"Exactly." Mari grinned, glanced over at him. In the orange of the flames and streetlights he looked brighter, radiating life. His smell of mint and woodsmoke was even stronger now than it had been in the enclosed space of the library, and it made Mari inexplicably light-headed. This close, she could see the faint goggle lines pressed into his tan skin. "So how long have you had your salvage shop?"

"Fifteen years," Julian said. "I considered selling it, a few years ago. But it ended up not happening." He paused just past Jo's line to let a gaggle of children tumble through. "I'm glad for it," he continued.

"I love the work. It's pretty amazing the ways we're able to really help people. The things we're able to get back for them."

"So why were you going to sell it?"

"I was very close to leaving Boston," he said. He glanced at her, then away. "Personal stuff."

Then Mari remembered what Evangeline had told her. "Evangeline mentioned your ex-wife," she said quietly. "I'm sorry things didn't work out."

He stilled, studying her. "Yeah," he said after a moment. "Just wasn't meant to be. We went into it way too fast."

"What happened?" She winced at her own lack of tact. "If you don't mind me asking."

"There was someone else," Julian said. "Someone from her past. There were signs, I just didn't want to see them. I should have been more careful."

"No wonder you're so cautious now," she said, half teasing to lighten the mood. "I've never met a salvager so obsessed with process."

He met her eyes as somber as ever. "Maybe so," he said. "Better safe than sorry." Then a smile quirked at his mouth. "But *I'm* sorry if I was harsh about that the other day."

"It's okay to be reckless sometimes," she said. "Cutting some corners is good for you. It shows you what the important ones are."

The quirk grew wider. "Yeah? A skeleton in your closet teach you that too?"

"My mom," Mari said, then added, "She died."

Julian's smile vanished. "Shit. I'm so sorry."

"No, it's okay. I just meant . . ." She shook her head. "Sometimes I feel like I have to do everything quickly. To make up for what she didn't get to do. To find things she didn't get to find. And if that means rushing into things, great. At least it means moving."

They had stopped walking, shunted several feet off the path to make room for everyone else, so close to the forest that Mari's back was grazing a tree. Julian filled the whole space in front of her, his dark eyes searching hers, and she felt a thrill of what she'd just been describing. Motion, headlong and bone deep. She opened her mouth—to say or do what, she wasn't sure yet—just as he stepped back, the moment doused in the cool night air between them. It was enough space for her eyes to flicker past him, caught by movement beyond Theo's fiery silhouette, and freeze. "Julian," she hissed, grabbing his arm. "Sam Beauregard is here."

"What? Where?"

"Last tent. Behind Theo."

"Let's talk to him," Julian said at once. "If we explain the situation, maybe he'll let us finish diving on Swan Light before he moves on the wreck." And Mari could have laughed. Still upfront as ever.

"Hold on." Mari kept her grip on his arm. "What is he doing?"

Sam Beauregard was moving slowly along the street, something held up to his head. A walkie-talkie, Mari realized. He was listening intently. As they watched he spoke into it, his hand cupped around his mouth, and set off into the trees that led back to the cliff, away from the festivities. Julian and Mari followed.

Away from the fires and the noise it was immediately cooler, darker, and she heard a mournful yapping. A fox, she thought. Sam Beauregard had vanished. But as she pulled in a breath to call for him, a hand clamped down on her shoulder.

"Fancy seeing you two here," a deep voice said into her ear, one she immediately recognized as the man who'd talked to Julian over the radio from *New Providence*. She turned to see a hulking man with a black eye and a sneer.

Julian recovered from the surprise more quickly than she did. "Hi there," he said amiably. "I'm Julian Henry. I think we spoke on the radio. We have a misunderstanding to clear up with Sam Beauregard."

"Oh yeah?" the man said. "And what's that?"

"We were chartered by a local resident to help find a lighthouse that fell off those cliffs," Julian said, pointing. "You all are obviously looking for something else in the same area. We promise to stay out of your way, if you'll give us a few days to bring the rest of the lighthouse up first. Sound good?"

"Doesn't sound good at all, I'm afraid," came a new voice, and Sam Beauregard emerged from the trees, smiling. His face was hard, the darkness throwing his hooded eyes and jaw into sharp relief. The scar on his eyebrow danced red in the splotchy light. He looked much older than he had when they'd met.

"I should have told you that first day," Mari said to him, and his eyes slid to her. "I get that lying about diving gave the wrong impression. But we only want the lighthouse, like Julian said." Teach must have lost their legal claim, she realized, probably because they had not been able to definitively prove that whatever they'd pulled from the water had come from *Saint Gray*; since Teach had been searching the wrong side of the cliff, it probably hadn't. If Teach had won the rights to the wreck, there would have been no reason to approach Mari and Julian at all; they would have just slapped *Shanty* with a lawsuit for diving in their water.

"'Bring the rest of it up,' you said," Sam Beauregard said. "So you found this lighthouse?"

"Most of it, yes."

"Did you file a claim?" Beauregard asked.

"We don't need a claim," Mari said. "It's not a wreck. We're just salvaging—"

"If you didn't file a claim, then it's open water," Beauregard interrupted. "You can't ask us to stay away."

"Relax," Mari snapped, annoyed. "There's no reason to start a turf war over this."

"Is that right?" Beauregard said, stepping toward her so quickly she almost flinched. "Because I don't believe you. You've been talking to people. You were asking Gerald Cooper questions, snooping around about the Normans."

"That was only because—"

"And we saw you back on the water yesterday," Beauregard barreled on. "From the top of the cliff. If you found this lighthouse like you say, why are you still mowing?"

"She told you, we haven't found all of it," Julian said, but Mari was distracted. Teach had been at the top of the cliff? The thought of them so close to the keeper's house, to where Swan Light had once stood, made her irrationally angry. They had no business there, no right.

"We're not looking for trouble," Julian said.

"How's this for trouble," Beauregard said, leaning toward Julian's face. "You stay away from the water until we're done. If you don't, you'll have Teach to deal with." He stepped back and shifted his jacket enough for Mari to see the gun at his waist. And both men turned and moved off into the woods.

Their words stayed with Mari as she and Julian rejoined the oblivious chatter on Highs Street. Between Sam Beauregard's youth, arrogance, and cowboy attitude, it was hard to take him seriously. But he was armed and clearly felt threatened, and she'd seen wreck wars get ugly much more quickly than this. The promise of millions in shipwrecked treasure was no joke. Beauregard didn't believe that Mari and Julian weren't there to steal his find, and if *New Providence* and *Shanty* were both on the water tomorrow, she worried about what they'd do.

Julian seemed to be having the same thought. "I want to go check on *Shanty*," he said. "Otis should have brought everything from today to the barn already, but I don't trust these goons to leave it alone."

The harbor was quiet, moonlight freckling the water. *Shanty* sat empty in her slip.

At least, mostly empty.

When Mari swept her flashlight over their ship's bow she saw it immediately, a shiny square taped to the pilothouse window. Julian gingerly lifted it free, its silver Sharpie letters coming into focus under the light.

STAY AWAY FROM SAINT GRAY

Mari almost burst out laughing, it was so dramatic. But the reflex died on her lips as she realized what the warning was written on.

It was a glossy photograph, the Sharpie showing up bright against the black that covered most of it. What wasn't darkness was a window, a sliver of light behind lace curtains. And seated at a table, her face old and lined, illuminated in the glow, was Evangeline Devon.

Clara, 1913

Clara Vettrey wasn't supposed to see them.

She watched from her bedroom as her father left for the harbor, his cart clattering loud enough to wake the dead. Gloucester Harbor was walking distance from their home. But getting there, she knew, wasn't the point. The point was the clamor, the announcement that a ship from Vettrey Shipping was on its way to sea. Soon one of them would be steaming for the horizon, *Westyard* or *Gloucester* or *Saint Gray* or *Luxca Deep*, and Clara imagined, as she did every time, what it would be like to trade this prison of trees for belching coal and raucous sound and wide-open ocean air.

She tiptoed barefoot down the hall, past her stepmother Anna's closed door and her stepsister Lowell's open one, and as soon as she touched the dirt of the garden she started running. She made good time through the five-mile stretch of woods that separated the south water from the north, across their awkward stretch of land that stuck out from Massachusetts like a knob, the stunted sister of Cape Cod below, and emerged at the mouth of the Annisquam River just as Mags limped out of her house and fixed Clara in a glare. "You're late."

"I'm not," Clara said, holding her arms out in an exaggerated stretch. "I got here early and took a lap waiting. Nice of you to join me." She and the old woman grinned at each other. Mags's face was dark and weathered, laugh lines like feathers and frown lines like currents, teeth yellow and fingernails black. She was Clara's best friend. Together they hefted the oil drum and made their way along the river to the lighthouse perched at its end. Clara thought it was lovely, with its shining brick and its red-roofed supply house, but Mags always scoffed. She'd seen three lighthouses here, each rebuilt over the same foundation and each, she said, uglier than the last. But she'd been an assistant keeper for every one of them. It had always seemed odd to Clara to have a lighthouse on the bay, shining back toward mainland Massachusetts instead of out to sea. *Sailors can find shore on their own,* Mags liked to say. *Sometimes they forget when they get here that it's more dangerous than the ocean.*

That was hard to imagine today, the river quick and cheery, so clear she could see the oysters at the bottom like the backs of dented silver mirrors. Jack was already at the lighthouse, perched on a railing to clean the windows. "You didn't have to do that," he called, scampering down to lift the oil keg from them.

"Needed the exercise," Clara said, and Jack blushed when their fingers met.

"I saw a steamer's getting ready," the keeper's son said. Clara nodded, watching Jack heft the oil into the supply room. Jack Davis had tan skin and thick hair and beautiful brown eyes, and he'd gained what seemed like two feet this past summer. He no longer looked anything like the scrawny boy she'd grown up with, back when their whole ragtag group of children would race through the river, Clara always ahead of them, before the others got jealous and started to pull at her ankles. *Slow down,* they complained. *It's just a game.* But Jack had never tried to hold her back.

"Yes," she said as Jack finished moving the barrel and stood. "It leaves tomorrow."

"Good riddance," Mags sniffed.

"That means you can come for dinner," Jack said hopefully.

It did, Clara thought. Dinner and even longer. The whole world was wide open to her now, for the next two months, until Nathaniel

Vettrey returned from Halifax. He didn't always sail on his own ships, lost instead in the elaborate planning and scheming of running his empire. But even when he was lost, he was always home. This time, he was leaving.

This time, she wouldn't miss her chance.

Anna wouldn't care, wouldn't miss her, and Clara could spend her days with Mags and with the Davises, Jack's lighthouse-keeper father and silly younger brothers. There would be no rabbits to skin or clothes to scrub or ledgers to carry to and from the governor's house while avoiding the governor's gum-tooth smile. No father watching her stir the stew, pinching her arm and twisting hard when it took too long to boil. Nothing but nights memorizing Mags's maps, tracing their curves and dreaming of the day she could see their places for herself; running along the river, moving too quick for anything to catch her.

And suddenly the trees that had always felt like cages felt more like the veins of spread-wide wings.

~~~

After the day had passed in a crawl of sunlight Clara ran all the way home before dinner, too eager to wait. She'd bring all her clothes, she thought, the maps she'd traded Anna's comb for and her strings of beads from the harbor. When she reached the yard, Lowell was in the garden. Clara squatted next to her sister, who threw dirty fingers around her neck. "Hi, Lowie. What are you planting?"

Lowell was the good daughter, the dark daughter. Crow-haired as Nathaniel, with the same clear brown eyes. Nothing like Clara, who'd come out blond and blue-eyed to a mother who'd vanished right afterward. *She ran off with him*, the town had whispered. *The witch's boy.*

The witch.

Mags.

It was Clara's dearest secret, these days spent at the hut in the woods. A place she'd avoided for years before curiosity got the better of her, and then, immediately, the only place that had ever felt like home. She kept these days tucked tight to her chest, looking over her shoulder, always tensed and ready to flee if the wrong pair of eyes came across her. She didn't need to think hard to imagine what Nathaniel would do if he found out. He didn't need another reason to make Clara pay for her mother's crimes.

Lowell held up a carrot, then wrinkled her nose. "Your hands smell funny."

Clara grinned. "I'm sure they do. I was carrying oil this morning."

"What's oil?"

"It's smelly water that helps fires burn."

"What did you burn?"

"It's for the lighthouse on the other bay," Clara said. "I'll take you there soon." She let the promise linger on her tongue. *Soon.* She grinned even wider, watching the sun sparkling in the leaves as she stood and swung through the door.

And into the back of her father's hand.

Clara stumbled backward, stunned, barely catching hold of the frame to stay upright. Lowell squeaked in alarm. Nathaniel Vettrey cocked his head, absently rubbing his knuckles. "Where have you been?"

"Nowhere," Clara managed.

"*It's for the lighthouse on the other bay,*" he mimicked. He fixed her in his dark gaze, and though she always tried not to, she cowered. "I know where they keep the oil for that lighthouse, Clara."

"It wasn't—" Clara said, automatically hunching, placating. "I just meant—"

"Dada!" Lowell said, scampering inside. "You're not on the big boat."

"I'm not going on the boat this time, sweet," Nathaniel said, scooping her up, his eyes still on Clara. "It's leaving in the morning, but Dada has important things to do here." Clara felt the sunlight inside her shatter. "Run along and get ready for supper, now. The governor will be joining us." He put Lowell on the floor, where she threw a concerned look at Clara before skittering off to the kitchen. Her father cocked his head. "You just meant what?"

A long time ago, at her very first day of school, a teacher had asked Clara who she wanted to grow up to be like. Before the whispers about her mother and the witch's boy had ever reached her ears, she'd thought of Nathaniel's commanding presence, the way he could talk anyone into anything, and smiled.

She knew now that she was nothing like Nathaniel. But hated how much she still wanted to be.

"We were just talking," she said, her voice small, and his silence in response was its own kind of threat.

The governor's cart interrupted them, but Clara knew it was a temporary savior. Dinner was extraordinary, pheasant and lamb and potatoes so tender they melted on her tongue, and Clara didn't taste a bite. *That means you can come for dinner.* Jack's family and Mags would be having slimy ham and biscuits so hard they could knock a tooth out, and Clara would have been so happy. The ache in her throat overwhelmed her, and it was all she could do not to scream. She felt her father's eyes on her, and the governor's; heard their laughter; heard *witch*. After, she slept, her last hazy thoughts of the impossibly far horizon and its far-off worlds that had to be kinder than this one.

〜〜〜

A long time ago, at her very first day of school, a teacher had asked for Clara's name. "Clara," she'd said, and a smile had played on his face.

"Clara what?"

"Vettrey," she'd said, breathless and proud, and the teacher had laughed in her face.

She knew, then, how a name that fit one person so perfectly could hang off another like old, tattered clothes.

~~~

Clara woke in darkness and guilt, her father's eyes burning every time she closed her own.

Wide awake and itching for fresh air, Clara slid out of bed and into her coat, padded out of the house. As she started running, the winter night flooded her brain and her lungs, cleansing her. She took the path to Mags's without thinking, intending vaguely on a wide loop to the lighthouse and back to bed. But when she reached the little hut, she froze.

There was a jagged black space where there should have been a glimmer. A window, shattered. And below it, painted dripping red: WITCH.

Clara's stomach seized. And she knew in a moment of clear and chilling clarity that it was never going to stop. That she was never going to be enough to defend Mags, or even herself. That this wasn't her own window only because of her father's cruel mercy, in whatever supply he had left. This wasn't her own window, yet.

Then a sound cut through her own beating heart.

The long-drawn blow of a ship's horn.

And it was enough to wake her.

Her father wasn't going to Halifax.

But his ship was.

She ran until she thought her feet were bleeding, on and on and on until she burst out into the clearing of Gloucester Harbor and saw the steamship waiting at its docks. It wasn't the towering, graceful *Westward* as she'd expected, the pride of Vettrey Shipping, but *Saint Gray*, the newest and smallest, squatting catlike at the end of the wharf, her mast-head lights bright as tiny suns. Clara moved so quickly, her movements bold and sure, that no one tried to stop her. She crept along beside a cart, and as the man driving it slowed to pull onto the gangway she leapt aboard, hoisting herself into the only tiny free space. The cart was piled with cardinal-red boxes, SAN FRANCISCO BANK stamped on their sides, that were unloaded from the cart into the hold under cover of darkness so that no one would see them, by which time Clara was long gone.

Clara wasn't supposed to see them.

And then with a roar of coal fire and a bone-deep shudder, *Saint Gray* was heading east to the ocean, Clara crouched in her belly, bound for anywhere but home.

〜〜〜

Now she looked down at the once-proud ship, crushed and sagging against the mouth of the cove, as she waited for Lou Roland. Which meant, since she was sitting with her legs over the edge of the cliff, heels bumping against the rock, that she had to turn every few minutes to make sure he hadn't arrived and was just too afraid to get closer. She couldn't understand it. If she'd grown up in a place like this, as free as Lou had, she would have danced along the cliff every chance she got. She wouldn't have been afraid of anything. When the doctor from Norman Cliffs had asked her name, she'd answered without thinking. But here, saying *Clara Vettrey* hadn't gotten a laugh. It had gotten respect. People heard *Vettrey* and knew *power*. They didn't know anything further, and they didn't need to. For once, her last name did what she'd always wished it would.

"Hello, there." Clara turned to see Lou standing behind her, a predictably safe distance from the edge, eyeing the lighthouse apprehensively. It clucked at him, but he didn't seem to hear it. Clara clambered to her feet. "I have everything you asked for," he said, handing her a piece of paper. It was the sketch he'd showed her before, now more carefully laid out. "All the measurements, and the list of equipment we'd need to move Swan Light."

"Thank you," she said. "Do you think Cort caught on?"

"No," Lou said. "Not yet, at least. I've told people to drop notes in the suggestion box at the bank if they can help. He'll never look there."

"Good."

Lou was squinting up at the lighthouse, leery. "Have you spoken to Swan about any of this?" he asked. "Is he aware that a town's worth of people will be showing up to move the light?"

"Of course not," Clara said. "It's a surprise."

"I'm not sure it will be the good kind," he said. "Especially if it doesn't work."

"It will work," she said.

"Cort is going to see that something's happening eventually," Lou said dubiously. "And I'm not sure it will keep him from coming around to bother Swan about the deed again. He really needs that money. And if he sees that Swan is deliberately going around the bank—"

"Lou," Clara said, frustrated. "Shush. Everything is going to be fine. At least we're trying, unlike your bank."

"Okay." He settled awkwardly onto the ground beside her. "What will you do afterward? Write to your father for another ship home?"

"No," she said, still annoyed. "I'm not going back there. I'm not like you. My father won't just *send a ship* for me." She froze at her slip. As far as Lou knew, she was exactly who his brother thought she was: wealthy, entitled. A Vettrey. And she trusted him, at least enough for this task, but she didn't need him knowing the truth just yet.

But Lou was frowning, thoughtful. "So where are you going to go?"

"I don't know yet," she said. "Stay here, if Mr. Swan lets me? At least for a while."

"You want to be a lighthouse keeper?"

"Well, we don't all want to be bankers."

"I don't really want to be a banker either." He was looking at her now, and she got the uncomfortable feeling that he understood exactly what she wasn't saying. "If it makes you feel better, if I were trapped in Gloucester, I'm not sure my family would send a ship for me either."

Clara couldn't help chuckling, but then forced her eyebrows down. "Still," she said, "you might not want your family's influence, but at least you have the option. Not everyone does." Waves lapped far below them. Somewhere at the other end of this water was Lowell in the garden, and Jack's family eating ham and biscuits, and a river filled with oysters bright as mirrors. And a house with a broken window, maybe fixed now. At the other end of this water was everything she'd left behind.

"Fair enough," Lou said. He looked like he was going to keep talking but stopped and shook his head. "None of this solves the most important problem about moving the lighthouse," he said. "It still takes a lot of money we don't have. Unless you're planning on robbing my bank."

"No," Clara said. "Even better." She lifted the leather bag that sat beside her. After this morning, her fifth or sixth dive, it was heavier than ever. She thought back to something Abigail had said to Gable Strauss at dinner, trying to impress him: *No daughter of Nathaniel Vettrey's is a stranger here.* She smiled at Lou's face when she opened the bag. For better or worse, Nathaniel had given her this name. And he'd given her something else too.

"Clara," Lou said, his voice strangled, as he looked down at the golden half eagle coins that stuffed the bag to its brim, shiny as the day they'd been cast. "Where did you get that?"

"You know where," she said. "You were with me." She turned to look back down at the jagged black hull, remnants still bobbing around it, wrenched free on every wave. A tangle of netting. A brown boot. A splintered plank from a room full of cardinal-red boxes no one else knew was on board. "Down there," she said. "There's so much more."

∼∼∼

The second part of her plan, Lou couldn't know about.

Clara walked to town just after dusk, after Lou had gone and she'd lit the tower and fed Stay. The Norman mansion was brightly lit, loud with children's laughter inside. "Mama!" one cried, delighted, and Clara paused, picturing Lowell in the garden, dirty and happy. She set her jaw and kept walking. Norman Bank, by contrast, was silent. Clara raised her fist and knocked.

It took a moment for Cort to answer, and when he did he looked surprised. "Miss Vettrey," he said. "Please, come in."

It had begun as a seed before she'd even met him, when she'd seen the way Mr. Swan looked at the lighthouse. The same way Mags had. He didn't have anyone to defend him either. And Clara hadn't been brave enough to stick up for Mags, but the night of the wreck had changed something inside her, as if the rock and the waves were now inside her spine. She'd survived worse than Nathaniel in just one night. Cort would be nothing.

"Forgive me for dropping in like this," she said. She tried to mimic Nathaniel's speech, his easy, haughty cadence. "I wanted to apologize for my behavior during dinner the other night. I acted rashly. But I think your grandmother was right. There's a lot our two families could do for one another." Cort looked bemused, and she made herself stop. *Don't oversell.* Another thing she'd heard Nathaniel say. *Right to the point.* "I'd like to talk to you about that deed in New York City."

At that, eagerness bloomed in Cort's blue eyes. "Has Swan said something?"

"No," Clara said firmly. "I don't believe he still has it. He didn't understand its importance. He's not like us," she added, watching him closely. She was relieved when he nodded. "That's why I'd like to make you a different offer instead."

His head tilted. "I'm listening."

She took a deep breath. Thought of Mags, and *witch*, and Nathaniel commanding a room without fear. And lied. "I work closely with my father on business matters," she said. "We've been building connections with bankers in New York. Due to recent events, as I'm sure you know. The Federal Reserve and the centralization of the bank." She tried to say it as casually as Lou had, even though she had no idea what any of it meant, and was rewarded by Cort's eyes going brighter as he nodded again.

"Good on your father," he said charitably. "I know firsthand what a challenge it can be."

"Yes," Clara said. "The thing is, he doesn't currently have any partners outside the United States. And I'm sure he'd like one." She paused again, letting the implication sink in. Cort was practically radiating excitement.

"Well, we'd certainly be interested in that," he said.

"Good," she said. "Then don't worry about Silvestre Swan, or this deed. I'll write to my father and he'll send money for twice the land Swan's deed would get you, so you can expand in America faster. You can be his first British partner."

"He's raising a smart young woman," Cort said.

Then a door beside them opened. "Papa?" It was a girl, the same one who'd been on his wife's lap at dinner. She was small and wan, dark sickles under her eyes, her breath a soft wheeze. Clara saw a small, blanketed cot sitting among the boxes in the room behind her. "Papa." Cort was at her side at once, and Clara felt a fissure of uncertainty. She'd known this plan would work because of how quickly Cort had reminded her of Nathaniel, but this was a side she'd never seen of either of them. Cort knelt beside his daughter, a hand tracing small circles on her back.

"My youngest," he said, looking up at Clara, and the fissure she felt deepened at the softness on his face. "My other children are too loud for her sometimes, so I bring her here with me when she's up to it. She went to Dr. Wright's earlier and is a little tired now, but she was very brave, weren't you?" This last question directed back to the girl, who curled her chubby fingers in his shirt. Clara teetered, on the edge of leaving them in peace.

Then she thought again of Nathaniel, of the way he'd been with Lowell. Cradling her with one hand, a rock ready in the other. *Witch.* Clara stiffened her neck and closed her eyes. She pulled the bag of gold from her pocket. "Here," she said, handing it over. "This can serve as a gesture of good faith until I write to my father."

He didn't second-guess it, didn't act like she wasn't the type of person who should have gold at the ready.

He smiled, thanked her.

For better or worse, Nathaniel had given her this name.

And Clara left feeling braver than she ever had before.

Mari, 2014

If Mari were ever informed that a group of gun-toting, gold-hungry treasure hunters were spying on her, she hoped she'd handle it half as well as Evangeline Devon did.

She and Julian rushed to their sponsor's house as soon as they found the note on *Shanty*, and Mari explained their night while Julian took a lap of the barn to make sure Teach hadn't tried to get inside. In all likelihood, she'd realized in dismay, the fact that Sam Beauregard had found Evangeline was Mari's own fault. When he'd introduced himself at the library, it had been right after Mari had ended the phone call with her sponsor. He'd overheard the bit about needing a ship to the cliffs; he'd probably overheard Evangeline's name, too, and ferreted out just where to go to try and blackmail Mari and Julian away from his wreck. Mari felt as deeply uncomfortable as when she'd learned that Beauregard had followed her to Horizons Community and Gerald Cooper. Beauregard probably didn't see any of it as threatening, just making a statement and marking his territory. But if he really believed in a shipwreck full of gold, those lines could get blurred quickly. And if he thought that Mari and Julian were there for the wreck, then he thought Evangeline was too. That made all of them targets.

But Evangeline listened to her story and at the end of it said only, "Well, that explains the footprints in my garden, then. Would either of you like tea?" So, even though she herself was still rattled, Mari crossed the lawn to the barn to get the blueprints and photos that would show Evangeline their progress.

"They haven't touched anything in here," Julian said when she stepped into the purple gloom. She joined him beside the tank, looking down at the ghostly remnants of Swan Light's giant lens. The bath was just starting its work. Iron-brass edges had begun to emerge from the mess of salt and sea rock, glowing dully through the water. It really was beautiful. In the excitement of finding and researching *Saint Gray*, she'd almost forgotten to pay attention to the lighthouse. Julian felt it too, she could tell, standing with his hands resting on the edge of the bath, his eyes on its lines. For a moment they just stood staring, taking in this chunk of metal and glass that had guided people home above the sea and survived a century below it, until Julian nudged his shoulder against hers and they turned to go back to the house.

Evangeline's kettle whistled merrily, with cookies in the oven and a fire crackling in the fireplace. She'd put on music, a quick, soft Irish-sounding tune fuzzed with static. Outside rain dripped and puddled onto the porch, thunder rumbling low in the distance. The old woman leaned close to the table as Mari spread Keya's blueprint across it, Julian holding the other side to weigh it down. Mari narrated it line by line to Evangeline, starting with the tower and working her way up. For the most part, they had no way of knowing which of their finds had come from which parts of the lighthouse. Keya had determined, from the few more pictures she'd found, that Swan Light's tower hadn't had windows below its lens, so each piece of stone was indistinguishable from the next. But from the sheer amount they'd found, especially the three largest pieces that still had iron spines, they guessed they'd collected about seventy percent of the tower. They'd done even better with the lens's clockwork mechanism, which was now fully reconstructed, and they'd found several pieces of the roof and railing, a fully intact lantern-room window frame, and most of the rest of the lens. Evangeline pored over all of it, her face unreadable.

"Evangeline, I have to ask you what comes next," Mari said finally. "This might be as much of Swan Light as we're able to pull up, especially with Teach in the mix now. We can be ready for a court battle if it comes to that, but first we need to know if you even want us to keep diving."

Evangeline shook her head. "You can stop diving on the light, for now," she said, and Mari's heart fell. The old woman ran a finger along the letter from Amos Wright that Keya had found. "This girl, though. Clara Vettrey. What have you found about her?"

"Not much more than that," Mari said, gesturing at the page.

Evangeline was still except for her eyes tracing patterns back and forth across the blueprint and the stack of papers. "Keep looking into her," she said finally. "Her and Silvestre Swan. That's what I'd like from you now."

"Okay," Mari said, sending a quick text relaying this to Keya. The archivist was already scraping the bottom of the barrel on information about Silvestre Swan, she knew. But there was no harm in doing a final pass. And selfishly, now, part of her was thrilled. Looking into Clara Vettrey meant looking into *Saint Gray*, the ship she'd arrived on. Whether she'd meant to or not, Evangeline had given them permission to explore the shipwreck.

~~~

Mari woke to a crack of thunder the next morning and rolled over to her window to see the bay frothing and frantic. She let out an involuntary growl so loud it made Beddy leap from her bed. At least *New Providence* was still moored, her hull larger and redder than anyone else's. If the weather ruined Mari's dive day, at least it ruined Teach's too.

She decided to use the time to return to Silvestre Swan's house to take a round of pictures for Evangeline's exhibit. The storm felt right for that, with the kind of dark skies and blurry seas that would have marked Swan Light's strongest moments. She tucked her umbrella into her dive suit as she pedaled Jo's bike along the muddy trail to the cliff. The wind was still July-warm, the rain turning to mist the higher she climbed from town, and she sucked in a breath when she reached the house, the wet air refreshing in her lungs. The part of the house that was still standing kept her dry, its inside the same as the last time she'd been here. The flowers were brighter, though, their pinks glowing through the gloom. Mari snapped their picture first, entranced.

"Hey," someone called, and she turned to see Julian, a green umbrella stamped with BERGY BITS in his hand, his hair flat with rainwater despite it. "Jo said you'd be here." He whistled and ran a hand down the crumbling doorway. "Wow. That's unfortunate."

"I know," Mari said. "How's Otis?"

"I don't think he slept a minute," Julian said, ducking under the doorframe to stand beside her. "He's installing cameras on the ship and in the barn now, so if Teach tries anything at least we'll have proof."

"Not really what the poor kid signed up for," Mari said, and Julian grinned.

"No," he said. "But that's true for all of us now."

They settled into a comfortable silence, Mari photographing every inch of the house while Julian sifted through the debris for anything she missed. All the while, rain clattered on the water ten feet ahead of them and eighty feet down. In Silvestre Swan's time this house must have been a comfortable distance back in the woods, with a lovely view of the lighthouse and the water. Now the view was far too much of the water as the cliff continued to erode. In another hundred years this would probably be gone too. The thought made her ache.

"Has Evangeline seemed off to you?" Julian asked, and she looked over. He was holding a bar of dripping wet firewood in his hands.

"Off how?"

"Just . . . older than usual." He grimaced. "Don't tell her I said that. I just can't help worrying. She says she doesn't care about Beauregard, but this is a lot of stress for someone over a hundred years old."

Mari had almost forgotten how old Evangeline was. She didn't seem it, and didn't seem any older to Mari now than when they'd started. She thought back to last night, how intently Evangeline had pored over Mari's research, matching her page for page well into the night. "I think she's tougher than we think."

Then her phone rang. It was Keya, her voice quick and excited. "Check your email," she said. Mari put her on speaker and pulled up her email as Keya kept talking. "We found them by accident. I've had my coworker looking into Nathaniel Vettrey's bank records, to see if there's any truth to the gold *Saint Gray* might have been carrying. He had another daughter, Lowell, who ended up inheriting his money, so we looked into her too. She was a bit of a photography enthusiast, and someone later digitalized her collection. But look at what ended up with them." There were two black-and-white photographs attached to Keya's email. Mari opened the first one and sucked in a breath.

It was taken from nearly the exact spot she was standing now.

In the foreground was a windowsill, a head of hair blurred on the other side from someone just out of the shot. And in startlingly clear focus behind it was a lighthouse, textured white stone with a single iron railing around the top, crisscrossed windows with a single open pane separating it from a domed black roof. The second picture was taken down the side of a cliff. But instead of waves at the bottom, there was the battered half hull of a steamship lying on its side, its deck flat against the rock.

"Lowell Vettrey took these?" Mari asked, stunned.

"No," Keya said triumphantly. "Her sister, Clara, did. It's written on the back of the lighthouse one. In pencil, so it never would have showed up in a digital search. *Love, Clara.*"

Mari stared at the photos, blown away. They'd known that Silvestre Swan had helped *Saint Gray*, but these pictures showed more than that. Clara Vettrey had come back to the lighthouse afterward, in the beautiful weather of these photos, had been inside the keeper's house. She wasn't just a faceless crew member to Silvestre Swan. He'd known her personally.

"There are more," Keya said. "Tracing those photos led us to a list of sixteen photos and a diary by Clara Vettrey. But that's where it got weird. The rest of it is blocked in what looks like an academic journal archive, but we couldn't figure out how to access it. It's registered to a group that actually reached out to us about Clara and the Normans a few years ago."

Mari and Julian looked at each other. "Let me guess," she said. "Teach."

"That's right," Keya said. "They only ever called us the once. They were creepy. But there's one good thing. Their site has a legal line saying the location of the physical version of their archive is on file with the New England Maritime Foundation. So I called *them*, and I got an address. Teach's headquarters are at 15 Salt Street in Boston. That's where the rest of the pictures and Clara Vettrey's diary will be."

"15 Salt," Julian said as they hung up. "I know where that is. Give me a minute." He stepped toward the cliff, taking out his own phone.

Mari sat on the windowsill and refreshed her email reflexively, her thoughts racing. So *this* was how Teach had drawn the connection between the Normans and Swan Light. They'd had Clara's photos and her diary all along, locked away, probably ignored after they didn't give the exact location of *Saint Gray*'s wreck. If you didn't already know this cliff, there were no details in the two pictures that identified where it was. And Clara's diary might not mean much to Teach, but it could hold the key to the story Evangeline was looking for.

She had several new emails below Keya's, and in her distraction it took her a moment to realize that one of them was from Hector. She opened it, her mouth suddenly dry.

Hey, Mar, it started. I've got some bad news.

Well, two pieces of bad news. The team lost the ROV last night. Tim is hopeful he can pull her out. But bad news number two is that they'd already searched most of Ursula when they lost it. Mari, it's not looking good. There's more to the hull that we missed because it read as debris on the sonar. It's about eighteen feet longer than *Californian*. They grabbed some stuff and I'm looking it over but I really think we got this one wrong.

Mari dropped her phone into her pocket without reading the rest. Ursula wasn't *Californian*.

She felt suddenly nauseated, dizzy at the whiplash between Keya's news and Hector's. Part of what had made her so sure about Ursula was the size of the target's hull, the same as *Californian's* down to the foot. There were plenty of things that could make a hull shorter after an explosion and decades underwater. There was nothing that could make it longer.

She'd been wrong.

And that meant that the whole project, ten years of waiting and hoping and losing, came down to Skyline, a target they might not even have time to search.

She rubbed at her forehead, Keya's note and Hector's clashing in her mind. Was this how it was meant to be? To come so far only to be foiled by a long hull and a group of treasure hunters? To have the one thing you needed always barely and hugely out of reach? Mari felt her years of certainty quaking on their foundation, and in a flash she was back in her childhood nightmare, right after her mother's death, a shipwreck watching her from the darkness like a monster she could feel but couldn't see. A monster that didn't care whether or not she found it. It didn't care about her at all. And this time, she was in far too deep to find the sun.

"Okay, Keya's right," Julian said, returning, pocketing his phone. He stopped at the look on her face. "What's wrong?"

"My other wreck," she said, trying to rearrange her face. "We found out our prime target can't be *Californian*. The wreck site is too long."

He leaned forward, eyes taking in her face. "Are you okay?"

"I just . . . we found this target five years ago," she said. "Ursula. And this whole time, I've been so sure that it was *Californian*. I was fine doing my due diligence, searching our other hits, but I *knew*. And I was wrong."

Julian considered that for a moment, then sat down beside her on the ruined windowsill. "Maybe you weren't."

"Maybe *Californian* somehow grew twenty feet underwater?"

"No." He shifted toward her. "You said you had to leave another target before you finished searching it, right? Because Evangeline needed you here?"

She was surprised that he remembered that. She barely remembered telling him, their first day on the water. "Yeah."

"So maybe it doesn't matter how promising this one was," he said. "Maybe it's just proving you need to revisit an old target instead. Like Edison."

"Edison?"

"Yeah." He nudged his shoulder against hers. "The whole inspiring quote about lightbulbs: he didn't fail a thousand times to make one, it just took a thousand steps. You found the wrecks that were wrong. Now go find the ones that weren't."

Mari nudged back, grateful. He was right. She'd spent so long engrossed in Ursula that she'd almost forgotten the day Skyline had appeared on their sonar, not even a week later. And she'd written off Cherry, maybe too soon. There were so many reasons to stop looking, to stop caring, to give up. But maybe there were more reasons not to.

Then she realized something else: how odd it was that she'd brought this up with Julian at all. Back in Greece, she hadn't told any of *Mercury*'s crew about Stuart Noble pulling their funding. They'd been interchangeable, indistinguishable, all of them only there to do their jobs. Her fully included. Her at the top of that list. But working with Julian had been different from the start. He approached it differently than she did, true, glued to the ship while she talked to Gerald Cooper, still and steady while she raced along as usual. But unlike with *Mercury*'s crew, it hadn't even occurred to her to hide her bad news from Julian. He felt like a teammate in a way that none of her other salvage partners had, not even Tim. In his own way, this wasn't just a job for him either. "Why did you agree to work with Evangeline again?" she asked.

If he was thrown by the change in direction, true to form he didn't show it. He rubbed his chin, thoughtful. "I like Evangeline," he said. "She's what I hope I'm like at her age. She's never stopped asking questions. And I was a little too distracted by my personal life on my last dive for her to answer those questions as well as I could have." He shrugged. "This was a chance to do it right."

"I get that," Mari said. "I don't think she feels you owed her anything, though."

"I know she doesn't," Julian said. "But I do."

"How so?"

He shifted his weight on the wall, his jacket brushing against hers. "When my marriage was ending," he said, "on Evangeline's last project, I wanted to give up on diving completely. It just seemed so . . . trivial, I suppose, compared to this real-life stuff that was happening. What you said about feeling as though you had to do everything quickly after your mom died—I had the opposite reaction. I almost shut down."

Mari nodded, listening closely, and for a flickering moment as Julian took a breath to keep talking she thought back to herself at her mother's funeral, hands full of other people's food, numb and aimless. The speed had come later. The shutting down had come first.

"I thought about that dive a lot afterward," Julian continued. "Evangeline's had a hard life; I don't know how much she's told you.

She was sick for a long time. And to her, funding these projects is a way to pay it forward. To give other people the chances she didn't get. I used that mentality to get back on track. I guess this dive is my way of thanking her for it."

Maybe it's just proving you need to revisit an old target instead. Julian was right, Mari mused as she ran her eyes along the gray horizon. There was no right way to do this. And that meant there was no wrong way either.

"Thanks for telling me all that," Mari said. "I needed it, I think." He leaned his shoulder against hers again, hard, a beat too long. And there was that feeling again, the racing in her bones. "And thank you for not pointing out that I could have avoided this by just moving more carefully with the *Californian* targets."

He grinned. "You'll find it," he said. "No matter how fast or slow you need to move. I really believe that." His phone chirped, and he glanced down at it. Mari tried to ignore the fissure of disappointment that bubbled up when his eyes left hers.

"What were you going to say before?" she asked, nodding at his phone. "What was Keya right about?"

He tilted the phone toward her. "15 Salt," he said. "Teach's headquarters. It's a corporate workspace; I have a friend in the same building. He said it will be closed this weekend because his company is hosting an event there, some kind of gala, which is a bummer. I was thinking about calling Teach to see if we could pay them for the photos and diary or something, but if it's closed they might not have—"

But Mari's pulse was quickening again, an idea blooming fully formed. A fast idea, a reckless one. So reckless it just might work. "Julian," she said, cutting him off. "Do you trust me?"

He met her eyes. "Yes."

"Okay." She stood and held out her hand, and he took it. "If you get to suggest something careful, then I get to suggest something wild. How far are we from the airport?"

Swan, 1913

To Swan's annoyance, though not entirely to his surprise, both of his guests had extended their stay.

As with Clara, he'd expected Lou to leave the morning after he'd arrived. And as with Clara, he hadn't. Instead, they were both making themselves quite at home. The cliff now skittered constantly with their comings and goings, the icebox packed with the misshapen berries Clara took pity on and brought back from the woods, the kitchen table covered in driftwood from the cove, the kitchen perpetually loud with their arguments about how close was too close to the sea. They brought books and sundries from town, the most distressing of which was a boxlike camera Clara had wheedled from Dr. Wright and now took joy in snapping in Swan's face when he least expected it. If it weren't for how happy Stay and the tower seemed to be at all the new attention, Swan would have barred the doors on them long ago.

Clara was the most energetic person Swan had ever met. Newfoundland prided itself on slow and steady, on measured, on thoughtful, and even its most stormy-headed sailors didn't run around the way she did. Swan was convinced that one day she was going to run right off the edge of the cliff and even more convinced that, if she did, she'd simply pop back up at the bottom and try to do it again. Lou was her opposite, quiet and watchful, wary of the water and the light and the cliff. They made an odd pair. But their extra hands, at least, were helpful. With the two of them taking on the maintenance of his property, Swan found himself sleeping earlier and later and better every day, though his body kept its reflex of waking throughout the night to check the oil. Clara fixed the oil shed and the broken side-room window, and Swan was amazed at how much more light it let in. She navigated the tower's wilting iron with caution and care, and in return its stone hummed more lightly than it had in years. *She'll know,* Swan thought. *When the end comes, she'll feel it as much as I do.*

Because there was no saving it now. He'd caught himself thinking it a few days ago, sitting in his chair on the back porch, pressing his fingertips into its wooden whorls, and he'd wondered idly where he was meant to go after the tower fell. Would he stay here and watch the sea without it? Could he bring this chair to Peter's? Could he stomach living anywhere else?

Then he'd realized it was the first time he'd thought *after*, not *if*.

He hadn't been able to stop thinking it since, and for once the light didn't protest. Maybe some part of both of them had known it for years, even as Swan wrote letter after letter to Norman Bank. Maybe some part of both of them was tired of pretending. It was simply too late. The tower was going to fall. And Swan found that accepting it made the remaining days sweeter, even with his two new guests.

It was nice, near the end, not to be alone.

And so two weeks passed and Swan learned to live around them, gruff and guarded and waiting for the moment when the tower finally tired of their constant ruckus and sent them all plunging into the sea.

One evening he found himself sitting in his chair while Clara lit the tower. It was nice, too, to watch this from a greater distance, to see the flame flicker and leap and the lens start churning. He didn't notice Lou Roland sliding into Peter's chair until the boy cleared his throat. "Am I interrupting you?"

"No more than usual," Swan said, and Lou grinned.

"Good," he said. "I have something to tell you, but you can't tell Clara I did." Swan squinted at him.

"I don't like the sound of that."

"No, it's a good thing," Lou said. "When she goes into town every day, she's been talking to everyone she can find about helping move the lighthouse. So you won't need the bank at all. She wants it to be a surprise, and I haven't said anything because I don't want to get your hopes up in case it doesn't work. But I . . ." He picked at his hem. "I just thought you should know how many people love you down there. How many people are on your side. She's very convincing; I think she's even got Gable Strauss warming up to you."

Swan watched the tower, torn between feeling humbled and heartbroken. A moment ago he'd been resigning himself to the end. Now, Lou was right. A stubborn flare of hope. Inside the tower Clara called something out, unintelligible, and she and the stone both laughed. A moment later she skipped out the door toward them. "One of the muntins is about to break," she said. "I'll talk to the smith tomorrow about a new one while I'm in town."

Still overwhelmed, Swan could only nod, and as Clara looked between his face and Lou's sheepish one, understanding dawned on her own. She reached out and smacked Lou in the arm. "Lou! What did I tell you?"

"I'm sorry," he said. "I thought he should know."

"I'm glad to know," Swan said. He looked up at Clara. "And I'm very glad for you to try. But why?" The tower tutted at him in reprimand. "Why are you doing any of this?"

She stared at him, uncomprehending. "Because I owe you. You saved my life."

"You don't owe me anything for that," Swan said.

"Yes, I do," Clara said. "I wasn't even supposed to be on *Saint Gray*. I snuck on because my father hurt my friend, to punish me. I didn't stay and help her. I just ran. But if I left only to let someone else get hurt too, what was the point? I should sit back while it happens again?"

She was so very young, he thought, so fierce. So very much like Nico. And maybe that was what this cliff had always needed. *I'll get it, Soph.*

Maybe this cliff had always belonged to people like her.

"You can't stop every bad person in the world," Swan said after a moment. "Or every bad thing. But it's very admirable that you want to try."

"I don't need to stop *every* bad thing," Clara said. "Just this one. If I don't, I abandoned Mags for nothing."

Swan didn't need another stray. He emphatically didn't need two. But now Clara had her head on Lou's shoulder, these two children who didn't fit their worlds, who had made the tower their home the same way Silvy Swan had so many years ago when everything else around him had fallen apart. Who knew without being told that these cliffs were so much safer than they looked, that as long as the tower stood shining nothing else could hurt them, no matter how the storms came in. Swan didn't need a stray, but maybe they weren't so different after all, Silvy and Clara and Lou. The light would fall, or maybe it wouldn't. For now it was swinging around above them and the waves were crashing against *Saint Gray* below. And in this single dusk-drenched moment, it was enough.

Mari, 2014

Mari's gala dress, rented sight unseen from a shop in Boston, looked like it had been made for this very occasion. It was silver-black and sequined, inky and fluid, and as she examined herself in the hotel mirror, nerves jangling and stomach tense around the protein bar she'd forced herself to eat, she considered that if she had to carry out a heist in the impracticality of a dress, at least it was one that made her feel like a sea creature.

Julian was equally tense in his dark green suit, drumming his fingers against his phone throughout their several-block walk from the hotel to Teach's headquarters. Mari was as shocked that he was still going along with this as she was sure to her core it would work. She couldn't explain it, this throwing caution to the wind. It had been easy so far, to get Julian's friend's building card, to rent the clothes. This brick building was all that stood between her and Clara Vettrey's story. It was born of frustration at Teach and *Californian*, of the thrill of throwing something just to see it fly. And it was a dozen photos and a diary—how long could they take to read?

And as the elevator door opened onto the seventeenth floor, Mari felt herself fly even higher.

Because this was her kind of gala.

The company hosting the event, Dodd Seawhether, was a maritime equipment manufacturer. On a normal night this room in their corporate headquarters was probably a typical banquet ballroom: an open floor with beige walls and a scatter of high-top tables, a shiny square dance floor at the end, floor-to-ceiling windows looking out into the heart of Boston. But tonight the overhead lights were masked with blue glass, the floor strewn with sequins, the tables met by delicate golden spirals that draped down from the ceiling. And the windows had been covered end to end with fish tanks glowing an eerie teal, shimmering every few feet with the city lights behind them. More tanks had been set up in pillars sitting throughout the room, and Julian nudged Mari and pointed at the closest one as they stepped into the room. "I think we've been out-shipwrecked," he said.

Mari leaned close to peer into the water. Instead of toy castles or treasure chests, the pebbled bottom was covered with three startlingly realistic miniature ships, a schooner and a sailboat and a steamship. Some of the other tanks held similar replicas, but some went a step further, full of what might be real wreck artifacts. Mari spied a pocket watch, and an arrowhead, and the curling lettering of a passenger manifest encased in a plastic sleeve. The hundred or so other guests seemed to have gotten the theme memo. Mari saw men wearing vintage-looking first officer epaulettes, women in early-1900s-style dresses, and multiple attires patterned with Jolly Rogers. Mari grinned watching one man refasten the fake parrot tied to his shoulder, then realized that she knew him. "He's worked with Scripps before," she said to Julian, turning her face away in case he recognized her. "He's looking for *Mount Temple*. She was one of the ships that came to help *Titanic*, but she was too far away."

"Not as scandalous as *Californian*," Julian said.

"Not quite," Mari said. "She's a cooler wreck, though. She sank with all these dinosaur fossils on board."

"You're kidding."

"Nope," Mari said. "Twenty boxes of million-year-old bones on their way to the British Museum, scuttled and sent to the bottom of the sea in World War I. Along with seven hundred live horses."

Julian winced. "Damn. They must have been terrified."

"Yeah. Whoever finds *Mount Temple* is going to have a really weird time."

The man didn't even glance her way as he passed, too intent in his conversation, but still Julian stepped closer to block her. Mari had to forcibly restrain herself from reaching out to touch him, the muscle of his arm a soft swell under the green of his suit. It looked good on him in a way it wouldn't have on most people. They'd hardly exchanged more than a glance on the flight here, a wordless agreement to focus on the task at hand. But under these swiveling lights it was harder, the shape of him a comfort as much as a thrill. It was the fact that if she were to start talking about Silvestre Swan and Bergy Bits and Mettle House he'd be the only person in the room who would know what she was talking about. The only person who knew the way the moonlight caught on the foam of the sandbar, the way the weather changed without warning, the way the water pulled things into the cove. She was astonished how quickly and fully Norman Cliffs had started to feel like a home to go back to. That Julian was here meant that all of it was real.

Soon a woman stood up and signaled the DJ, who let out a pulse of sound and then cut it off for a low background track. "Good evening, everyone," the woman said into the mic. "And thank you for being here as we celebrate twenty years with Dodd Seawhether Enterprises, and our first annual CQD Ball!"

"Showtime," Julian whispered.

Every eye was on the woman speaking. No one even looked over as Mari and Julian slid into the stairwell. And Mari's nerves roared to life as the applause faded into silence.

Teach's office was four floors above Dodd Seawhether's. The stairway exit door clicked open at Julian's keycard, and they stepped into a dark space lined with messy cubicles, papers overflowing from plastic bins, half-eaten food still littering some of the tables. A quick lap of the floor showed nothing resembling archives or storage. Julian walked along a row of closed conference rooms, sticking his head into every one until he said, "Bingo."

The archive's linoleum floor was hidden by dozens of boxes stacked haphazardly on top of one another, overflowing to lean against the computer in one corner and the tall metal supply cabinet in the other, its doors open to reveal yet more boxes. Julian and Mari pulled on their gloves and got to work. Thankfully, Teach's organization was better inside the cardboard than out of it. The contents were sorted by location, and it didn't take long to find C. CANADA—N&L. "Here," Mari said, pulling it open. And, like a miracle, everything they needed was sitting at the bottom. She pulled out a small leather book, a stack of photographs, a sheath of newspaper clippings, dozens of other loose brittle pages. Nathaniel Vettrey's bank records, letters to Halifax, photos of gold. Adrenaline shot down her spine.

"Here's our boy," Julian said, handing her the stack of newspapers. The words LIGHTKEEPER SWAN sat at the top of the first page like a beacon. "I'll take this one." He gingerly pulled open the leather journal and began snapping pictures page after page, not stopping to read. Mari did the same with the newspapers and other sheets, and had just turned her attention to the photos when there was a clatter from the glass front door and the harsh static feedback of a walkie-talkie.

They both froze. "Hurry up," Mari hissed. But Julian was only half way through the journal. And now there was a new sound: footsteps, getting louder.

Julian moved to the vertical supply cabinet, but the boxes stacked inside left no room to fit. "Back here," he whispered, flattening himself against the wall behind it and pulling the door open all the way to hide himself from view. Mari squeezed in beside him, so close her shoulder was pressed against his chest. She could feel his heart beating through his suit. Mint and woodsmoke, as always. But above that, something new. Had he put on cologne?

He was definitely wearing cologne.

This was definitely the wrong time to be noticing it.

"It will take a bit to pull the tapes," the walkie-talkie buzzed as the footsteps got closer. "All we know is something tripped the alarm. Keep an eye on the stairs and the elevators."

"I'm only one person, boss," a real voice said, right outside, and Julian tensed.

"Stay where you can see them both, then," the radio voice said, irritated. "Adrian and Park are on their way." The footsteps passed them, pausing at each door, then proceeded back around the corner, the static fizzing away.

"Shit," Julian breathed, reopening the journal. He set his camera to video and held it over the book as he flipped quickly through the remaining pages. "That was fast. We can grab stills from this later. It'll have to be good enough."

Mari pushed the articles back into their box but held on to the photos, torn. There was no time to take pictures of them. Would Teach really notice them missing? Even if they did—if there were security tapes like the man on the radio had said, Mari and Julian were already in huge trouble. What was one more crime?

And before she could think better of it, she tucked the black-and-white photographs into her purse.

Back in the main office a man was standing just outside the open glass door to the elevator bank, his back to them. The down button was already glowing white.

"Under there," Mari whispered, pointing to the desk closest to the stairs, and together they crouch-ran across the room to hide beneath it. Mari picked up a sunglasses case sitting on top of it and took aim for the conference-room doors. The sound of it hitting the glass seemed riotously loud in the silence, and as the man at the door dashed around the corner Mari and Julian burst into the stairwell and down the four flights to the gala.

"Whoa, there," a woman said, jumping back as Julian swung the door into her. But her glare gave way to a good-natured eyebrow wiggle as Mari slid, panting, up beside him. "There's a hotel down the street, you know," the woman said, grinning. "You two might be a little more comfortable."

Julian stared blankly, and Mari elbowed him. "Look at him in this suit, can you blame me?" she slurred, wrapping her arms around his waist, and Julian caught on and draped an arm over her shoulder. The woman chuckled as she rejoined the dance floor, clearing the way for Mari and Julian to be swallowed up into the crowd.

Time that had seemed to pause while they were upstairs unspooled in a rush now, and Mari felt suddenly unsteady. Julian's arm was still around her shoulder, and she gripped his hand as the last ten minutes—was that all it had been?—came crashing in. "We have to *run*," Julian said, but the same triumphant glee was dancing in his face and he didn't let go of her hand. She couldn't get the sound of him saying *Here's our boy* in reference to a long-dead lighthouse keeper out of her head. He was warm and solid, the only solid thing in this room. A piece of iron on a shifting seafloor. And he'd said the word *run* but neither of them had moved an inch, his eyes dark on hers, their fingers still twined together, and suddenly no wreck in the world was as important as leaning forward and kissing him.

He pulled away almost immediately. It gave her enough time to think about how she'd once compared him to a British guard, serious and immovable, and how kissing one of them mid-crime-spree was probably a terrible idea too. But then his arm tightened around her shoulders and his other hand moved to her jaw and he was pulling them back together, his lips catching hers. And then what she'd thought was solid iron was alive with silt and sunlight, and Mari felt their giddy euphoria giving way to something else right in front of her, the heat of the moment turning to the inexorable churn of the sea. She pulled him closer and it wasn't close enough; bit his lip as he made a sound into her mouth, careful Julian Henry from Bergy Bits with his fingers curled into her hair and her arms tucked under his, and the only coherent thoughts in her head were a combination of *Why haven't we been doing this the whole time?* and *Well, shit.*

"Ladies and gentlemen, may I have your attention for a moment," the DJ said, and Mari felt a gut-deep stab at the security guard's raised walkie-talkie, and then a second, stronger, at the look on Julian's face.

Careless.

Reckless.

Run.

"Come on," Julian said, grabbing her arm. They snaked back to the front door while the crowd was still quieting and made it into the elevator before the guard had said a word. They didn't stop running until they'd made it the four blocks home.

〜〜

The rest of the night passed in a blur: the cab to the airport, the frantic ticket change, the gate. Moving quickly had never felt so unnatural, time jerking ugly from A to B to C. Julian wouldn't look at her and there wasn't time to talk about it, and Mari flipped Clara Vettrey's photos over and over in her hands until she worried they would tear. "What did you *do?*" Julian hissed when he saw them.

"Teach has the digital copies," she said, defiant. "I should have taken the journal too. It should all go to Evangeline."

"Then we should have asked Teach, like I wanted. Mari, this is a *crime.*"

"Well, it's already done," she said shortly. "Can we talk about what just happened?"

He met her eyes for the first time since they'd kissed. "No," he said quietly, and that, more than his anger, flooded Mari with shame. "I think I've had enough for one night. Let's just see if we got anything to make this worth it."

Her skin prickling, Mari looked down at the photos in her hands. And thumbing through them, her irritation faded. Because one frame at a time, Clara Vettrey's time at the cliff came alive under her fingers. There again were the shots of *Saint Gray* at the bottom of the cliff, of the lighthouse seen through Silvestre Swan's window. There were more of the lighthouse and more of the sea, several of a dark-haired boy playing with a Labrador dog. There was Highs Harbor, glutted with ships. There was a pile of misshapen berries. And then—Mari caught her breath. Then was an old man, his hand a blur in front of his face but not quite enough to cover it. The emotion of it caught her off guard. After a century forgotten, here was Silvestre Swan again.

"There's another connection," Julian said, snapping her back.

"Between what?"

"The Vettreys and the Normans." He tapped the screen. "Clara married one. Lou Roland. I skipped to the end. They lived in St. John's, and she's talking about him volunteering for World War I. She says, loosely quoting here, that she hopes his penchant for doing the right thing doesn't get him killed."

Mari frowned. She'd looked into Cortney Roland, but they'd never found anything about a Lou. "Does it say anything else about him?"

"She noted his regiment number; let's see." Julian switched screens from the video of the journal to Memorial's database. "His unit deployed to Greece in 1914, to assist with war efforts in the Mediterranean. The next record is when part of the regiment departed for Marseilles the following November aboard the—" He stopped, his eyes going wide.

Mari felt it before he spoke. Greece to France in November. It was a route etched into her core. A bright blue sea shattered by an underwater gun. *It can't be.* She made her mouth move. "What?"

He looked up at her. "Aboard the chartered British troop carrier SS *Californian*."

Swan, 1913

November was almost over. It took Swan several days to notice, as Clara had taken over writing the logbooks in her own journal, tearing out the last few pages of Swan's for her own reference and pressing them carefully into a small leather book she'd found in town, interspersing the typical straightforward observations with her own musings on things she saw around the cliff. Subtly and steadily the air had grown raw and hostile, the wind sharp and bitter and strong. And one early, especially gusty morning, the tower let out a sound louder than anything Swan had heard from it before.

It was just after dawn and Clara had just put out the light, Swan awake by habit but still in bed. The sky out his window was as pale as the tower stone, the air heavy and iron-tipped with frost. Swan reached for the bit of glass from *Saint Gray* that he left beside his bed, the tiny bull's-eye that Clara had brought him that first morning, saying it was like his own tower lens. It was icy to his touch. He ran his finger along its edge, thoughtful. It reminded him that he should bring the pickaxe back up to the lantern room from its place in the shed. Soon enough it would start to snow, and they'd need it to break ice from the windows. And then the tower shuddered with a keening sound that was more animal than stone, high and guttural, cutting off with a snap that echoed out over the water.

As it faded the whole cliff seemed to shudder too, the gulls quivering where they sat on the matted grass, the waving branches cutting sharp lines across the sky. Stay barked. Swan rose and pulled aside the curtain into the kitchen to find Clara there tinkering with the black box, only the slight quiver of her hands giving away that she'd heard the sound too. "I need to take more pictures of the cliff," she said briskly, without looking up. She raised the camera and set off a burst of light directly into Swan's eyes.

"What?" Swan yelped, pressing a hand to his face. Lou emerged from the side room, his hair unruly.

"What on earth was that?" he asked.

"She's blinded me," Swan said.

"No—before that," Lou said. "The lighthouse. Is it okay?"

And Swan felt the room get colder still.

In all the time the two children had been here, it had been Clara carrying on conversations with the tower, Clara who understood its sounds. Never Lou. For him to have heard it now meant that the tower's distress was even worse than Swan had thought.

Swan leaned against the window as Clara and Lou went outside with the camera, studying the tower. It seemed to be sagging, its base shriveling like a rotting vegetable where it met the cliff. The rail around the lantern room was no longer quite parallel with the horizon, and its plaque was slightly angled, its words dipping toward the sea. He pressed a hand to the windowsill, dizzy. Thinking about the tower falling was one thing. Watching what came before it was quite another.

But he forced himself outside and into his chair. And he stayed there until Clara tired of scampering around with the camera and collapsed into the chair beside him, opening her arms for Stay to jump into her lap. "I'm going into town again," she said. "Will you be okay to get the light going?"

"'Course I will," he said gruffly. "I'm not that soft yet."

She grinned. "Good. You should do some work around here, for once." Swan couldn't help grinning back. Clara lifted the camera and snapped it in his face.

He held his hand in front of his eyes just in time. "Could you stop that? You're not going to town to get another one of those, are you?"

"No," she said, then stood. "Come take a proper photo. Just one. Please?"

"Fine," Swan said.

"Lou," Clara called. "Go stand by the lighthouse."

Lou frowned at her. "No, thank you."

"Come on," she wheedled. "If Mr. Swan can take a photo, you can stand a little closer to the edge."

Lou and Swan stood at the base of the tower, right below its plaque, Stay stretched between them. And once she'd taken the photo Clara wavered for a minute, then launched forward toward Swan and threw her arms around him. "Thank you," she said. And before Swan could summon any resistance she was skipping back to the house, looking for all the world as if this was where she'd always been.

᠊᠊᠊᠊᠊

When Clara and Lou had gone and dusk started gathering in the treetops, Swan climbed the tower stairs for the first time in days. He relished the cool press of the air in the stairwell, the way it ballooned downward when he opened the hatch to the lantern room. But in the lantern room he found himself unable to look away from the water. Was it closer than it had been yesterday? Would the tower fall in one piece, or hit the cliff and crack? Would it hit *Saint Gray*, still lying down there at the bottom? Would the waves push it into the cove the way they did everything else? Or would it be like that orange stone from his childhood, there and then simply gone?

They were terrible thoughts, and he made himself stop before the tower got angry with him. But its stone was silent, and he realized that other than that snap in the morning, it had barely made a sound all day. It worried him. He pressed both palms to the lens, studying the bull's-eyed pattern. "Soon, my friend," he whispered. Nothing. Not a murmur. And Swan knew it, deep in his bones.

The tower would fall tonight.

Mari, 2014

"Evangeline has to have known Louis Roland sailed on *Californian*," Mari said for the dozenth time. "*Has* to. How else do you explain that a random man from Newfoundland ended up on the same ship I've been researching for twenty years? It can't be a coincidence."

For the dozenth time Julian nodded without looking up. She knew he agreed, that she didn't have to keep saying it. But at this point she was repeating it for her own sake, because a full twelve hours after the gala she still couldn't believe it. It was too convenient to be true. But if she was right, if this was why Evangeline had wanted her for Swan Light, how would she have expected Mari to make the connection? Mari never would have looked into the Normans or the Rolands or the Vettreys, never would have heard about them at all, if Teach hadn't been here asking about them.

Mari felt her brain was trying to move in too many directions at once. She itched for the plane to fly even faster. She had a lot of questions for Evangeline.

But at least her constant questioning had so far kept the journey from being awkward. Julian still wouldn't meet her eyes. Mari was willing to chalk their kiss at the gala up to adrenaline and the heat of the moment and carry on being friends, but evidently her dive partner wasn't. And now Mari couldn't stop thinking of Vanessa—or, more accurately, couldn't stop thinking of Julian thinking of Vanessa, the other faceless diver she was sure he was comparing her to. So she forced herself out of it with thoughts of *Californian*. Its manifest had been lost in the explosion, but other records were very clear that only one person had died when it sank: a fireman named Harding. Whatever had happened to Louis Roland, he hadn't died on that ship. She thought about Ursula's shape appearing on the sonar, the edges and scatter of something once magnificent that had been ruined. But no, not Ursula. Ursula with the too-long hull, Ursula that put them back at square one, with nothing from the other targets but iron and coal and—

And gold.

The odds were so slim it was laughable. But the rest of this had happened, hadn't it? A needle in a haystack in a barn full of haystacks under four thousand feet of water. Maybe, sometimes, you found it.

Mari pulled out her printed copies of Hector's notes and flipped through them until she found the assessment of the gold they'd found on Cherry. It had been cast in 1899 in San Francisco. That was all they knew. Its very existence on the Cherry wreck site had been a strike against it in Mari's eyes, because there was no reason for there to have been American gold on a British ship. But was it so unlikely to think that Louis Roland had kept some of it with him when he'd deployed, that it had gone down with *Californian*?

There was only one way to find out.

She flipped through Hector's notes until she reached her own, and the mag chart that had first shown them *Saint Gray*. They'd never done a proper sweep, since Julian had insisted that the wreck was outside their purview and he was the one controlling the boat. But from what they did have—hits smeared one over the other in a vaguely straight pattern—she guessed that what they'd found was an edge of the ship, not part of the middle where it had torn open, like they'd seen in Clara's photos. The specie room, where the gold most likely would have been stored, would have been toward the center of the ship, deep in the hull. But when the ship had hit the cliff its gold could have gone any- and everywhere. Mari studied the chart, thinking hard. One hundred years in rough waters. Unlike the stone lighthouse, gold wasn't heavy enough to sink right into the sand. Especially at the tail end of a storm, it would have been buffeted out into the bay, at the mercy of the current . . .

Mari felt a thrill run through her.

The current. It took everything near the cliffs to the same place.

The cove.

Next to her, Julian was frowning, peering at the mag chart in her hands. At least he was finally looking in her direction. "What are you doing?"

"We found gold on one of our wreck sites," she said. "Cherry. We didn't finish exploring it because we had to move on to Ursula. But what if this is why Evangeline wanted me to find *Saint Gray*? What if I can compare the gold from Clara Vettrey's wreck to the gold on the ship her husband later sailed on?"

"Are you serious?" Julian asked. His voice was so low and rough that she looked up, startled. "Evangeline didn't ask us to find *Saint Gray*. She hired us to look into Swan Light. Even if they're tangentially related, diving *Saint Gray* because of *Californian* goes way beyond our scope. It has nothing to do with the lighthouse."

"Our scope?" she repeated. "If you had your way, our scope would be us sitting in *Shanty* with no idea about Gerald Cooper or Clara Vettrey or *Saint Gray* or any of it. Evangeline told me to find the full story."

"About Swan Light. *Californian* happened two years later."

"Sorry, I didn't realize historical discoveries had to stick to your personal timeline." Mari sat back, frustrated at herself as much as him. She'd asked too much of him, pulled him along too fast. Thrown too much caution to the wind, and now she'd lost him. In more ways than one.

"What happens if you do find gold on *Saint Gray*?" Julian asked. "You go running back to Cherry. Then what? What about Evangeline? What about—" He stopped himself, rubbing a hand over his jaw.

"I'm not running anywhere," Mari said, stung. "Some of us can care about two things at once, Julian. But if you want to go back to just steering a boat, fine. Have fun."

They spent the rest of the flight in stony silence. And the moment the plane touched down in St. John's and her service returned, her phone exploded with texts and voicemails, most from Zoe at Scripps. She cursed and dialed as Julian walked toward their car without looking back. Her project manager answered after half a ring.

"What did you do?" Zoe yelled.

Mari dug her fingers into her browbone. "Good morning."

"Is it?" Zoe asked. "Because I spent the night fielding calls from treasure hunters looking for confirmation that you're employed at Scripps. They have security video of you breaking into some building in Boston. How did you end up in *Boston*?"

"Okay," Mari said. "To clarify: it was just a room, not a whole building. The building was open. We even had an invitation."

"Really, Mari? Did you have an invitation to take files from a secure system?"

"No," she admitted.

"Teach is furious," Zoe said. "They're dangerous, Mari. I've been looking into them, and they have a horrible reputation. There's no telling what they might do."

"They're not going to do anything," Mari said. "They were just trying to scare us away from the wreck."

"And now they know it didn't work," Zoe said. "They have you on camera stealing their information about *Saint Gray*. I'm serious, Mari. You should keep an eye on your ship, and maybe have Evangeline Devon stay at the inn with you awhile, in case they try anything. You don't want other people getting caught up in this." Zoe sighed. "What happened to you out there? This was supposed to be a quick job. Where's the Mari who follows the rules and the facts and doesn't break into buildings?"

First Julian, now Zoe. Mari was suddenly bullish. "I don't regret it," she said. "We needed that information. It's not just about *Saint Gray*, it's about Swan Light, and this was the only way we could get it. Evangeline wants us to find the whole story."

"Once the story involved breaking and entering, it wasn't your call to make," Zoe said. "You're not a contractor anymore, Mari. You can't drag Scripps into this."

"Deny it, then. Say you had no idea I was there."

"We *did* have no idea you were there. But it doesn't matter; it doesn't work like that. I'd be shocked if Luke doesn't pull you out of there."

Mari remembered the thrill of warmth she'd felt standing in her hotel room looking at her dress, the way it had made her think of Norman Cliffs and how thinking of Norman Cliffs had made her feel at home. It hadn't been *Californian* that had made her go to Boston. It had truly been Clara Vettrey and Louis Roland and Silvestre Swan. And now she'd found a way that their story lived beyond that winter, how Clara had written about *Californian* in a journal she'd later send to her sister along with photographs of the town where she'd come ashore. Julian didn't understand that a story didn't stop just because its people moved away. And Zoe didn't understand how deep this story had gotten, that Teach would have taken all of it from them if Mari and Julian hadn't acted first. Scripps had been okay with her taking time off work for this job because it was meant to be quick, for easy funding. And maybe that's how Mari had thought of it too, at first. But this project deserved more than that. This was what scientists dreamed of.

If she was in trouble anyway, then she might as well make it worth it.

Back at Mettle House she called Hector, and he picked up right away. "Are you okay?"

She grimaced. "You heard?"

"Are you okay?" he asked again, his voice noncommittal.

"I'm fine," she said. "I need you to check something for me."

"You're in a lot of trouble, you know."

"I'll explain it all when I can," she said. "I promise we had a good reason."

He sighed. "That's what I told Luke when he came to me. I trust you, kid. You just need to be more careful."

Hector's words made her feel abashed in a way Zoe's never could. She was putting his time and reputation at risk too. And Tim's, still at sea on *Mercury*. "I know."

Hector was quiet for a moment. "What do you need?"

"The gold we found on Cherry," she said. "Can you pull it up?"

"Got it," he said after a minute. "Half eagles. San Francisco Mint, 1899."

"Can you look into other pieces from that bank? Anything that might have gone to Gloucester, Massachusetts, in 1913?"

Hector whistled. "You *have* gotten yourself into something, haven't you?"

"I think so. I hope so." Her call waiting beeped in her ear. It was Julian. She sent it to voicemail. "Can you take another look at everything else from Cherry, too?" she asked Hector. "We cut early to get to Ursula, I know nothing was conclusive. But knowing this, I want to give it another pass. Do you know if they got the ROV back?"

"Yeah, they have it," Hector said. "They're repairing it now, they're still anchored on Ursula."

Her phone beeped again, and she impatiently swiped Julian away. "Hector, I think *Californian* was Cherry all along," she said. "And I think I know where the gold may have ended up here. If I find some and send it to you, you can match it against Cherry." She was thinking quickly now. She'd barely noticed on the ride back, wrapped up in her calls, but the sky out her window was slate-gray and heavy, thunder rumbling faintly behind the cliffs. *New Providence* was in the harbor, moor lines taut in the reaching waves. She had a chance, right now, to search for the gold while Teach wasn't looking, in a place they might not know to look. To take a piece of wreck and get the salvage rights, Julian's sense of scope and morality be damned. And if he wasn't going to help her, she'd do it the way she'd always worked best.

Quickly, and alone.

"Hector, I have to go," she said. She grabbed her dive gear and moved quickly down the stairs and out the door. Highs Street was empty, as was the harbor. She wondered briefly whether Otis would still be keeping watch on *Shanty*, but she saw no sign of him as she approached. She leapt aboard, grabbed the metal detector from its lockbox, and was halfway to the Zodiac when she saw it.

Another note on the pilothouse window.

She froze, Zoe's words about Teach in her ear. *There's no telling what they might do now.* She approached it cautiously, holding her breath. It was another photograph of Evangeline's window, silver Sharpie across it, the same handwriting as before. LAST WARNING, it said this time. And this time, Evangeline wasn't making her tea, sweetly oblivious to the camera.

This time, she was looking straight into it, mouth open in surprise, lined face slack with fear.

"Shit," Mari said softly. Behind her thunder rumbled again, ominous and getting closer. Her window for the gold was closing.

She slung the metal detector to her feet and pulled out her phone.

"Where *are* you?" Julian barked when he answered.

"*Shanty*," she said. "Julian, there's—"

"I've been calling you," he said. "I'm at Evangeline's."

Relief fizzled through her. "Is she okay?" she asked. "Teach left another note. I was going to ask you to check on her."

"No," Julian said. "That's why I was calling. I went by and the door was unlocked. There was tea spilled everywhere. None of her neighbors have seen her today."

Mari's fingers went cold. "What do you mean? What are you saying?"

"Mari . . . Evangeline is missing."

Clara, 1913

"Hurry *up*," Clara hissed, bounding past the overturned dory that marked the edge of Norman Cliffs.

"Slow down," Lou countered from behind her, panting. "No one will be ready yet, Clara."

"You don't know that."

"Yes, I do." He caught her as she reached the top of the hill and they both stopped, breathing heavily. "I know because I told them not to come to the bank until they had everything together. No one was ready to move a lighthouse at a moment's notice."

"Then we'll have to make do with whatever *is* ready," she said. "Did you hear the noise it made this morning? We're running out of time, Lou."

"And if we do it wrong we'll make it worse," Lou said. "We can't just grab a hundred people and some rope. I know you're worried about him, Clara. But bringing a bunch of people up to the cliff will just get his hopes up when there's nothing we can do."

She whirled to face him. Mags's window flashed behind her eyelids, black and shattered. "We can't just give up," she said. "It's my fault. I should have been faster."

"It's not," Lou said firmly. "What you've done this quickly is remarkable, even if it doesn't work. You don't have to prove anything,

Clara. Swan Light was always going to fall. And give Swan a little credit. He'll be okay."

"He's lived there since he was my age, Lou."

"I know," he said quietly. "And we'll be there for him, when it happens."

She wavered. Was he right? If she didn't help Mr. Swan, she was giving up. No amount of justifying could make that go away. But maybe he was right about something else. Maybe she wasn't only doing this for Mr. Swan. She closed her eyes and sucked in a breath. Nathaniel's face swam in front of her. Mags's broken window, WITCH painted red. But everything was going to be fine, this time. Mr. Swan would be fine. He would still have the house, far enough from the edge of the cliff. He would still have town, would still have Peter and Sophie and Will and everyone else who was ready to drop everything to help him. And he would still have Clara too. Maybe this could be a place she could be happy. *You don't have to prove anything.*

"We have to at least see if there's anything we can do," she said, opening her eyes. "Please, Lou. I need to try."

His eyes only searched hers for a moment before he nodded. "Then we'll try," he said. "Let's see if anyone has been by the bank."

Norman Bank was still open, its lights on and its door unbarred, but there was no teller behind the desk. Cort and Lou's office was empty too. Lou cast a cautious glance down the hall before stopping at a thin bookshelf beside it, opening the slotted box on top. SUGGESTIONS, the front read. Lou sifted through them for a moment before looking up at Clara and mutely shaking his head. She felt her insides shatter like Mags's window.

"I'm sorry," Lou said. "Truly. There are notes: one of Will Mettle's cousins has wheeled platforms we can use, and the blacksmith from St. John's is bringing his horses down in a few days. We just need a little more time. The lighthouse has held on this long. Maybe it will still surprise us."

Clara shook her head, not trusting her voice, not knowing how to explain to him that the lighthouse's chatter had become dimmer and dimmer, until this morning all it had done was groan and slur. Not knowing how to explain the way Mr. Swan had looked at it, as if he was already saying goodbye.

There was a creak outside, and they both froze. Clara tiptoed to the window. But even before she pressed her eyes to the glass, she heard the coughing. The high voice, struggling for steady air. Cort's daughter. And Cort.

"Hide," she said, her heart thumping, but no—Cort was lifting his daughter into a cart, leaping on it himself. And then they were gone, swallowed up by night, heading away from town. She felt something in her stir, uneasy. "Where is he going?"

"He came from the direction of the back door," Lou said. "We must have just missed him."

"What's at the back door?"

"The accounting room." Lou frowned. "Let's look." The room held only an empty desk, a candle burning above a few scattered pieces of paper. "That's not like him," Lou said, pushing the flame farther away and spinning the note closest to him to read it. Clara saw his eyes widen, his jaw clench. "Oh no."

"What?"

He handed her the paper. *Mr. Roland,* she read. *Norman Bank is not a good candidate for investment at this time. Best of luck with your future endeavors. Gable Strauss.*

She shrugged and handed it back. "Gable Strauss didn't seem very nice anyway."

"But we needed his money," Lou said. He rubbed a hand over his forehead and sighed. "Norman Bank is almost completely broke. That's why we couldn't help with the lighthouse. Cort has been skimming off the top ever since his daughter was born, for her medicine. He said he'd repay it once she was better, but she's only gotten worse."

Clara heard her own breath in her ears, sharp and unsteady. "I didn't know that," she said. "Why didn't you tell me that?"

"Why would you want to know that?"

Clara dropped her eyes, her face warm. And even in the wavering flame she caught sight of the page beside Gable Strauss's note and felt her heart squeeze.

It was a telegram.

At the bottom was the name NATHANIEL VETTREY.

Clara seized it, raced her eyes over it, missing half the words in her panic. She saw DON´T TRUST HER. She saw NO PARTNERSHIP. She saw STOLEN GOLD.

She saw WITCH.

She dropped the paper. "Oh my God," she whispered. "Cort knows."

Lou's face was dark with concern. "Knows what?"

"I've been lying to him." Her hands were shaking. "That's why he never came back about the deed. I gave him gold from *Saint Gray* and told him my father would partner with him and send him more. I just wanted to stop him from bothering Mr. Swan."

"Clara!"

"Lou, I didn't know." Clara felt as if she could hear the roaring ocean, even through the stone and the space between them. She'd thought she was so smart, using Nathaniel's name and money for something good. So brave.

So foolish.

Mags's window swam before her, spiderweb cracks in the darkness.

She'd only wanted to help.

She'd only ever made things worse.

"That's all the money Cort was counting on, gone," Lou said. "He'll blame you. That must be where he went just now, to find you. And that means . . ."

He didn't need to finish.

They ran.

Swan, 1913

Silvestre Swan stood with his hands on the iron rail of his lighthouse, watching the water and wondering how much time was left.

It was almost cruel how beautiful the evening was. The sky was cerulean blue, the water calm and diamond-tipped. The air was sharp with the lingering scent of rotting metal from *Saint Gray* far below. Two sailboats were anchored farther down the cliffs, their occupants tied to the sea with the fishing lines in their hands, and at the horizon a single steamer crawled along, trailing smoke behind it like a kite. It was a fair bit of irony, Swan thought. To stand through so many storms and go down on a night like this.

He stood there watching until his fingers were numb with cold, until evening gathered in a purple bruise at the horizon. Then he turned his back on the sea and lit a flame to the oil reservoir, the flame leaping up behind the lens and throwing golden bull's-eyes across the glass windows, filling the room with warmth. In the clockwork room below he set the mechanism turning, gears crunching together and making the ceiling shudder as the lens creaked to life. He descended the stairs slowly, the tower vocal now around him. But this was a different noise still, the cracks and whispers replaced by a constant strained humming. It was as if the stone had been seized by something primal and older than itself, a kind of language Swan could no longer understand, made of the same formless vowels as the waves and the wind. Swan stood at the bottom of the stairs for a moment, letting it fill him. And then he took the final step out the door.

He pulled his chair from the back of the house farther along the cliff, as far as he could go without falling into the cove, and he sat and watched. He'd missed Clara and Lou more than he'd thought, as night had fallen. But now, this felt right. Now he was glad he was alone. From here, even in the dark, he could see that a large chunk had fallen away from the cliff right below the tower, leaving a corner of its base hanging over the edge. He leaned forward, gripping the chair, Stay silent and tense at his feet. And together they watched the light as it spun, spun, spun. Doing what it was meant to, no matter the cost, shining through the night. Picturing the cliff without this light was like picturing half a whale, or a bird without its wings. Clara would be devastated, of course. But it had been that way once before, he reminded himself. For many long, languid years there were five of them, watching icebergs from this empty bluff. Nico and Silvy Swan, Peter and Sophie Mettle, and Abigail Norman, all running as fast as they could.

The tower wall keened. Not long now.

The tower door slammed.

Swan blinked, roused from his memories. For a moment, he thought he might have imagined it.

And then a human-shaped shadow passed between the fire and the darkness outside.

Swan jolted to his feet. It couldn't be Clara, not this time. She'd know the danger right away. He stood and crossed the lawn, and as he passed his house Stay barked, veering off toward the door. Swan looked over to see a girl watching them. "Papa?"

Swan stopped. The girl was tiny, barely old enough to stand on her own. Sickly, coughing, frightened, her bright blue eyes on the light. And Swan remembered her.

He squatted down in front of the girl, his hands on her shoulders. "You're Cort's daughter, aren't you?" Swan asked. "My name is Swan. What's yours?"

The girl was shaking, her hands clenching and unclenching her red coat. But despite her wheezing, her sky-blue eyes didn't waver. Abigail's eyes, watching him still. Maybe watching him always.

"Evangeline Roland," the girl squeaked.

Mari, 2014

Evangeline wasn't in her barn, or at Bergy Bits, or at Mettle House. Each new empty place tightened Mari's chest. And as she and Julian returned to the harbor, she couldn't stop wondering when, exactly, it had happened. When had Sam Beauregard knocked on the cottage door, rousing Evangeline from her tea, bringing her shuffling to the door with her hand pressed to her side, probably expecting Mari or Julian? While Mari was scrolling through pictures of *Californian*'s gold? While she was kissing Julian on the dance floor?

"They'll have to head in soon," Julian said, his eyes on the storm-dark cliffs. "They must have a Zodiac too; there's nowhere else they could be." But even from here Mari could see that the bottom of the cliff was empty. Could Teach be hidden away in the cove? Would Mari have already been too late to look for *Saint Gray*'s gold there?

"I don't see—" she started to say. Then, against the dark clouds massing at the top of the cliffs, something caught her eye. Tiny beams of light swinging across the gloom.

Flashlights.

"They're at the top," she said, grabbing Julian's arm.

His jaw tensed. "Otis's rental car," he said, starting forward. "I have the extra key, let's go."

They raced up the hill and through the scrubby pines, the darkness growing denser the farther they got from town. When the trees were too close together to continue, Julian pulled over and they continued on foot, and as they emerged from the woods Mari saw five men strung along the cliff. "Hey!" she yelled out, and they turned. And even from a distance Mari could see Sam Beauregard's ugly smirk and his gun.

"Well, well, well," he said, striding toward her. "Enjoy Boston?" One of the other men had a piece of paper in his hands. A photo, she realized. Clara Vettrey's, the shot of the broken *Saint Gray* at the bottom of the cliff.

"Where is Evangeline?" Mari asked. Beauregard's gun was loose in his hand, but she hardly glanced at it. "If you hurt her—"

"She's fine," Beauregard said. "Got your attention, did we?" His eyes were bloodshot, the skin below them purpling and paunchy. "Doesn't feel good to have someone messing with your things, does it?"

"I'm sorry we broke in," Mari said steadily, keeping her eyes on Beauregard's face. "I know you're upset. But it wasn't about the wreck. Clara Vettrey stayed in Swan—"

"*Upset?*" Beauregard interrupted, his voice rising. "You know I'm *upset*? Do you know how long I've been looking for *Saint Gray*?"

"We're not—" she started, and he stepped forward, raising the gun.

"I was the one who found Nathaniel Vettrey's backdoor deals," he hissed. "I was the one who searched through twenty goddamn years' worth of bank records. I was the one who tracked the gold across two *goddamn* entire provinces. Two elitist techies and some old woman are not going to show up at the last minute and stop me. Don't you tell me I'm upset."

"Let's all just stop and talk about this," Julian said, his eyes on the gun, and Beauregard turned toward him.

"No," he said, his voice cracking. "No more stopping. I'm done listening to you lie. You're going to take me to the gold, or so help me I will push both of you over the edge right now and you can join your precious lighthouse and be done with it."

Mari's heart was thumping. Thunder clattered above them, echoing over the bay. If Teach had swept the area they'd seen Mari and Julian searching, and if they'd figured out that this was the cliff from Clara's picture, they must have found the wreck already. That wasn't what Beauregard was asking. He wanted the gold, specifically, somewhere down among all that metal. Any salvager worth their salt would have known that Mari and Julian couldn't have located and excavated it all in the three short weeks they'd been here. But Teach weren't salvagers, and Beauregard wasn't thinking straight. Again she thought about her hunch, the cove, the currents that could have pushed the gold to safety a century before. If that gold matched Cherry's, she could prove it was *Californian*. If Teach found it first, she'd never get the chance. If Teach got the salvage rights, this water would be locked to her forever. But could she afford not to tell them, with Evangeline in danger?

Beauregard was forcibly moving Julian forward, and for a wild moment Mari thought he was serious about pushing them into the sea. But he turned at the edge farthest from the keeper's house, toward the dip in the rock that led to the cove. Mari followed them, another member of Teach close behind her, and peered over the edge. Julian had been right: Teach had their own Zodiac boat waiting at the bottom.

The climb down was silent and endless, rain starting to drip frigid around them, and at the bottom Beauregard hefted his gun. "All right," he said to Julian, his eyes glittering. "Start talking."

"The wreck is just past the opening," Julian said carefully. "Closer than twenty feet to the surface, according to our mag. That's all we know for sure."

Beauregard's face went still. "What did I say about lying, Mr. Henry?"

"I'm not lying," Julian said. "It's a huge wreck, and it's made of metal. You're just going to have to start looking."

Beauregard stood motionless for another few seconds. Then he stepped forward and drove the butt of his gun into Julian's stomach.

Julian doubled over, wheezing, and Beauregard pressed the barrel into his shoulder. "Then let's start looking," he said, pushing Julian toward the Zodiac.

And seeing the gun pressed into Julian's arm, Mari made her choice.

"It's not in the wreck," she said. Beauregard and Julian both looked up. "At least not all of it. The current pushes everything in here and buries it. There should be pieces in the cove."

Beauregard released Julian and stepped forward. "Are you lying to me too, Adams?"

"No," she said steadily. "We haven't found any of it. But based on the current, this is where I'd look."

Beauregard jerked his head to another member of his team, the only one dressed to dive, who had a metal detector over his back. "Watch them," he said over his shoulder as the two of them climbed into the little boat, and the tall man Mari and Julian had found in the woods took a step closer.

Mari held her breath, her back against the cliff, as she watched the screen in Beauregard's hands bathe his skin in a yellow-white glow. It was responding to something, faint and steady. The minutes stretched on, the diver invisible underwater, Beauregard tense and hunched above it. After about ten minutes the diver reappeared. He had something in his hands. But it wasn't gold. It was an iron rod with a long screw in it. Mari immediately recognized it as part of a steam engine's propeller shaft, water-worn but discernable, and her heart sank. With that, Teach would get the salvage rights for *Saint Gray*.

"Check the sand," Beauregard said tersely, and the diver waded out of the water to pad across the sickle of sand. The other members of Teach moved aside to let him sweep around them. All the while the monitor in Beauregard's hand let out a steady trickle of noise. It wasn't the staccato that pieces of gold would have caused. And even though she hadn't wanted Teach to find it, Mari couldn't help her disappointment. Maybe she'd been wrong. Maybe the gold wasn't here after all.

Julian cleared his throat, and she glanced up at him. He nodded toward the arched opening of the cove. She frowned, but a moment later she heard it too: a low humming on the water outside, audible over the now-clattering rain. A ship.

Was it someone from Norman Cliffs? Or was it *New Providence*? There was no way to tell. But they'd have to risk it, Mari thought, sucking in a breath to yell out. The longer Teach kept them down here, the more danger they and Evangeline were in. But before she could make a sound Beauregard's head snapped up. "Someone's coming," he said. "Everyone into the boat. You too," he said, grabbing Mari's arm, and she met Julian's eyes and nodded.

"In here!" they both yelled, and Beauregard recoiled. The tall man clamped his hands around her and she twisted and lashed out with her elbow, nailing him in the ribs, and he released her with a startled grunt.

Beauregard looked toward the mouth of the cove, to where the purring was getting louder, and cursed. "Leave them," he said. "There's no time, let's go." The five men leapt into the Zodiac and puttered over the choppy water and through the arch. A moment later another hull nosed into view, and the purring engine cut. Mari sagged with relief. It was *Shanty*.

"What was all that about?" Theo van Gooren called, squinting in the direction Teach's Zodiac had gone. Bill Baxter was beside him, Otis at the wheel.

"Teach," she said. "They were looking for the gold. Theo, they took Evangeline. We have to call the police, have to find her."

"No, they didn't," Otis said, pushing his hair back where the rain had loosened it from its bun. "I've been calling you both; you didn't answer. Evangeline's in the hospital. We only just found out. She fell while making tea last night and called nine-one-one. She didn't have an emergency contact, but they finally called the inn, and Jo called me."

"Is she okay?" Julian asked.

"She's fine," Otis said. "Come grab the line. We'll take you up to the hospital."

Mari stood motionless, letting the news wash over her. Evangeline was safe. Mari and Julian hadn't put her in danger. She found that she couldn't stop shaking, a combination of the cold water and her adrenaline wearing off. Now that Evangeline was safe, the reality and defeat of what had just happened was crashing in. Mari and Julian hadn't put her in danger, but they could have. Julian had as good as called her selfish, and now she felt it. *Look for the people,* Evangeline had said, *not just the wrecks they leave behind.*

And what a wreck she'd made of this.

~~~

The twenty-minute boat ride to St. John's passed in a blur of pitching waves and soaking rain. The hospital was warm and wan, its panel lighting illuminating plastic green chairs and beeping machines and hand-painted cards pinned along the hallways. Evangeline was stable, but unconscious—medically induced, her doctor told them, to get her blood pressure under control. A minor stroke, he said. Probably not her first. Energetic, ageless Evangeline now looked every bit her hundred years, maybe even older, frail and withered and held down by tubes. Mari pulled a chair beside the bed and took Evangeline's hand. It was translucent, blue veins glowing, and so thin she was afraid she could snap it. "Evangeline?" she said softly. Beeping was the only reply.

There was a woman in the room, in her fifties, a drawn face framed by wild dark hair. She smiled softly at Mari over Evangeline's bed. "Keya Talley," she said. "I came as soon as I heard. It's nice to finally meet you." All Mari could do was nod back. Julian sank down beside her. He looked terrible. His gray T-shirt was black with water, a cut on his collarbone seeping blood into the fabric. "We talked all the time," Keya said, pulling up her own chair. "She asked me not to say anything, but I called her with all the same updates I gave you. She said she didn't want it to seem like she didn't trust you, like she was going around you to talk to me, but I think she just wanted a friend." The archivist's brown eyes were warm and sad.

"I wouldn't have minded," Mari said, though of course that wasn't the point.

"I sent one more thing to you that I wasn't going to send to her," Keya said, pulling out her phone. "Just a few hours ago. Here." The photograph on the screen was of a bleak-looking building, a large family standing in front of it. A man and a woman and six children, the youngest on his mother's hip. The mother looked worn, the father young and handsome, with dark hair and eyes so light in the black-and-white photo that they must have been bright blue. Cortney Roland to open Norman Bank in Charleston, South Carolina the newsprint caption read. Pictured at the site March 3 1914 with his wife, Ruby, and their children Philip, Abby, Francis, Lester, Evangeline, Gabriel.

Evangeline.

Mari held the phone so close her nose almost smudged the screen, staring at the second-smallest child. Her hands were bunched in her dress—the only one of the children whose eyes looked directly into the camera. It made her seem older. As if she knew something her family around her didn't.

"Evangeline Devon is Cortney Roland's daughter," Keya said softly. "Devon is her middle name, her mother's maiden name. She dropped the Roland a long time ago."

Cortney Roland's daughter. Mari sat back in her chair, stunned. Evangeline had much more invested in Swan Light than a curiosity in local lore and a promise to a friend. She was tied up in all of it: in Cortney and Louis and Clara and *Saint Gray*. In looking into Swan Light's history, she was looking into her own.

But one piece of the puzzle was still missing. In arriving in Charleston by March of 1914, Cortney Roland must have moved his family from Norman Cliffs several months before. Which meant that they'd left right after Swan Light fell. All of them had, as if Swan Light had been the only thing holding them here. Cortney Roland to Charleston, Louis Roland to St. John's and then to the war. And what about Silvestre Swan? Where had he been, this night that had sent them all adrift? A cold weight settled in her stomach. She thought about Clara Vettrey's diary in Julian's phone, the image frames from the video he'd taken still being digitally sharpened enough to read. What had happened that night? And what had brought Evangeline Devon back here to finish out her life in the same place she'd started it? *I was here once,* she'd said when Mari had asked her why she moved. *When I was very young.*

Evangeline stirred, the beeping speeding up, and they all leaned forward. But after a few seconds she relaxed, her mouth going slack again, the beeps resuming their steady count. Keya pressed a reassuring hand to Mari's shoulder, then gasped. "You're soaked," she said. "You must be freezing."

"I'm okay," Mari said automatically. But as soon as she did it was as if the cold finally reached her skin, and she found that her hands were shaking.

"I'm getting you rooms at the university," Keya said, taking her phone from Mari's hands. "It's right down the street. You've both been through a lot. Evangeline will be asleep until morning, at the least, and you'll be nearby if that changes."

"I'm not leaving her," Mari said.

"You're no help to her if you catch pneumonia," Keya said firmly.

"But—"

"I promise I'll call you the instant anything changes," Keya said. "You'll be right down the street. Go."

Keya's colleague met them outside a stately-looking duplex, student housing that, here in summer, was empty except for them. "I left clean towels and bathrobes for you," the man said. "And food is on its way."

Mari only made it a few steps into her room before everything about the day crashed in, her calls with Zoe and Hector and finding Evangeline missing and Teach at the cliff and the gold and the bitter summer rain. She was so cold her stomach clenched, and she fumbled with the old radiator, turning it up as high as it could go before getting into the shower and standing motionless under the water until her body went from red to white to something vaguely resembling skin. When she finally left the bathroom in her robe, the heater pipes were clanking and the room soggy with fog, heat so thick she could taste the ocean in it. She had a text from Julian. They brought us food. Left yours at your door.

This was ridiculous. After what they'd been through, they couldn't even eat together? Mari scooped the takeout bag from her doorway and crossed the first-floor entryway to Julian's room. He answered her knock in his own robe, his clothes drying on the radiator behind him. "Hi," he said.

"Hi." She pushed past him and put her takeout bag on his wooden table. "Look, can we talk?"

He studied her for a minute, hand on the still-open door, before softly shutting it. "We don't have to if you don't want to," he said. "We found everything Evangeline asked for. The project is done. Otis is taking *Shanty* back to Boston on Saturday. I'll stay until we know Evangeline is okay, of course. But you should leave soon too. You'll lose your diving window in Greece."

"Of course I'm not leaving yet," she said. "Why do you keep talking about *Californian* like that?"

"Like what?"

"Like I'm abandoning all of this to run back there. Like all of this didn't matter."

He stepped around her to open their food. Matching sandwiches and fries. Whoever had put the bags together had added in Band-Aids and bandages as well, and Tylenol, and thick wool socks. The thoughtfulness of it made Mari's throat tight, these bags made by total strangers, at a moment's notice. "Did it?" he asked softly. "Matter?"

"Of course it did," she said. "Swan Light mattered. *Saint Gray* mattered. And if you'll recall, I was never the one who acted like they didn't. 'I'll stick to steering and flying a towfish,' remember?"

Julian threw up a hand, frustrated. "I'm not talking about Swan Light, Mari," he said. "I know you care about that. You care more about wrecked things than anyone I've ever met. I'm just trying to figure out if you care about un-wrecked ones too."

A month ago she'd have been so excited to wake up on *Mercury* again, under a ceaseless and predictable sky, guided by numbers and plot points and her own two hands. But now she could hardly picture any sea but the one dark beyond the window, sharp and gray and wild. There was something about this place, she thought. Something Julian knew too, something that made you not want to abandon it. And now she couldn't imagine a world without it, without Jo flipping four burgers at once while an old fisherman juggled fire nearby, Reggie Cooper taking the jacket from his back when she'd said she was cold, Daniel the librarian and Keya the archivist dropping everything to help her, all of the Theos and Bills and Geralds and the stories they had to tell.

A world without, of course, Julian.

Maybe it had been right, to cut it off before it began. They were returning to different oceans. It was safer this way, not to get attached. Safer to let him join the ranks of her forgotten dive partners, the rotating faces behind dive masks and air tubes. Maybe in five years she wouldn't remember Clara Vettrey's name, or *Saint Gray's*, or the way the light hit the top of the cliff at sunset. Swan Light would be just another notch in her belt.

The thought made her dizzy.

"I care," she said, holding his gaze. "I promise. I know I'm reckless with things. But I don't want to be reckless with you."

His eyes were oceans, dark and endless. She could still smell the salt on his skin. He took a step closer, so close his hands brushed her own, then her waist. "I wouldn't go that far," he said, his breath warm in her ear. "A little reckless is probably okay."

She grinned, and warmth rose in his eyes. He pulled her against him and the world spun bright. Evangeline was in the hospital and Teach was on the run and the gold was gone but here was one thing that felt good, that felt safe and solid and sure, her hips under his hands and her palm against his jaw, his fingers snaking under her robe and her teeth at his neck. A shifting seafloor, a thunderous wave, bringing everything around it close and pulling it under.

Mari, 2014

The days started unfolding like cresting waves, cold white edges giving way to cheerful blue mornings and clear dark nights. The bramble leading to the cliffs went tawny with July dryness and the scent of berries was suddenly everywhere, a sharp citrus carried in the breeze and the chimney smoke that gave the world a soft purple hue. Evangeline hadn't woken up. They stayed another night in St. John's before returning to Norman Cliffs, and as they came around the bend in Theo van Gooren's car to see the expanse of the slope and its scattered houses bathed in rusty orange, Mari felt something in her loosen again with the feeling of coming home.

And Saturday came, and went, and she and Julian stayed.

There was progress to be made, still, despite Julian's proclamation that the project was over: his colleagues had descended on Evangeline's barn to run their gauges and tests on the remains of Swan Light, filling the dim, cold space with bubbles of cheerful conversation and filling Keya's blueprint piece by piece by piece. Back in Boston, another colleague was almost finished pulling still frames from Julian's video of Clara Vettrey's diary. Some sections were in much worse shape than others—no telling which section of her life they'd receive next. But the memories did come, in bits and pieces, and together Mari and Julian swam through the tantalizing fragments, slowly putting the story together. How Clara Vettrey wasn't Nathaniel Vettrey's daughter at all, but the daughter of his wife and the man she'd fallen in love and run away with. How Nathaniel had vandalized that man's mother's home. About Nathaniel's shady business dealings and the gold that had kept them going. How Silvestre Swan had saved Clara from *Saint Gray*, climbing into the cove in a storm, and how she'd made an enemy of Cort Roland in trying to repay him.

But so far there had been nothing about the night Swan Light fell. Julian cautioned her that maybe there wouldn't be, that maybe the wound was too fresh or too strange or ultimately too small for Clara to remember. But Mari, who felt that she knew this headstrong girl more and more in every piece they got back, felt deeply sure that it was coming, that the answer was somewhere in the still-missing pages. Her room at Mettle House became their command center, maps and notes spread over the floor and taped to the walls as they put the story together, Julian on the floor surrounded by maps; Mari at the desk deep in the archives; Keya calling at midnight with one more thing, one more, one more. And then falling blur-headed into bed in the buzzy silence of the rising sun, meeting each other warm and eager and spent, her hands in his hair, his breath in her ear, their eyes going soft in the darkness. *One more, one more, one more.*

And in this way, every day pinned to nothing but sunlight, she could pretend that their time here wasn't ending.

Teach had filed their claim on *Saint Gray* but hadn't been back to the site, and despite the APB out on both *New Providence* and his skiff, Sam Beauregard had vanished. Without them, Otis had been running stealth operations in the Zodiac, ready to call himself an independent contractor to anyone who asked. He brought up several new slices of Swan Light and, at Mari's wheedling, ran several tracks over *Saint Gray* and the cove to look for any remaining gold. But every attempt came back either empty or too full of ship pieces to tell if there was gold among them, the start of a much larger endeavor they didn't have time for. The gold, and its connection to *Californian*, was still out of reach.

It was a fact that had nettled under Mari's spine. That much gold didn't just vanish. Even if most of it had gone down with the ship, trapped in its iron innards, even if Clara and Louis had salvaged hundreds of pieces, there still should have been *something*. Some errant wave pushing out a fistful, several dozen scattered several feet below the sand. It was the long hull on Ursula all over again, a miss made worse by being so close. She could resign herself to a quest ending, because they were supposed to end with proof, with knowledge. Not like this. Who was she supposed to be now, if she didn't know?

Mari sat at the edge of the cliff one afternoon looking down at the water, wishing she could see straight through it. From here there was no shipwreck, no lighthouse, no hint at all of the seafloor. Only the white-spiked waves on the rock and the calm gray pool of the cove. There was so much this sea had seen, and from here you'd never even know to look for it. It was a strange twist of human curiosity, she thought, that pushed people to want to look anyway. That pushed them to dive into waters despite their darkness. That made them search for things they might never find. She leaned back on her elbows, picturing Swan Light standing above her. The old lighthouse had seen other wrecks, she knew, names besides *Saint Gray* that she'd read twice now in the archives but still found she couldn't remember. The lighthouse had come so close to being forgotten entirely itself. But thanks to Evangeline, it wouldn't. And it wouldn't just be remembered for the ships it had lost. It would be remembered for the people it had saved.

There was a crackling noise in the woods behind her, and she tensed as she turned, so lost in the daydream of a towering Swan Light that it was almost a shock to see Silvestre Swan's house still decrepit in the shadowed woods behind her. For a moment she could swear she felt eyes watching her. Strange, unfriendly eyes, lurking somewhere beyond sight, beyond time. Mari shook her head and turned back to the ocean, thinking for a moment back to the malicious fairies Bill Baxter had claimed lived among the cliffs, back to her own first impression of

Norman Cliffs as wilderness waiting to swallow something whole. But there was nothing unfriendly about this town. At its wildest it was all of it, teeth and a fairy and a wave, capable of crumbling and shattering and leaving for dead. But at its wildest too it was a white stone tower and a ball of flame, was an old man unafraid of the sea despite everything it had taken from him, was a ship willing to sail into the storm. And maybe knowing that was enough.

Mari let her eyes rest on the sandbar, more invisible than usual in the high tide, its foam white-green and lethargic below the catching waves. It looked beautiful, innocent, glowing against the dark water and forming a gentle ring around the town. In everything that had happened with *Saint Gray*, she'd almost forgotten that Swan Light hadn't actually been built because of the danger of the cliff. It was built because of the bar, Nico Swan's *Hazel* running up on it like so many ships had before her. *Forget shipwrecks and stories,* Mari thought. *That little patch of sand and rock will outlive us all.*

Hazel hadn't had a light to follow at all, but *Saint Gray*'s crew had followed a light they didn't understand. They'd thought they were in Halifax, Clara Vettrey's journal had said, as they rounded the cliffs from the southern side, hundreds of miles off course. They didn't know where Swan Light was, much less what it meant. Any lighthouse could be a welcome or a warning. *Saint Gray* had guessed which Swan Light was, and had guessed wrong. But what other choice had they had? They'd found a light and prayed it meant shore, with no idea in the darkness, in the chaos, that following that beam was going to mean coming up on the—

Holy shit.

Mari scrambled for her phone, her mouth going dry as she pulled up Keya's notes on *Saint Gray*. The steamship was just under two hundred feet long, sitting with a twenty-foot draft—deep enough to bring her into more of the sandbar than any fishing schooner. And she had something else these numbers hadn't accounted for: thousands of extra pounds of gold sitting in her hold, weighing her down. Mari stared at the numbers, her hands shaking. Everything they'd found had said that *Saint Gray* wrecked at the cliff. But what if that was only where she'd landed?

What if the cliff wasn't what broke her?

What if she was already broken?

With the ship sitting that deep in the water, the sandbar would have plowed right through *Saint Gray*'s hull on her way toward Swan Light, the force of the waves battering her back and forth across it, sawing open the hole that would soon force her to break in two. Maybe they didn't find the gold because it hadn't sunk with the ship. Most of it never made it that far. *Saint Gray* hit the bar and it opened her up on the spot. Wounding her. Dooming her. And emptying her hold long before she reached Norman Cliffs.

Right into the sandbar that had been shifting, moving, absorbing ever since.

Mari wasn't even aware of dialing, but suddenly Julian's voice was in her ear. "Meet me at the harbor," she said, running for the cove. "I think I know where the gold is."

~~~

Thunder was rattling the sky by the time the Zodiac hurtled around the corner of the cliff, but for once Mari didn't care. Julian dropped the metal detector overboard and began a careful sweep, his fingers tight on the wheel as they skimmed just above the precarious line of the shoal. Mari could hear it creaking and moaning with every wave that passed over it, a monster lurking just below their feet. They were safe from its grasp in the Zodiac, with its flat hull and its light weight, but they were also less protected from the strength of each wave crashing against the underwater rock. Luckily, it didn't take long. Halfway down the ocean side, farther than she would have thought from the cliff, the detector let out a keen that didn't stop until they'd travelled nearly thirty feet. She and Julian looked at each other, triumphant. Tracking the bay side would be almost impossible. Diving on any of it would be dangerous. But still. *But still.* One piece. All she needed was a piece, and she'd found it.

Julian cursed as he wheeled the Zodiac around to face the cliff. "We've got guests."

"What?" Mari looked around them at the empty ocean. But Julian was looking up. She followed his gaze and saw them: two figures, one large and one small, watching them from the top of the cliff. Mari's hair stood on end. And then the silence was shattered with a gunshot.

"Jesus," Julian said, pulling them back from the bar. The shot didn't make it anywhere near them. But then there was a whirring, loud and getting louder, and to her horror *New Providence* swung out from a gap in the wild shore farther past the cliff, a red dragon barreling straight toward them.

There was no point in trying to make it back to the harbor. There wasn't time. Julian veered hard, slicing away from the bar, but then Teach was there, cutting so close to them Mari could feel the cold radiating off their hull. "They're going to wreck their own ship," Julian shouted, fighting to control the Zodiac as it floundered between the waves on the bar and the larger boat's wake. Sam Beauregard was watching them over the rail with fury in his eyes. *New Providence* veered around and made another run at them, and as their Zodiac swung close to the bar there was a loud crunch below them. Julian winced. "There goes the metal detector."

"This is insane," Mari yelled. "They're going to—"

But before she could finish predicting it, two things happened in quick succession. The Zodiac finally crossed the groping, moaning sandbar, coming up so hard against a wave that Mari's feet left the deck as their bow pointed up at the sky. The force of it yanked the little boat back like a dog on a leash and they sat snagged there for a frozen instant, exposed.

And then *New Providence* plowed into them from above.

Swan, 1913

Swan didn't take his eyes from Cort's daughter, her face wide and slack, her eyes reflecting the light as it swung close and past, bright and dark. "Evangeline, look at me," he said. "Did your father go into the lighthouse?" The girl nodded. Behind him the tower snarled and gnashed, its temper returning with its unwelcome visitor, and as Swan stood there was a thunderous crack, and he turned in horror to watch as the tower slid several inches from its foundation, the force of the impact driving the door off its hinges.

Evangeline screamed. "Papa!"

"Evangeline, I need you to listen," Swan said, grabbing her arms as she tried to wobble past him. "It's very important to your papa that you do just what I say." She looked at him, her face scrunched in tears. Swan put out a hand for Stay, and the old dog raised his head to meet it. "This is Stay," he said, guiding the girl's hands to his collar. "He's going to keep you company. I need both of you to wait inside the house, and don't come out until I come to get you. Do you understand?"

"Y-yes," Evangeline squeaked. Swan pushed them toward the door but Stay resisted, whining under the girl's tiny hands, straining to follow Swan.

"Stay," he said gently, and the dog gave him a last frantic look and turned away, pulling Evangeline inside.

Swan limped as quickly as he could across the grass to the tower. For all his worrying about the edge of the foundation that hung over the edge of the cliff, it was the other side of the base that had cracked, splitting down the middle under the weight of being pulled off course. It had righted the tower's tilt, drawing the lighthouse straight again, but the rock below him was rattling ominously. There was not much time left at all now.

Swan pried open the battered door and climbed the stairs in the darkness, running his hands along the walls. *It won't go anywhere without telling me,* he'd told Peter. Not yet, he thought. The stone sighed around him. He passed the churning clockwork-room mechanism and pushed open the trapdoor into the lantern room.

And there stood a madman.

Cort was shiny with sweat, wet-haired and wild-eyed, the bull's-eyed glass sending shapes dancing red and black across his face. He had a pickaxe in his hand, the one Swan had just brought in to scrape ice from the windows, and he was driving it into the base of the lens with wild abandon. When he saw Swan he stopped, snarling. "Where is she?"

"Cort, stop this," Swan said. "You're in terrible danger. Didn't you feel the stone crack?"

But Cort was lost in his fury. Cort couldn't read the tower. Couldn't speak its language even as it choked to death around him. He hefted the pickaxe at Swan, panting. "Just tell me where she is."

For a bewildered moment Swan thought he meant the deed. All this for a piece of paper. "I've told you I don't know." But then he thought: *she.* Clara.

"Liar!" Cort said. The tower keened.

"Okay." Swan held his hands out, placating. "She's in town. Come outside, and we can talk about it."

"No." Cort turned back to the lens, driving the pickaxe into the floor. "I've done enough waiting and listening to lies. I'll tear down this godforsaken lighthouse and—"

The tower keened again, louder this time, in pain, and Swan felt a crest of anger followed by a rush of fear. Maybe the tower wouldn't wait after all. The sound gave way to a wrenching creak, and Cort looked up as dust ballooned down from the ceiling. For the first time, fear flitted across his face. "What was that?"

Mari, 2014

There wasn't time to move, time to breathe, time to think.

One minute Mari was flying, the Zodiac tilted below her. The next, everything was black.

The bay here was nothing like the still, shallow water at the cliff. The riptide pressure of the shoal grabbed her and yanked her down, her arm scraping along its length, sending blood blossoming upward, filling the space between her and the sun.

The shoal moaned, greedy and thunderous, towering above her, holding her tight at the bottom. She thrashed and kicked but its hold was too strong, the soft sand below its rock absorbing her feet when she tried to kick against it, bringing her deeper the same way it had brought the pieces of *Saint Gray* and Swan Light.

Sand could keep things safe for a century, or it could kill them in minutes.

Mari grabbed at the rock, trying to pull herself free.

Below her fingers, the rock just laughed.

Swan, 1913

"Where is she?" Cort asked. But his eyes were uncertain now, darting to the ceiling in fear, and in the glow of the lens Swan saw Arthur van Gooren in his face. A boy standing by a roaring fire, complaining about the water dripping onto his shoes.

"Cort, please," Swan said, and Arthur van Gooren's features resolved back into Cort's. Those blue Norman eyes met his as the tower shuddered again, another loud crack echoing below their feet. This time the jolt was so pronounced that Swan and Cort both stumbled, and the ocean tilted closer before Swan's eyes. The breath left his lungs. But again the tower stopped, sagging at an eighty-degree angle, leaning like a broken limb toward the water.

Cort was holding on to the iron base of the lens. Oil was dripping onto his feet, but the fire still burned, the lens still spun, the room for all the world unchanged except for its view. It wouldn't last long. Soon the angle of the fire would start to blacken the lens, filling the room with smoke and the windows with soot. The stone whined.

And Swan thought—knew—that he still had time to run.

He could leave Cort here and get himself out. Make sure Evangeline and Stay were safe, and let the tower go. Cort was the one who shouldn't be here. Cort was the one who had charged in, who hadn't listened. By all rights Swan should have been asleep in his own house by now, shouldn't have known there was anyone to save. Certainly not this specter of Arthur, high in a lighthouse that Nico had never seen.

"Cort," Swan said. One last try. But Cort was frozen, the pickaxe loose in his fingers, his eyes on the slant of the sea. It was no use. He'd been beyond reason, and now he was terrified. And Swan leaned forward, clinging to the rail for balance, and pried the axe away.

He lifted it high.

And he slammed it into Cort Roland's head.

Mari, 2014

The sandbar gnarled and gnashed as Mari's vision went blurry. She pushed against it, expelling precious breath in a flurry of bubbles. Her nerve endings felt like they were on fire, her fingers hyperaware of the press of the stone. Everything was dizzyingly clear, the seafloor more real than it had ever been from behind a mask. Was this what it felt like to drown?

She pushed her hands into the rock as hard as she could and finally it freed her, freed her to drive fingers and toes into its cracks, to climb it like an underwater cliff. Higher and higher.

And then her childhood nightmare sprang from the darkness.

It was so quick she almost missed it, so real she almost let go of the rock. There among the swirling silt below her, beckoning like fingers, were three cracked timber beams.

The rip current swelled and they were gone, washed back below the sand. But Mari stayed frozen, her little remaining air dying in her lungs. Her vision was darkening at the edges, the glass-clear world going blurry, and still she couldn't bring herself to move, paralyzed by the weight of the shape beneath the sand.

Another gust of water came in, exposing a second row of wood lined like stunted, gruesome teeth along the bottom of the rock.

And perched at the end of it was a boy.

Swan, 1913

Swan descended the stairs slowly, heart thudding, arms shaking under Cort Roland's weight. The man was taller than Swan, heavy in the best of circumstances, even more so when he was unconscious. His head sagged against Swan's shoulder, already swelling where Swan had hit him with the pickaxe. He'd hear about that from Abigail, Swan thought ruefully. But it was the only way to get him out of the lighthouse in time.

The tower groaned around him and dropped again, and Swan lost his footing and stumbled into the wall. And when he and his unwieldy cargo reached the bottom of the stairs, he saw to his horror that the stone arch of the doorframe was nearly half a yard lower. The force of the drop had crushed the door diagonally in its frame, leaving a large gap at the top and an impossibly small one at the bottom. Swan dragged Cort the last few steps down and, using the momentum, hoisted the man high enough to shove him through the opening. He heard the man's body land on the other side. Safe.

And his legs gave out from under him.

Swan sank to the floor, his entire body shaking. "Stay," he called reflexively, before remembering that he'd told the dog to wait in the house. Wheezing, he tried to hoist himself through the gap. He collapsed again before his feet even left the floor.

The door loomed above him, insurmountable.

But it was only wood. If he couldn't climb it, maybe he could break it.

Swan went back up the stairs hand over hand, crawling like a child. The mechanism in the clockwork room was straining now, gears grasping for purchase across their new angle, and the panes of the lantern were steadily turning black. The pickaxe had slid from where he'd dropped it, resting handle-first against the wall. Swan hefted it, gagging on the smoke, and pushed open a windowpane to suck in the cold, clean air. Outside, moonlight shone on the waves hitting the bar, giving the impression of something dancing across the darkness.

The tower groaned.

Mari, 2014

Mari wasn't aware of letting go of the bar, of drifting back downward, of her fingers going warm and numb. There was only the shattered wooden spine below her and the boy with his fingers reaching out.

He was going to pull her into the wreck. This was how it was always meant to be, she thought. She could do it. She could follow him down into those twisted ruins and let the darkness swallow her deep. She was warm and she wasn't afraid. The lines in the sea had been a dream, but never a nightmare, not really. They were like the lighthouse. A welcome or a warning. You chose what you saw in it. And you followed it as best you could.

She followed it down.

The boy's fingers met hers, and he was pulling her upward, his calm face suddenly intent, almost angry. He pushed her, hard, away from the wood. "Ow," she murmured, and closed her eyes. They rose higher and higher until there they were, the gold pieces from *Saint Gray* spread out above them like stars. Mari's mouth was full of salt and slime and she didn't care, and the boy gave her one last push as the golden circles expanded. Bright and bold, their edges sparked and blurred until they were glowing, a single bright beam painting the water, pulling her home. But when she reached up to touch it, it was gone.

Swan, 1913

The tower groaned.

And then stopped.

In its place rose a new sound, a single musical note, crystal-high and pure. And Swan knew that this was his warning. The light's goodbye. It was waiting for him, would hold as long as he needed to get out. He pressed a hand to the stone. His throat was tight with tears that suddenly, painfully, pushed their way out. "You've been too good to me, brother," he whispered.

Francis Norman's words came back to him again. *What would a lighthouse have done to help? Given them something pretty to watch on their way down?* But then the other words were there too. Old and new, good and bad, the complicated mess of trying to help and coming up short, trying not to and coming up shorter. Words unspooling, distilling, into what was and always had been enough.

I don't need to stop every bad thing. Just this one.

Here, Soph, a gift from the cove.

He thinks it's an invitation.

I'm going to name her Count Your Lucky Stars.

Your brother was a good man, Swan.

Silvy! You want to swim home, then, yes?

Storm coming in, I'd think.

His heart was racing, impossibly heavy, stopping and starting, out of time, out of sorts, and there was a tearing pain in his left arm. He took a step and it overwhelmed him, the world spinning sideways, and he sank to the stone floor. And from his knees, his forehead pressed to the glass, he heard it. A voice screaming through the darkness, still far away but getting closer step by step. "Mr. Swan!"

Clara.

If she reached them, he knew, she would find a way in. She always did. And there wasn't time for that.

He'd thought he couldn't be responsible for another life out here.

He'd been wrong.

But he couldn't be responsible for another death.

And there it was, the one thing he had always been able to give. Something pretty to watch on the way down. But also something bright enough to want to watch at all. Something that could fight the darkness. Something that could make it disappear. Swan closed his eyes and uncurled his hand along the window, his raging heart finally, mercifully, motionless. This was going to be enough.

It was time to let go.

Rose-Olive Cooper, 1913

At the edge of Norman Cliffs, Rose-Olive Cooper knelt on her bed with her window wide open, both arms crossed on the sill and her chin propped against them, heedless of the winter chill. She'd seen a crow in the garden that day as they'd walked to church, her and Mama with new baby Gerald tied cooing to her chest, and it got her thinking of phoenixes and the way maybe they only hunted at night when no one could see them. Now she couldn't sleep and was dreaming awake of great beasts roaming the skies; staring off into the darkness, humming, her eyes pleasantly out of focus as the great warm beam that had watched her all her life swung past . . . past . . . past . . . She was staring away from the cliffs, out into the velvet of the ocean, when the line of light painted against it dipped abruptly, as if someone had picked up the lighthouse and pointed it downward, and she turned her eyes to the brilliant circle in time to see it dip again, flare brightly, and then go dark.

Mari, 2014

Drowning was warmer than she'd imagined.

Louder too.

Mari flinched as a flurry of beeps went off beside her, afraid to open her mouth and have seawater pour back in. The shattered bones of the shipwreck gaped behind her eyelids, broken beams rising from the sandbar to pin her and pull her and swallow her whole. She murmured as the beeping got louder, louder—"Dr. Adams?" the shipwreck asked.

Mari opened her eyes.

"I admire your commitment," the voice said. "But there were easier ways of visiting me than getting admitted to the hospital yourself."

"Evangeline!" Mari propped herself on her elbows, ignoring the bandage on her arm and the pounding in her head. The old woman smiled from the bed beside her, her face pale and drawn but her blue eyes bright. "You're awake! Are you okay?"

"I've been better," Evangeline said. "But I was feeling much sorrier for myself before you got hit in the head with a boat."

That explained the throbbing. Mari raised her non-bandaged hand to her forehead and felt a lump swelling tight under her fingers. The rest of their room was empty, the sky dark through the window. Mari thought back to the water, but hard as she tried she couldn't summon up any memories past those wooden beams on the seafloor, the gold pieces in the bar, the boy keeping watch over all of it. The boy hadn't been real. So how much of the rest had been? "What happened?" she asked.

"As I understand it, a member of Teach hauled yourself and Mr. Henry aboard after they wrecked your boat," Evangeline said. "A big fellow with a very deep voice. Evidently he draws the line at murder. Mr. Henry was thrown into their ship's path while you were pulled under by the bar and came up right underneath it. But the doctors assure me you'll both be fine."

Mari remembered the golden light, her body drifting upward toward the sun. And then, through a throb, she remembered what she'd known for a week, the week Evangeline had slept through: *Pictured at the site March 3 1914 with his wife, Ruby, and their children.*

"You're a Norman," she blurted. Evangeline settled back into her pillows, eyes unreadable. "You're Cortney Roland's daughter."

"Very good, Mari," Evangeline said. "Even Teach never figured that out."

"But I still don't understand," Mari said. "Why go through all of this?"

"Silvestre Swan," Evangeline said. "Did you find any record of him after 1913?"

"We're still going through Clara Vettrey's diary," Mari said. "The later pages about her life with Louis Roland are clear, but the early pages are in bad shape, and that's where her record of that night is more likely to be. We still don't know what happened to Swan."

For a moment the room was silent, nothing but the beeping of the machines and the hum of the wind outside. "I do," Evangeline said softly, closing her eyes. "I was there. It's my first memory, I think."

Mari's breath caught. "At Swan Light?"

Evangeline nodded, eyes still closed. "I didn't know. Not until later. We moved to the United States when I was very young. I didn't learn about Norman Cliffs until after my father's death, when my brother Philip and I went through his things. We found letters between my mother and father from when he came to Charleston before the rest of us, to set things up. The first one was from December 1913."

"Right after the lighthouse fell," Mari said.

"That's right," Evangeline said. "In the letter he wrote about a man who'd saved his life, a man named Swan. And that's when I realized."

Mari twined her hands in her blanket, so tight her fingertips turned red. "Realized what?"

"His eyes," Evangeline said, and the quiet room seemed to go even quieter. "He had very sad gray eyes. He told me his name was Swan. 'I need you to listen,' he said. And I did. I sat in that house with his dog and I didn't move. I've always remembered that moment. But I didn't know where it came from, not until the letter. I sat with it for years, wondering, and eventually I couldn't live with not knowing for sure. That's when I tracked down Katherine Mettle and heard the legend of the lighthouse keeper." She pulled in a shaky breath. "I don't know why I was on the cliff that night. But I think Silvestre Swan saved my father's life. And I worry it may have cost him his own."

Mari's fingers were going numb beneath her twisted blanket, but she pulled it even tighter. "You're saying you think Silvestre Swan was in the lighthouse when it fell?"

"I don't know," Evangeline said, her voice a near whisper. "Where was my father while I was in the house? Why did Silvestre Swan make me wait inside, and where did he go? Why did my father come back, but there's no record of Silvestre Swan at all after that night?"

"There might be," Mari said. "Evangeline, why didn't you just tell me this at the beginning? We could have gotten Clara Vettrey's diary sooner if you'd told us what you were really looking for."

But Evangeline was already shaking her head. "It was a childhood memory, so many years later," she said. "I didn't know which parts were real and which parts were in my mind. I needed someone who didn't know anything at all to be the one to find out. Someone who wouldn't pander to my theory to get my money but would find the unbiased truth. Although," she said, and a smile quirked her mouth, "I imagine you've discovered why you were the one I reached out to?"

"*Californian*," Mari said. "You knew your uncle was on it before it sank."

"I did," Evangeline said. "And I meant what I said: I admire your work looking for it. The shipwreck sponsor circle is not large, and your friend Stuart Noble has been bragging about you for a while now. But I'd planned on needing to tell you about the *Californian* connection, as a motivator to look into Uncle Lou and find Aunt Clara. And then you ended up making the connection on your own."

"You wanted someone who wouldn't stop looking," Mari said. "*Californian* was a carrot you could dangle to make me look deeper."

Evangeline smiled. "That's one way to look at it, yes."

"But why now?"

"Nearing the end of your life has a tendency to make you reevaluate what came before it," Evangeline said, waving her hand when Mari tried to protest. "It's the one small thing I can do," she said. "To make sure that the man who saved my father's life won't be forgotten. This is the least I can do."

～～～

Before long a doctor came to check on both of them, declaring Mari free to go and fussing over Evangeline before whisking her away to see an internist. "I'm fine," Evangeline said, waving Mari away as she tried to come along. "I'm one hundred and four; I assure you my internals aren't any worse now than they were when this started."

Mari gathered her things and went along the hall until she found Julian's room. He looked terrible, bandages wrapped around his head and one shoulder and a leg up in a sling, but his eyes lit up when he saw her. "Come here," he said, and she slid into the narrow bed beside him.

He draped his free arm over her shoulder and pulled her close. "Are you okay?" he asked. "Have you seen Evangeline?"

"We're okay," she said. "They took Evangeline to run more tests."

He nodded, then rested his cheek on her head, and she moved closer, breathing him in. And here, safe, she let herself think about the boy she'd seen on the ruined beams on the bar. A figment of her imagination, obviously, something her oxygen-deprived brain had summoned in shutting down. And yet . . .

And yet she knew a ship that had wrecked on the sandbar, and the captain who'd gone down with her. *Hazel* and Nico Swan. And if it was all in her head, the boy and the wreck should have been the last thing she ever saw. The pressure of the bar had been immense, stronger than a person could fight. It should have killed her. How had she been able to kick her way up if she hadn't had help?

"What's wrong?" Julian asked, and she smiled.

"You should probably have Otis take *Shanty* back to Boston," she said, twisting to touch her fingers to his shoulder. "This looks like it could take you out of commission for a while, Captain."

"Otis is already on his way," Julian said. "I think he actually left me for dead and claimed the ship for himself, but I'm trying not to feel too offended."

Mari laughed and immediately regretted it, pressing a hand to her head. "He doesn't want to wait to see Evangeline's finished display?"

Julian hummed noncommittally. "Oh, he'll be back. I just wanted *Shanty* under maintenance as soon as possible. She's got a big trip ahead of her afterward."

"Yeah?" Mari asked. "You booked another project already?"

"You could say that." He traced a zigzag up her arm, and heat shot through her.

"To where?"

"I was thinking Greece."

Mari sat up. "What?"

Julian tilted his head, studying her with one fresh eye and one purpling one. "I know you have Evangeline's funding now. But you should put every cent of it toward finding *Californian*, and proving it. So I figured a free boat and equipment couldn't hurt."

"Julian, that's . . . you can't even move your leg."

"Nope," Julian said, but he was grinning. "No chance I'm going. Anyway, it's not my dream. It's not my wreck. But *Shanty* is yours if you want her." He leaned his forehead against hers. "So's her captain."

The offer, both parts of it, stayed on her mind as she returned to Evangeline's empty bed to wait. For the first time, she had a clear path to what she'd wanted since she was five years old. She had a path to *Californian*.

But for the first time, it would hurt to go back.

Evangeline had chosen Mari on purpose, had moved to Norman Cliffs and into a house with an exhibit-ready barn on purpose, had found Katherine Mettle and Keya Talley and all the rest on such steady purpose that it made Mari wonder whether Evangeline had actually dived on Swan Light herself, found what she was looking for, and then just been nice enough to put it all back. It wouldn't have surprised her. Mari remembered arriving in Norman Cliffs and feeling sorry for Evangeline, sympathetic to exploration reduced to phone calls and payments. But she'd been wrong about that too. Exploration was more than pulling stone from sand or dates from books. Stories weren't only found on the seafloor.

Back in the empty room, Mari noticed Evangeline's tote bag sagging against a chair, a corner of paper peeking out of its top, and knew exactly what it was. Katherine Mettle's drawing of the lighthouse on the cliff, creased and worn from years of unfolding and folding and unfolding again. But this time, as Mari opened it, knowing Evangeline wouldn't mind, there were more: Swan Light through the trees, drawn from somewhere down the cliff. A receipt from Isabel's Grocery. A piece of broken china, a pattern of roses along its side. A stack of letters starting *Dear Silvy* and signed *Love, Grace*. A sketch of a tower on a cliff surrounded by equations and doodled pulley systems, dotted lines and numbers keeping it forever tethered to its perch.

Mari sat on the bed, spreading the pieces of Silvestre Swan's story out around her. Swan's story, but Evangeline Roland's, too, and her father's. The story of a whole town. Mari remembered wondering, early in the project, how she would know when the story was over. How she'd know when she'd found everything there was to find. But maybe that was the point. You could never know, not really. This was something science couldn't touch. There were as many parts of a story as there were people who remembered it. Mari lifted each thing carefully, photographing the drawings and letters and china from every angle. They were perfect for the exhibit. They told a story. And she smiled as she thought about the very first conversation she'd had with Evangeline, over a satellite phone an ocean away.

Is there a whole story here, Evangeline?

There's only one way to find out.

Mari, 2014

Evangeline Devon's funeral was held on a rainy morning in the yard beside her barn.

Gulls wheeled across the gray of High Harbor, past ships' lines snapping in the wind. Beyond them the waves on the bar glowed pale through the fog, the only light in the slate-gray water, and the cliffs looked down craggy and muted and watchful from above. Under the patter of rain came the bellow of a far-off foghorn. Mari closed her eyes and listened, her fingers numb on the handle of Julian's Bergy Bits umbrella. The noise was deep as the water, dark as the sky, somber as the people around her.

The people of Norman Cliffs stood scattered across the yard and the street and the gravel, bubbling with respectful conversation. Keya Talley, Jo Cooper, Reggie and his men, Gerald Cooper and Beth the manager and a host of silent seafarers from Horizons Community, Theo van Gooren and Bill Baxter and Daniel the librarian and many other people Mari had never seen before were all ringed around the barn to pay their respects.

When the brief ceremony ended the little crowd thinned, some lingering below umbrellas and others retreating to cars and porches. Julian made no move to leave, his eyes on the barn, his fingers threaded loosely in Mari's. The rain was soaking his bandages and the boot on his leg, which he didn't seem to mind. Neither had he minded his doctor's express orders not to leave the hospital, for which Mari was grateful. At least, they'd told her, Evangeline hadn't suffered. That day in their hospital room was the last time Mari had seen her. When she'd woken the next morning, Evangeline Devon was gone.

"This is what she would have wanted," Julian said, tilting his gauze-wrapped head toward the barn. The rest of his team was inside with Swan Light, and as one of them pushed the doors open a stream of remaining townspeople funneled inside. Mari watched Gerald Cooper bend to lift up a little girl in pigtails and a muddy dress, hoisting her to peer into the murky bath of the lens.

"Yeah," she said quietly. "It is."

By early evening the rain had given way to a dazzling peach sky, and after returning Julian to the hospital Mari opened her window at Mettle House and sat looking out down the slope of town, Beddy purring in her lap. The cliffs stood stark and strong now, the water below them empty. She'd heard from Theo that the Coast Guard had found Sam Beauregard and *New Providence* sheltered in a cove across the island and had arrested him for reckless endangerment. But *Saint Gray's* wreck was registered to Teach, not to Beauregard himself. The water wouldn't be empty for long.

Mari raised her eyes to the cliff, tracing its familiar lines until she landed, as always, at its empty top. Something Keya was working on now was a scale likeness of Swan Light on a transparent sheet, one that could be pinned to Evangeline's barn window to show what the cliff would have looked like with the tower at its peak. Mari couldn't decide if that was better or worse than the empty cliff. The outline seemed to drive home, in some way the stone itself didn't, the fact that Swan Light was gone. It had been there and then it had fallen. It was stone and then it was story. Tracing outlines on the air above it only made that fact more real.

But in most ways, what they were building in the barn was hopeful. It was a testament to a man and a tower, one that Mari knew Evangeline would have loved, and she hoped the old woman would have forgiven her for moving some of her *Californian* money to support this endeavor instead. This was the story of Silvestre Swan, the story of two shipwrecks and all the things they cost, of a sea that stole and stole and that sometimes gave things back. Of a man who wanted to forget in a town that wanted to remember, and the two people he'd brought together in his wake. It was the story of the wrecks that hadn't happened, of the lives people got to keep living because of a light in the darkness and a long line of pilots and a harbor full of ships ready to sail into the storm, all these saints of shallow waters that kept the sea from taking its dues.

So she'd go back to Greece on *Shanty*, take another shot at Cherry. Keep doing the work that would have made her mother proud, keep looking for the things she'd never had time to find. And then, whatever happened, she'd come back here. *Saint Gray* could rot. But someone should look for *Hazel*, she thought. Nico and Silvestre Swan deserved that much. Then she thought about the boy on the sandbar, his ferocious eyes and his arms willing her upward out of his wreck, and she smiled. Maybe not. Maybe sometimes the sea deserved to keep what it claimed. Maybe it was enough to be the one who remembered. Maybe it was enough to know it was there.

But before she left, she had one more thing to do here.

It sat printed on her desk, the email from Julian's coworker with the rest of Clara Vettrey's diary. The early pages that, as Mari had hoped they would, told the story of the last night Swan Light had stood on its cliff. How Clara had entered a battle of wits with Cortney Roland that she was always going to lose, over a deed long lost to time, faded unceremoniously from any record. How she'd tried anyway, to protect the man who'd saved her, going up against Cortney with her lies and smiles. And gold.

The gold she'd kept for herself to start a new life, and had hidden under Silvestre Swan's kitchen floor.

The floor she'd never returned to after collecting Cort and Evangeline Roland the night the lighthouse fell.

Once, Mari would have raced to it. But now she let the idea sit, fluttering in her ribs. It was possible that Clara and Louis had returned for the gold; after all, Louis still had pieces of it with him on *Californian* two years later, taken to start his new life. It was possible that some adventurous kid from Norman Cliffs had found it in the meantime, running through the woods searching for ghosts and fairies.

And it was possible that the gold was still there, sitting below the rotting floorboards a century later, shiny as the day Clara had pulled it from *Saint Gray*'s ruined hull. Just as the rest of it still sat below the sandbar.

If the last one was true, her proof for *Californian* had been waiting below dirt and water for a century. It could wait a little longer. And if it wasn't, if she couldn't tie *Saint Gray*'s gold to Cherry and prove it was *Californian* . . . well, she'd just have to prove it another way. She was a scientist, after all. She'd think of something.

Mari rolled Beddy off of her lap and stood to look at the email, then at the prints beside it, the two of Clara Vettrey's photos she'd kept for herself. The first one was a wedding, a boy with a kind smile standing behind a girl grinning wildly in a white dress, seated with a Labrador dog's graying head cradled between her hands. The second was a cliff on a clear-skied winter day, the same boy beside an old man, the same dog curled between them. The young man was looking into the camera, the old one out to sea. Silvestre Swan's face was stern and weathered, his shoulders hunched, his white hair windblown. But he was smiling. And behind him, diamond-crisp, was a sturdy white stone lighthouse with a black iron railing, the dedication on the plaque below it thin but clear:

CAPTAIN NICO SWAN LIGHT
BUILT 1849
IN LOVING MEMORY

Mari lingered a moment, her eyes on the old man's face in one last private tribute. Then she turned and walked out the door, toward the cliff and the keeper's house and the sea, the dusk-rose of sunset smeared like a thumbprint above it. Toward a past, and a future, through salt-wet air that smelled, very faintly, like hyacinth.

ACKNOWLEDGMENTS

Writing a book is hard, and getting it into the world is much harder. Neither would have happened for me without the following people—I'm grateful for, humbled by, and lucky to have all of them.

My agent, Lori Galvin, who saw the heart of this book right away and championed it fiercely at every turn.

My editor, Alicia Clancy, whose vision perfectly matched my own, and whose sharp guidance pushed the story to get there.

The entire publishing team at Lake Union for all of their work in front of the scenes and behind them.

Michelle Brower and Danya Kukafka, who saw something in it first.

Constance Renfrow, whose early enthusiasm and above-and-beyond feedback blew me away.

The wise minds I leaned on for research—though any errors, exaggerations, or oversimplifications are mine—for all things wreck diving and conservation: *Ship of Gold in the Deep Blue Sea* by Gary Kinder, *The Shipwreck Hunter* by David L. Mearns, *Cleaning Coins and Artefacts* by David Villanueva, the work of Global Marine Exploration, and the work of Donny L. Hamilton at Texas A&M University; for lighthouses: *Brilliant Beacons* by Eric Jay Dolin, LighthouseFriends.com's accounts of the Cape Henlopen Lighthouse (on which Swan Light is based), the United States Lighthouse Society, and the US Coast Guard

Historian's Office; for life in Newfoundland in the mid-1800s: the Newfoundland and Labrador Heritage Website, and *History of the Great Fishery of Newfoundland* by Robert de Loture; for my approximation of *Californian*'s unknown wreck site: *British Merchant Ships Sunk by U-boats in World War One* by A. J. Tennent, and NOAA's Bathymetric Data Viewer; for information on *Californian*'s notorious encounter with *Titanic*: *The Ship That Stood Still* by Leslie Reade.

The earliest supporters of this book and/or the other one, who kept me going: Louise Walters, Jessica Olive, Mabel Gray, Amanda Shih-Goel, Lillian Beitzel, Liz Lunn, Len Boyette, and Emilie Troupe.

Brian, for telling stories with me as long as I can remember.

Mom, for everything, always.

BOOK CLUB QUESTIONS

1. The novel opens on Silvestre Swan remembering an orange stone he dropped into the sea as a child. How has losing things to the ocean defined his life? Why does he continue to live at the lighthouse, knowing he might lose that too?

2. If Swan's life is defined by what he has lost to the sea, Mari's is defined by what she is trying to reclaim from it. Which condition do you think is braver?

3. Before she knows of Evangeline's connection to Swan Light, Mari wonders if her sponsor is simply looking for new ways to spend her small fortune. If you were in Evangeline's position, what kinds of things would you put your money toward?

4. Abigail Norman and Cort Roland are presented as antagonists throughout the story. Do you think this is deserved? In what ways do they both find redemption?

5. Swan and Clara immediately gravitate toward each other. Why do you think this is? How is each of them changed

by knowing the other? How do you feel Clara's actions influenced the way the rest of Swan's life played out?

6. Though everyone around him does, Silvestre Swan himself never refers to the lighthouse as "Swan Light." Why do you think this is? How does the lighthouse function as its own character?

7. Mari's story involves the SS *Californian*, a real ship infamous for its inaction during the sinking of the RMS *Titanic*. What parallels to this do you see throughout the book?

8. At the end of the book Mari comes to the realization that proving things isn't as important as knowing them for yourself, and that finding things isn't as important as believing they're there. Do you think these are both always true?

9. Do you think there is still gold under Swan's floorboard by the time Mari goes to look for it?

ABOUT THE AUTHOR

Photo © 2021 Carrington Spires

Phoebe Rowe was born and raised in Wilmington, Delaware, and studied history and journalism at NYU. She works as a brand copywriter and resides in Brooklyn, New York. *Swan Light* is her first novel.